Drinking Poison
by
Irileria Muhammad

D1715683

Printed in the United States of America

Published by LericallySpeaking
LericallySpeaking@gmail.com

For my village.......

Drinking Poison

ONE-1

Nothing could have prepared Aysha (pronounced "eye-sha") for today's events. There was nothing abnormal about her morning. She followed the same routine that she followed every morning. She woke up at 5:05, and just lay in bed for 15 minutes before convincing herself by 5:15 that she did have to get up. There was something magical in the fat cells of a 30-year old that prevented them from going anywhere no matter how much exercise you did and how many calories you ate. She rode the stationary bike for 45 minutes listening to some rapper cuss about something or the other. She fixed the usual breakfast, an English muffin topped with egg whites and cheese, along with a piece of fruit. She took a quick shower and got dressed. Nothing unusual. Consequently, there was no way that she could have known that one day she would look back on today, May 4, 2011, as one of the best and worst days of her life.

Aysha Rutherford was a 32-year old school teacher, who taught Math and Science to sixth and seventh graders. After a huge life crisis, the catalyst for a career change, she'd finally settled in a school in the inner city of Houston. It was her whole world. She doted on the children like they were the ones that she'd hoped to have someday. Well, she could count the men she'd dated in the last five years on one hand. None of them ever panned out beyond the six-month mark; so, the hope of being a mother was dwindling. But she found comfort in the role she played with the children.

Who would have ever thought that she would be single and with no children at 32? She was beautiful, the kind of beautiful that made people ask her had she ever considered a career in modeling. She was intelligent in a down-to-earth, matter-of-fact kind of way. She seemed to have it all. And, really, she did, at least on the surface.

But today, none of that was important. She had gone on with her life, and poured all of her energy into her class. She took the girls on outings to the mall, and the boys to baseball games. They held cookouts and kickball games at the park near her home. She went to the graduations and debutante balls of the families whose children she taught. She had a full life and would not complain.

It took Aysha twenty minutes in the morning to get to work. Despite the fact that she loathed traffic, she used this time to catch up on phone calls with friends and family. Whoever invented Bluetooth should win a Nobel Peace Prize in Aysha's mind. It was well known that Aysha had a serious case of road rage because her friends and family were treated to her very colorful descriptions of her fellow drivers every morning. Today, Aysha was on the phone with Valerie. She and Valerie had gone to college together, and had maintained a friendship for the last 15 years. They were also sorority sisters, and worked on innumerable community service projects together. The only other person she was nearly as close to was her childhood friend, Kyra, who currently lived in Charlotte, NC. In fact, Valerie and Kyra were the sisters she'd never had. Well, except Aysha did have a sister, Jada. She just never spoke to her, unless her parents were around and forced her to.

Valerie was the founder and director of a homeless shelter. Her job was 24/7, and yet she still found time for her husband and three children. Aysha didn't know how she did it, but she also managed to find time to keep up with every detail of Aysha's life. She was certainly the sister she wished she had. This morning, they were laughing about some of the students' antics. Valerie also mentored some of the girls in Aysha's class, and they were laughing at one little girl who kept telling them both that she did not want to be "ghetto" anymore. Kassidy, an eighth grader now, decided that she wanted to be a professional, and developed a real and imagined allergy to all things "ghetto". She'd started dressing differently, changed the way that she behaved, and was badgering Aysha everyday with questions about becoming a vegetarian. Her most recent episode came when she was going to spend the night and babysit at Valerie's home and came to the car with a suitcase that only had enough items for one night, but could fit a week's worth of clothing for a family of four. When questioned about the suitcase, her response was, "What was I supposed to use? A grocery bag? No, that is very ghetto, and I am traveling with a suitcase from now own". Aysha was laughing so hard that it was hard paying attention to the road. She'd see Kassidy today; she would have to ask her about her 'travel plans".

As Aysha pulled up to the school, she let Valerie know that she was about the end their morning conversation. Valerie used this as a chance to push an issue that they had been disagreeing about for the last four years. "Have you spoken to your sister?'... "No, I don't have one". "Aysha, I still think that you should talk to her. Who goes four years without saying anything more than 'hi' to their sister". "Me, and we have been down this road. I have nothing to say to her. It is all water under the bridge. I have done the righteous thing; I have forgiven her and forgotten her. I showed up for her wedding activities, and that was pushing it. I will see her next month for Father's Day. She is taking my mom on a spa day since my dad is supposed to be going to the NBA Finals for Father's Day. She sent an email inviting me... HA, busy. That heifer can kiss my ass. I do good not to slap her in front of my parents, but to spend a whole day with her. No, ma'am. That dog ain't hunting. Anyway, I am at work. Need to change my mindset before I have to go and deal with my students. I get what you are trying to do, but I really wish you and the rest of the world would leave it alone. I will talk to you later. Bye". Aysha hung up the phone. She hated to be like that with Valerie, but she also needed Valerie to drop it.

When they were younger, Jada and Aysha were inseparable. Jada was two years older than Aysha, but she never treated her like a little sister, just a sister. In retrospect, Aysha could admit that Jada influenced many of her choices in life. She went to the same high school as Jada, she almost went to the same college as Jada, but ended up 30 minutes down I-35 at the state college as opposed to going to the university where Jada was. They saw each other almost every weekend, with either Jada or her friends coming to San Marcos, or Aysha and Valerie going to

Austin. They both graduated with degrees in Business Management, with Jada graduating a year before Aysha. Jada even convinced Aysha to move to Charlotte with her after Aysha graduated. It was there that she lost her sister.

In Charlotte, both Jada and Aysha got a job working for Bank of America. In fact, it was Jada who recommended Aysha for her position. Aysha excelled. Within 6 months, she received a promotion and her supervisors recommended she go and get her Master's in order to position herself for better opportunities. As Charlotte was new to her, she didn't have a life outside of Jada and an occasional trip to Atlanta to see some college friends. Getting her Master's seemed like a great way to pass time, meet people, and lay her career path. It had taken her three years with such a crazy work schedule that started to include her traveling to different locations for training and projects. Her lack of a social life would have been funny, except it was during that last semester of graduate school that she'd met the person she thought was the love of her life. Aysha started dating Jaylon Flowers, a point guard for the basketball team in Charlotte.

Jaylon and Aysha met in a restaurant across the street from the bank. Aysha had gone out to get some lunch after a particularly stressful meeting. She was so busy replaying the meeting in her head that she did not notice the very attractive man staring at her the whole time she ate. Finally, not used to being ignored, Jaylon got up and came to her table. "Hi, my name is Jaylon, and I think you are a very beautiful woman. You really should smile more," he said. Aysha was so caught up in her own thoughts; it took a few seconds for her to process his words. "Oh...uhm.... er..... I am sorry, what did you say?" He repeated exactly what he said, and Aysha started to blush. She was a bit embarrassed. Her friends and family always teased her about the tense expressions she often wore that hid the softness of the person she really was. Jada always told her that she looked like she was "waiting on a fool to start something". "I'm Aysha, and thank you for the compliment, and you are right I should smile more". Then she glanced at him again, 'Wait, I know who you are. You play basketball here in Charlotte." Jaylon later told her that he was afraid that she was the type of female that would only see the money and go for it, but he thought she was so beautiful he thought he would at least take her out. Of course, he had every intention of sleeping with her. "So, are you a fan?" he asked. "I used to be", she replied. When Aysha was in college, she spent a lot of time keeping up with sports, but since she'd moved to Charlotte, with work and school, she didn't have the time anymore. In Houston, they went to the games a lot because her dad bought season tickets every year, but in Charlotte, she and Jada had gone to a couple of games, and that was only when they got tickets from the bank, which had a set of passes that oscillated around the offices. "Well, would you like tickets to tonight's game"? "Yes, I would, but I have to work late and I can't make it". "Well, what about Saturday's game, and maybe we can get something to eat afterwards". "That would be great. I don't get out much here in Charlotte, and a basketball game would be just what I need to relax. Or, smile more as you say." "Well Aysha, two things. First, I need your last name and I will leave the tickets for Saturday at will call, and I will also need your phone number to call you about dinner".

When Aysha went back to work, she put the whole meeting with Jaylon out of her head. It wasn't like a professional athlete would be interested in her. In fact, she had her fill of bad boy athletes in college. Having dated players at her school and at Jada's she knew most of them had no intention of settling down for more than one night with almost any female that would let them in. One of her exes was an NBA all-star now, and whenever she ran into him in Houston, he told her how she was the one he should have settled down with. Too bad. Nope, she'd cried enough tears over that crowd to last a lifetime. But she was excited about going to the game, especially since she knew she'd have great seats. In Houston, her dad bought season tickets, and he had decent seats. A few times when growing up, her dad had gotten her courtside seats to see the Boston Celtics and the Philadelphia 76ers, her favorite teams for her birthday. Occasionally, he got tickets to the games when players in his clientele played in Houston, but usually her dad and her Uncle Rob went.

That Saturday had come a lot quicker than she expected. Jada was going to the game with her and running late as usual. C'mon Ja, I am ready. You know we gotta find a parking space, stand in line at the Will Call Window, and find our seats. Let's go". "Coming, coming... Wow, it is just a basketball game". Aysha had kept her usual Saturday routine and washed and flat ironed her hair after she ran this morning. She wore a Teal shirt with black jeans and silver shoes. She thought about wearing a team t-shirt but that was not really her style. Besides, she was not trying to advertise that she was there at Jaylon's request. Certainly, he had his own fan club of women there to see him.

It ended up that they arrived to the game while shoot around was still going on. She'd talked to Jaylon a couple of times on the phone. He seemed nice enough, but he was still a basketball player. He waved to her, and she caught him looking at her several times during the game. They'd gone to dinner afterward, and started dating almost immediately. Despite all of her apprehensions about dating an athlete, Jaylon had charmed his way into her life. They dated for almost three years, and in front of their friends and family, Jaylon had proposed to her. She'd accepted. The three-carat diamond ring was much smaller than what Jaylon wanted to buy for her, but he'd relented in the face of her protests about being at the bank with a ring worth more than the day's deposits.

They decided to get married the weekend after Father's Day in Houston. Jaylon's season would be over and they'd go on a trip, as well as get her all moved in. They'd picked out a condo in downtown Charlotte near the bank's headquarters, and were planning to close on it the before the wedding. During the week before the wedding, they would close on the house that they planned to live in when Jaylon retired in Houston. Jaylon was from Austin, and thought having a place near both of their families would be nice.

That morning had been like every other. It was her last day at the bank. Jaylon's team was in the playoffs and they were coming back to Charlotte for a home game. They were supposed to go and get the rest of her things packed up from the place she shared with Jada, and get it ready for the movers to come and get it. They were in the last 30 days countdown for the wedding. Surprisingly, when Aysha got to work, it seemed that every person she'd worked with, every customer she'd helped, and every client she'd ever secured all showed up for her going away party. Six years of transactions were all there. The entire lobby of the high-rise where she worked was decked out with a breakfast in her honor. Certainly, she'd expected a little cake and punch, but nothing so extravagant. For the most part, she went to work, and did the best job that she could, but she had no idea she was so appreciated.

After the breakfast, Aysha's supervisor informed her that they wanted her to go home because the company had rented out a suite for the last playoff game of the season and that would also be her going away party. Overwhelmed, Aysha needed help getting all of the gifts and flowers into her truck. She wished she'd driven Jaylon's truck. Her truck was much smaller than his. After she fit it all in, she decided to go by and see Jada. She had taken the day off. Aysha would wake her up like she always did, and make her help her pack.

The first hint that something was wrong was when Aysha pulled up to the house and saw Jada's BMW in the driveway. Jada loved her car more than life, and always kept it in the garage. That had been the center of many battles between them when Aysha was home more, as they only had a one-car garage for the townhouse they shared. Aysha just overlooked that, and walked up to the door. She put her key in the door and walked in. It was obvious that Jada had company. Jada was never the neat freak that Aysha was and if the townhouse was that spotless, someone had to come over. At the front door Aysha paused when she looked at the shoe rack. Something inside of her told her that she recognized those shoes. Anyone could wear blue and white running shoes, right? Her heart was beating fast, and yet at the same time, she was getting angrier by the minute. As she exited the foyer and headed towards Jada's room, she was petrified and furious at what she might find.

When she opened the door to Jada's room, she was shocked to find nothing. Well, relieved was more like it. No one, not even Jada, was in there. But that still did not answer the question as to where was Jada? She decided to just go to her room and start packing. Most of her things were already at Jaylon's, but there were a few things and pieces of furniture that she was taking with her. As she opened her room door, the life drained out of her. There was Jaylon and her sister curled up in her bed. Neither of them even realized that she'd open the door. Her mind was going 5,000 miles a minute. A spirit not her own took over her body. While she was furious enough to kill, there was a certain calm that took over. It was such a surreal experience; it was almost as if she was watching this from outside of her own body.

The anger flooded in. She was not even conscious that she was carrying the Snapple Bottle until she threw it against the mirror in her room. Glass shattered everywhere, and both Jada and Jaylon jumped up wearing nothing but shocked expressions. They both started stuttering and stammering, and Aysha simply turned around and walked out of the house. She went back to her car and got in it and headed to Jaylon's house. She just needed to get some of her things so that she could go.

She made it back to Jaylon's house, and went into the garage and grabbed one of his team travel bags. It was large enough for her to curl up in. Inside of the house, she grabbed as much of her clothing as she could. She would worry about toiletries later. She didn't know where she was going, but she was getting away from the both of them. At this point, she still was not feeling anything. Thank God breathing was an automatic reflex because her mind was void right now. It was on autopilot, and she could just think about getting away.

Just as she put the bag on top of all of the flowers and gifts she'd just received, Jaylon pulled up. She didn't say a word to him; she simply got in her truck and closed the door. She didn't even look to the side to see him. He'd pulled in behind her, but luckily for her, the driveway was circular and she could get out without having to ask him to move.

As she drove off, she saw him just standing there staring at her. She immediately called her cell phone's customer service department and asked to have her cell phone number changed. She didn't have to guess who the previous 47 missed calls were from. As she headed towards the highway, she had no idea where she was going. She wanted to go and check into a hotel, she wanted to go to the beach, but most of all she wanted to go home. She needed to talk to her parents. She punched her parent's address into the overpriced navigation system and headed home. She immediately called Valerie to let her know what happened. She didn't cry, scream, or yell. She was still rather numb. She did make an agreement with Valerie that she would deal with it as soon as she got to Houston. She also pleaded with her not to tell anyone, especially her family, what was going on. She wanted to tell her parents herself, in person. It would take her at least 16 hours to drive to Houston if she tried to go straight there. She decided to drive 8 hours to Mississippi, check into a hotel and rest and then go again in the morning.

She was still not thinking about what happened, but what she needed to do. She'd already quit her job. She decided to call her supervisor, and see if she could arrange something in Houston. She told her that for reasons she couldn't go into, the wedding was off and she was headed to Houston and would need a job. Her supervisor informed her that she had not processed her termination papers since she had 4 weeks of vacation time to use. She told her that she would talk to Human Resources about her simply transferring to Houston, but she had nothing to worry about for at least one month. That put her mind at ease. She did not want to live with her parents any longer than necessary. She would have to start over from scratch. Luckily, she was always waiting for a rainy day. Jaylon had started giving her a monthly allotment about six months after they started dating. Since she still worked and he paid for most of her expenses, she rarely used any of the money. She would be fine. She would land on her feet. In fact, her nickname with her family was, 'Kitty", because as a child she would jump off of anything, and land on her feet.

To keep her mind occupied while driving, and distracted from what she saw, Aysha called one of her line sisters, Jessica, who was a realtor. 'Hey, Soror!!!, "Girl, are you getting ready for the wedding". Of course, the wedding. Aysha did not want to begin to think how she was going to cancel a wedding that was happening in less than four weeks.

"LS, don't go there. I need a huge favor".

"Anything for you. All of the commission that you have gotten me from Jaylon's friends, what can I possibly do for you".

"I need you to start looking for a place for me." "For you, I don't understand". "Uhm, listen, I don't want to go into details, but if you bought a dress for my wedding, take it back. It is off and I am heading to Houston. I am not trying to stay with my parents any longer than is necessary."

"Stop! Rewind, diva, and push play again. What in the world is going on?"

"Jess, I haven't processed it all myself, so I really can't talk to you about it. What I can tell you is that there will not now, nor ever be a wedding between me and Jaylon".

This conversation was wearing on her heart. She could feel all of the emotions that I was suppressing coming to the surface. She didn't want to burst into tears on the phone, and she certainly didn't need to burst into tears while driving. She was going to need to be the master of compartmentalization if she was going to get through this. She needed to make a plan, and she could cry later.

"Look Jess, I am not ready to deal with my reality right now. What I do know is that I need a place in the next three weeks. You know me well enough to know what I like. As a matter of fact, you know what our, I mean his place in Houston looks like. I would like something very similar to that. I can't afford that neighborhood, but I like that style. I am trying to stay around $200,000, and I can close immediately. I work at a bank so I am sure I can get whatever paperwork you will need. I will be in Houston in the next 2 days, and I will be ready to go and look for a place, and put an offer in all in one day." "Okay, Soror, you know I got your back. If you need to talk, let me know. I am going to get on that immediately, and I have some ideas already. Call me as soon as you get here. I love you and you will get through this". "Thanks LS, I will talk to you when I get there".

When Aysha finally got to Houston the next day, her parents were surprised to see her. For once in her life, Jada did not run to them. No need to wonder why. They were then moved to a state of alarm when her dad looked out and saw the truck with North Carolina plates in the driveway.

"Kitty, did you drive here? What's going on?" He asked. At that moment, in the place where she felt the safest, with the two people who loved her most, everything that was bottled up flooded out.

"Daddy. Mom. Just sit down, and let me say this. For right now, just ignore my tears, because there is something I have to say to you."

"Oh my, where is your sister? Is she okay?" By the end of the statement her mother's voice was a shrill. Mrs. Rutherford was getting hysterical, and despite her tears, Aysha needed to keep her mother calm. Aysha's parents sat down on the large sofa and she sat between them.

"Mom, no one is hurt. That is, unless you are counting me. The wedding is off. I walked in on Jada and Jaylon". That was all she could say before she collapsed on the couch into her dad's arms. You could hear the gasp her mother took.

"What do you mean, sweetie? Please calm down, and tell us exactly what happened".

"I love you too much to tell you *exactly* what happened, but Jada and Jaylon were together behind my back. I walked in on them, and then I got on the road and drove to Houston. I was supposed to be marrying him. Him and Jada" Aysha was sobbing into her father's arms.

"Aysha, my dear, are you okay"? Her mother leaned back, relaxed into the couch, and started to cry. Her dad was silent for several minutes and then his anger erupted.

"I will hurt him. I told him that if he hurt you, I would hurt him".

"Daddy, please. What about your daughter? Are you going to hurt her too? I am equally angry with both of them. Actually, no, I am angrier with your daughter. I never would have expected that from her. I am putting you all on notice that there will be no happy family gatherings. I will not tolerate her unless absolutely necessary."

"Kitty, what did your sister say"?

"Mom, nothing. What could she say? I walked out without giving either of them a chance to say anything. And they were in my bed. My bed. We have three bedrooms in that townhouse, but they were in my bed. They are both dead to me"

"That is your sister. Don't say that". Her father said. "Nothing breaks up a family"

"Daddy, I love you and I respect you. That is your daughter, and in the interest of me staying here another minute, don't say anything else about sister. In fact, I am going to my room." Aysha stared at her father for a few seconds, silently challenging him to say another word. She was sure she had enough points at some hotel chain as a tradeoff for all of the travel she did for work to stay for at least a month, and that might be just what she needed.

Finally, in the safety of her room, Aysha broke down. She felt a pain that was indescribable. It felt as if someone was ripping out her insides; and in truth, the two people who should never have hurt her like this had ripped her heart out of her body. She didn't remember much about the next 24 hours. Her mom brought her food, and her dad would come in and watch the news with her. Neither of them tried to talk to her. On the second day Valerie came over, and made her up get up and get out of the bed. She reminded her that she had an appointment with Jess to look at houses, and that she needed to get up.

The irony of this situation would have been funny if it were not happening to her. She would always say if a man left her that she would cry for 5 minutes, and move on. Well, Valerie kept reminding her that this was a long five minutes. The reality was that Aysha did not want Jaylon back. She was hurt, angry, and sad, but the other 7 billion people on the planet were going on with their lives. She could mourn the death of her dreams, but she had better get about creating new ones.

After taking one look in the mirror, Aysha realized that vanity was a much better motivator than reason. She looked a hot ass mess.

"Val, I will be ready in an hour. Can you call Jess, and let her know, and find out where we are supposed to meet her while I get myself together? No man on the planet is worth me looking like Ms. Celie. You should have told me that I was giving Whoopi a run for her money. TRAGIC!!!"

The pain was still there, and Aysha doubted it would ever go away. However, she knew that life needed to go on. More than that, she knew that she needed to get out of her parents' home before they went in high gear on the "Blood is thicker than water" soapbox. If she was not mistaken, her dad said he spoke to both Jada and Jaylon. They both wanted to talk her. NEVER. She would take one thing to her grave. She was never speaking to Jada or Jaylon again.

Aysha was so excited that she found a place that she loved on the first day. Actually, it was the second place that they went to. It was a brand-new townhouse in a gated community in an area that didn't used to be the best place to live in Houston. If she could get a transfer to the downtown headquarters she would be close to work. She would be relatively close to her parents, (by Houston standards anyway) which would calm her father, but given the current situation at that time, that was not really a good thing. Being able to negotiate directly with the builder was an advantage, and she was able to get a place that someone reneged on, for $20,000 less than the market rate. She put her earnest money down, and filled out all of the paperwork. They notified her within the first 24 hours of what else she needed to do. She'd let them know that she needed to close as soon as possible. She basically had one month to order her affairs, before she would be reporting to work.

"Aysha, what are you going to do about the wedding? Everything is paid for. Invitations are sent."

"Well, I have an idea that I saw a few months ago on the internet that I hope you will like. A groom died before the wedding, so the bride and his family held a gala to raise money for his favorite charity since everything was already paid for. Since you are always struggling for the homeless shelter, I will send out notices to cancel the wedding and let everyone know that we are having a benefit for the shelter, and it can be a fundraiser for you. As a matter of fact, let's go to the same printer we used for the invitations. I will call some of Jaylon's friends who live here and let them know what is going on, and see if they will support us. I need to call Jaylon's mom. I just don't know what to say to her. She is more of a mother to me than my own, and I just don't know how to tell her this."

Aysha and Valerie had a late lunch after talking to the printers. They'd also called the decorators and the caterers and made a few small changes to the program. At the restaurant, Aysha had an episode. She'd been so distracted today trying to put her life together that she was blindsided by the sudden emotional rush. Sitting there, tears began to fall. This time, there was no anger, but a strong sadness. She'd lost so much in a short time. Her fiancé', her sister, her life, her dreams, her plans, were all gone. Although she was trying very hard not to let it debilitate her, she found that she was drowning in the sadness. Valerie just sat with her. They ordered tiramisu for dessert. This was Aysha's favorite, but today, it was like eating rice cakes, she couldn't taste it.

"Valerie, I don't want to go home. Can we swing by the mall, and let me pick up a few things for tomorrow? I will call my parents and let them know.

"The girls will be happy to see Auntie Aysha"

"Well, no offense, but I need some alone time. I am going to check into the Westin Galleria, and just take some time for me. Maybe go and blow some of the money that I have saved up on some impractical stuff, get my hair done, and pamper myself. My parents have smothered me, and I really need to put some things in perspective and just decide what I want to do."

"How will you get home? "

"Girl, I am not desolate. Sad and pathetic, maybe? But your girl does have a little change. I was employed. I can afford a cab".

"Cab!!! Cab, my ass! I will be by there at 2 p.m. tomorrow. Have yourself downstairs, ready to go, we need to look at furniture. And I don't care how sad and pathetic you are, if you go Angela Bassett from "Waiting to Exhale" and chop off all of your damn hair, there will be hell to pay." They both laughed. They'd watched that movie a thousand times together, and Aysha swore that she was going to do the same thing if she ever got divorced, but instead, she really wasn't feeling "The break-up chop". She thought she'd called the Beauti Bar Salon and see if her stylist couldn't fit her in. Maybe some highlights or something to give her a new look. She could not stop her heart from hurting, but she could stop the rest of the world from knowing how much it hurt.

"Yes, and I need you to do me a favor. I need you to fly to Charlotte with me to go and pack up my stuff. I know Jaylon's team plays tonight, and they are headed back to San Antonio, so I want to go and get my stuff out while he is gone. You can go to Jada's and get my stuff from there, and I will have a friend of mine put it all in storage and meet the movers to ship it back once I close on my place".

"Okay, when do we leave?

"I will let you know in the morning. I need to check the playoff schedule. I think they have two games there, so we can probably go Saturday." I think they play Friday and Sunday night, so they will probably fly back right after the game, but I will have all day Saturday and Sunday to get my things.

That night in the hotel was horrible. Aysha cried all night. This time, it seemed that she was crying for her family. She realized what her parents were losing. No more happy family times. No more family dinners. There would always be a glittering elephant with a pink rhinoceros in the room. There would always be a certain amount of tension in the air, but that was the route her sister chose. She thought of all the years that she wanted to be just like Jada. She wanted to measure up to her sister, and all along her sister had held some venom in her heart. How else could she explain sleeping with her fiancé? The questions began to spiral. So many times, she had to stop herself from calling both Jada and Jaylon. There was nothing that either of them could say that would ever ease the cross that she was now force to bear. She hurt in places she didn't know that she could.

Aysha decided to fly to Charlotte on Friday night. She and Valeria would stay in a hotel and go over and get her things Saturday. She was sure Jaylon wouldn't have changed the locks. Certainly, he thought she was in Houston, she was pretty sure someone had called him by now and let him know she was there. She was pretty sure her father had gotten a hold of him. That was his battle, not hers. Once they got to Charlotte, she would let Valerie handle Jada. She didn't know if she could be in the same room with her and not have to go to jail. They always said there was thin line between love and hate. That was not true with Jada. There was a wide gaping crater between her and her sister, and there was nothing but hate emitting from Aysha's side.

When Aysha got to Jaylon's house, it was just as she expected. He was gone and she arrived at the same time the housekeeper did. Ms. Dorothy was so happy to see her. Apparently,

Jaylon hadn't told her what happened.

"Ms. Aysha, sweetie, where you been? Is everything okay? I asked Jaylon where you were and he said you were on vacation before the wedding. Where'd you go? "She looked at Aysha with such concern that Aysha almost started crying all over again.

"Ms. Dorothy, I haven't been on vacation. I have been in Houston. The wedding has been called off and I am just here today to get my things."

"No wedding. My dear, what is going on? I knew something was wrong with Jaylon. Poor thing hasn't left out of that game room except to go to the arena for practice. I asked if he was okay, he said, he was missing you and nervous about the playoffs."

"Ms. Dorothy, I am doing a lot better than someone in my position should be. But, I refuse to give him and my sister the satisfaction of knowing that they destroyed me. Inside, they have, but I will never let them or anyone else see that face. I will be okay".

"Sister. Your sister. Wait a minute. Please tell me that boy ain't gone and did what I think you telling me he done gone and did? With your sister? That explains why she's been coming over here the last couple of days. He won't talk to her, though." Ms. Dorothy looked like she was ready to go against the devil himself.

"I ain't going to tell you what I really think because I imagine you already hurting, but you go on and do what you gotta do. Now, I gotta call Jaylon and let him know you are here, but you take your time. He won't be back until Sunday night after the game at the earliest."

"Thank you, Ms. Dorothy. The movers will be here this afternoon; I hope to have everything packed by then. By the way, you remember Valerie, my friend from Houston. She came down to help".

Ms. Dorothy had come into the room where Aysha's closet was and said that she spoke to Jaylon. He told her to tell Aysha that she could take whatever she wanted. Sadly, looking around she realized that she only wanted her clothing. She'd leave all of the memories right there in Charlotte. Ms. Doro-thy was nice enough to help them, so it took about three hours to get all of her things packed. Ms. Dorothy stopped and made them some lunch. While they were waiting Valerie called Jada.

"Hey Jada, this is Val, wassup"

"Val, I am surprised you are speaking to me. I am sure Aysha has told you what happened".

"She has, and honestly, while I want to kick your ass, that is between the two of you, and that is not why I am calling. Aysha and I are in town and she wants me to come and get her things from there, and I was just calling to let you know that I would be over there in about two hours to get her things".

"Okay. But Val, how is she?"

"I don't think I owe you an answer to that question".

"Val, please. I have been worried about her. Not even my parents will talk to me about her. I tried to ask Jaylon about her, but he won't talk to me either. She is my sister".

"Fine time for you to remember that. Look, I don't want to get into all of that. I just need to get Aysha's stuff and move around. You did what you did and the consequences are on you. I am not going to judge, but I am also not going to give you any informa-tion to help you sleep better. In fact, I think you should never have another restful night, but that battle is not mine"

"Val, I understand you and Aysha have been friends for years, and you know I love my sister.

'Ja, Ja, Ja, let me stop you. You have a jacked-up way of showing love. Besides, like I said this is not a discussion I want to have with you now, or ever. I will be there in two hours. I have Aysha's key so you can be there or not, but I will be there."

Aysha was listening to Val's responses and she actually felt sorry for her.... her...... Jada. She didn't know that she con-sidered her a sister any longer. She'd told her parents that shar-ing information about her life with Jada would get them cut out too. She didn't want to cut ties with her parents, but she knew they were used to telling her and Jada each other's business, a practice they'd engaged in since she was born. No matter, it was time for them to understand they had two daughters, separate and Aysha did not consider herself Jada's equal anymore.

After Aysha returned to Houston, she was ecstatic to find out she could close in ten days if she wanted to. She hadn't told her parents about her plans to move out. They would surely be upset that she wasn't staying longer. She was also excited that she'd gotten a call about a position at the bank's regional headquarters. Actually, she'd gotten a call about several positions. Her supervisor in Charlotte told her that she'd had no problem getting her interviews. Aysha had worked on several projects in Houston. That was her way of coming home to visit her parents without having to pay for travel, so she was well known in the corporate headquarters. She'd spend a few days learning about the positions and deciding which one to take.

For some reason, Aysha looked at her hand. Despite all that had transpired in the last 10 days, she still wore her engagement ring. For a moment, she got light headed as she started to try to reflect on why she hadn't taken it off. She decided it didn't matter. She removed the ring from her finger. Tomorrow she would ask her parents to put it in their safety deposit box. Returning it wasn't an option.

On closing day, Aysha was overwhelmed. She'd given Jess and the bank all of the paperwork they needed. Aysha was going to have her own place. She'd looked at furniture, but didn't want to buy anything until after she closed. This weekend, she would be like a kid in a candy store. Retail therapy was exactly what she needed and she would get more than enough trying to fill a new house with all of the things she couldn't live without.

After one month, Aysha was no closer to the pain being gone, but she was becoming a master at hiding it. She couldn't watch television. Jaylon's team won the championship and his face was plastered on every channel. She couldn't stand it. The cancellations had gone out. No doubt her parents' phone rang off of the hook. Thank God she'd changed her number. Small favors. The gala was on her wedding day, and she chose not to attend it, although it was the talk of the town. She started her new job the following Monday. Her life was not what she thought it would be, but it was starting anew, and for that she could smile, even if her heart still hurt.

That was a whole different life. It had been almost five years ago, and she wasn't sure that she was any closer to mending the hole that all left in her. She'd only dated one other man, Jonathan. However, his unwillingness to commit to marriage was more than Aysha could contend with. In retrospect, she was sure that although she voiced an interest in being married, she really wasn't. Honestly, she was still stuck standing in that doorway looking at the two people she loved the most lying in bed. But rehashing that moment was not on today's agenda.

After hanging up the phone with Valerie, and snapping herself back to reality, she remembered all that she needed to do at school. It was awards day at the school. Aysha was the sponsor for the Student Council, and was in charge of the event. The students had been meticulous in planning the event. It was the most exciting event of the school year. The best of the best in every possible category was awarded for their success, and they raised enough money that it was like the middle school version of the Oscars. They'd sent out nomination letters, and there was a red carpet and photographer. In the last two years, the students had even given awards to teachers. Aysha pled with the council members not to nominate her for any awards, but she was sure they would make sure that she got at least one.

Valerie's words replayed in her head all day. "Who goes nearly five years without speaking to their sister?" At what point do you forgive? She'd gone to Jada's wedding three years ago. It just seemed like more of a hassle to have to explain to friends why she missed her sister's wedding. After all, did she really want to have to keep telling the story? She missed Jada's baby shower by making sure she was scheduled to be out of the country. She'd sent a gift, a check made out to her niece, Lailani. Jada was pulling out all of the stops. Lailaini was Aysha's middle name. While that did soften her heart towards her niece, she still wasn't ready to be sisters, or even friends, with Jada. She hoped that when Lailani was older, Jada would let her come to Houston for the summer, and she could get to know her at her parents' home.

The day went as planned. The students had trophies, ribbons, medals, and certificates denoting their accomplishments. Aysha had a headache and swollen feet to show for another successful award's day. She'd smiled so much her face hurt, and shaken so many hands that she thought her wrist might be sprained. She headed to the parking lot, with a huge smile on her face. As tired and worn down as she was, she knew the program was a success.

TWO-2

Aysha almost broke out in a sprint when headed towards her car. Having signed out for the year, she was looking forward to the weekend. Well, most of the weekend. Her mother had roped her into brunch with her and Jada. She was lucky to get out of the other activities, although she would be at church on next Sunday to witness Lailani's christening when her father returned. Though she was sure that she still hated her sister, she had nothing but love for her only niece. Even Jada's husband seemed nice enough. Oddly, from what she'd been told he was a coach in the NBA, and Jaylon had actually introduced them. *How nice of him*, she thought. Use her up and then pawn her off on someone else. Hey, like her mother always said, "If they liked it, she loved it".

Apparently, Jada and her husband bought a house in Houston and stayed there in the off-season. Luckily for Aysha, she and Jada traveled in very different circles, purposefully. Most of their family members and mutual friends knew better than to try to get them together. Their paths had crossed at a couple of family and sorority events, but Aysha always made it her business to avoid Jada. Occasionally, they'd smile for the camera, but rarely were any words spoken. As for their parents, Aysha tended to go to her parents' home in the mornings for breakfast, and Jada typically went for dinner, so there was little chance of them running into each other. Over the last three years, she'd rarely been forced to sit at the table with her, but Christmas was unavoidable, but she'd found it surprisingly simple to keep her distance from her sister.

When she got close to the parking lot, there was a huge, black SUV blocking her car in. These parents had nerve. She was exhausted and prepared to go home, and even with all of the open spots, they chose to block her in. Before she could decide on a course of action, the driver's door opened on the SUV. Aysha noticed that the man getting out was very tall. From a distance, he looked like just the type Aysha would go for, that was if she was going for any guy. Somebody had already broken her heart, so that was not even an option right now. The guy started heading towards her. As he got closer her heart stopped.

"What do you want?" she asked with as much attitude as her stalled brain could muster.

"I need to talk to you. There's been an accident, and I need you to come with me".

"Do you smoke crack? I don't care if hell froze over. I am not going anywhere with you. Accident? Wait! What aren't you telling me? Why are you here?", Aysha yelled, as she was livid.

"Aysha, please get in the truck. I promise to tell you everything, if you will just sit down and calm down".

Aysha was in shock. She hadn't seen Jaylon in nearly five years, and here he was at her job telling her to get in the car. How'd he even know where she worked? How would she know what her car looked like? And, who in the hell sent him to come and get her? There were too many questions, and so far, no answers. At that moment, the Houston heat became overwhelming, and Aysha felt lightheaded. She did not want to, but it seemed getting in Jaylon's car was going to be her best option.

As she walked to the passenger side of the car, Jaylon took her bags from her and placed them in the back seat. He opened the passenger door for her. Without missing the opportunity to roll her eyes at him, she got into the vehicle. It seems it took him forever to walk around the car. She was fixated on the million-dollar question of how did Jaylon know so much about her. Who in her life was still talking to Jaylon? That was question number one.

"Okay, I am in the car, so start talking. And, how in the hell did you know where to find me anyway?" She asked. She did so without looking directly at him. She couldn't. She wasn't ready to see him. He'd always been the most handsome man she'd ever met. Being aware of her own weaknesses, she knew she could not look at him and maintain the anger that had been simmering within her all of these years.

"Aysha, I need to take you to the hospital. Your father had

a heart attack this afternoon, and the ambulance rushed him to Memorial Hermann in the Medical Center, and I need to get you there".

The truck started spinning for Aysha. She'd heard what Jaylon said, but she could not process the words. Dad. Heart Attack. Hospital. Fragmented words that were not making coherent thoughts were swarming in her head. For a second it seemed she was in a vacuum, as she couldn't see or hear anything. She was sure that Jaylon had begun driving, but the spiral that she was in had not yet stopped spinning. She didn't respond. She just sat back, and tried to make sense of it all. Actually, she sat back hoping she would wake up soon. Aysha in Wonderland. Yes, this was a dream. A horrible dream, but a dream, nonetheless.

As they headed towards Highway 288, Aysha felt herself merging back into reality. So much so, that all of her initial questions were coming back. She oscillated between ignoring Jaylon and getting answers. Surprisingly, he seemed content with just driving. So much so that it started to anger Aysha. Was he really sitting there ignoring her as much as she was ignoring him? Was he really unmoved by her? Maybe she was right in feeling like he'd discarded her for her sister. No time for that, she needed some answers.

"Please tell me what happened to my dad?" she coolly asked.

"He and I were at The Royal Oak Country Club having lunch after our weekly golf game".

"Hold up!!! You play golf with my father? Wait, you talk, no my father talks to you?"

"Aysha, your father and I have played golf for the last three years or so. We played every Friday that I am in Houston".

"I don't believe you. My father would have told me"

"Aysha, there is a lot of things your father didn't tell you, and I am not going there with you. Not right now anyway. While we were walking out to the car to leave, he said he felt pains in his chest, and I could tell that he was short of breath. We were close to the car so I got him to the car, and turned it on to get air, and had him sit down. At the same time, I called 9-1-1. I also ran back inside of the Country Club to get the Nurse on duty. By the time we got back, the nurse said she thought he was having a heart attack."

"Is he okay, will he make it?"

"Aysha, the doctors are not optimistic. This is the third heart attack he's had."

"WHAT ARE YOU TALKING ABOUT? Third heart attack... Jaylon, stop. How do you know all of this?'

"Aysha, your dad went to the All-Star game with me two years ago. He had a heart attack prior to the game."

Aysha was thouroughly confused at what Jaylon was saying to her.

"No, your dad had a heart attack the year you didn't play in the game. It was the first All-Star game I watched after we broke up, and the commentators mentioned it because you chose not to play."

"No, it was your dad. We kept his name out of the media. I still don't know who my father is. Your father was in the sky-box area, and he'd started a tab at a bar in the arena, and had given them his I.D. and credit card. He walked to the restroom, and collapsed on the way. You know he only carried his driver's license, cash, and one credit card with him, so he had no other I.D. Because the ticket he had in his pocket said, "Guest of Jaylon Flowers" and his age, I guess they assumed he was my father. They rushed him to the hospital, and the arena staff notified me during the shoot around, and I left the arena and went to the hospital to be with him. He made me promise not to tell. Even your mother does not know."

Aysha was on the borderline between hysteria and shock right now. How was all of this going on behind her back? Why didn't her father bother to tell her any of this? Just like her dad to try to keep stuff from her. He always told her that she'd been through enough sadness to last a lifetime. Why didn't he realize how strong all of that had made her? She was grown, and she was strong, but to him she would always be his little "Kitty".

They were nearing the hospital. Aysha's stomach had twisted up in knots. Her dad would be fine. Three heart attacks had to be hard on anyone, but her dad could beat anything and anybody. He would come through this just fine. Good thing she was now officially on summer break. She could come over and help her mom take care of him. Maybe she would even move in with them until her father was back up and on his feet.

As they pulled into the valet lane at the hospital, Aysha did not have a good feeling. Her intuition was telling her that she might be too late. She waited for Jaylon to come around to the entrance. He grabbed her hand and led her towards the elevator bay. She wasn't sure about Jaylon touching her, but she was sure that this was not the proper time to voice her displeasure. So, she sucked it up, and got on the elevator.

As the doors closed, Jaylon pressed the button for the 3rd floor. Aysha knew from previous visits to this hospital that the Intensive Care Unit was located on that floor. When they stepped off of the elevator, the first person Aysha saw was Jada. Jada was seated on a sofa holding the baby, and her husband was seated over next her. Aysha didn't really know Jada's husband very well, not that she should. She'd only met him once, at Jada's wedding and she had seen him at Christmas, and a few other family gatherings, but never did much more than wave and say, "Hi". Aysha found a reason and a way to miss all of the pre-wedding festivities, but under threat of death from her mother she was at the wedding. Although she refused to be in the wedding, she'd sat on the front row with her parents and Jada's godparents.

Jada stood and came towards Aysha. She put her arms up like she wanted to hug her, and Aysha stopped short before she could. "Jada." Was all she said. Aysha's head was swimming. This was too much for one day. Having her father in the hospital after having a heart attack, and seeing Jaylon and Jada were proving to be psychological torture. Where was Calgon when you really needed them to take you away, she wondered?

"Where is my dad?" Aysha asked the question to no one

in particular. She did not see her mom, and could only assume that she would find her mother wherever she found her dad.

"Kitty, dad is...", Jada started to reply.

"Excuse you, my name is Aysha" interrupted. She didn't understand why Jada insisted on trying to recapture their sisterly love whenever they were together. True, the fact they shared the same parents should have made them sisters, but the fact they had also shared the same man negated that. When Jaylon tugged at Aysha's arm, she realized he was still holding her hand. In an instant she was over both of them, and she snatched her hand away from Jaylon. She looked up at Jaylon, and rolled her eyes, ending with an empty stare directly at Jada.

"As you were saying, my daddy is where?" Aysha asked in a very challenging tone.

"He is in a room, but we can only go in two at a time. Momma has been in with him for the most part, but he keeps asking for you"

"He's asking for me? Did you see him?" Aysha was skeptical. She didn't understand why her dad was asking for her specifically.

"Yes, I saw him. But, he is the one that sent Jaylon to the school to get you. He didn't want us to call you and tell you what happened over the phone. He actually made us wait until after school was out". He is talking a little bit, but the only thing he really says is "Get Aysha".

When Aysha turned around Jaylon was walking back to her. Before she could say anything, he told her that he notified the nurse that she was there, and wanted to see her father. The nurse was going to get her mother so that Aysha could go in.

"I don't think I can do this. I can't see my daddy like this." Tears were streaming down her face. She was still wondering when she would wake up from this dream. There was no way on God's green Earth that all of this was happening in one day. No way.

"I will go in with you. Your dad asked to see us together" Jaylon responded.

"Us? Together? Why? I don't understand". Aysha's normally clear mind was a jumbled mess right now. Nothing had made sense since she got to the parking lot at school. She wished she could hit the rewind button, and go back. Certainly, she'd missed something. Certainly, she'd missed a whole lot of something because nothing about this was making sense right now.

Aysha was torn between her worry about her father and her anger with Jaylon. She didn't want him to go in with her. It was bad enough he was witnessing her crying, and really she didn't understand why he was here at all. This was not his family. But, she would honor her father's wishes, and go in with Jaylon. As she was wrapping her mind around that fact, she saw her mom walk in. She came straight to Aysha, and wrapped her arms around her. They both started to cry. There were no words to say. Her mom pulled back. Her mom looked as if she'd aged 20 years since Aysha saw her only two nights ago.

"Kitty, he is asking for you," her mom sobbed. "Jay, he wants you, too". There was nothing else to say. Jaylon grabbed Aysha's hand and headed towards the room. Aysha was moving, but she kept looking back at her mom. Before they entered, the nurse cautioned, "He is very weak. Please don't agitate him in any way. You will have 10 minutes and then the doctors want to come back to see him".

Aysha walked in the room. When she saw her father lying there with all of those tubes and machines attached to him, Aysha was grateful that Jaylon was there. Her legs went numb, and she found herself leaning on Jaylon. He'd placed his arm around her shoulder, and she leaned into him. This was overwhelming. Her father was a large man. He stood 6'5" to Aysha's 5'5", so he'd always towered over her. Seeing him in this bed reduced his stature, and made him seem most unlike the larger-than-life figure he'd always been in Aysha's life. Walking over to his bed, she couldn't help but remember all of the mornings when she and Jada would jump in the bed with her parents and beg her dad to come and fix them breakfast. He wasn't a great cook, but he had French toast down to a science. Even to this day whenever Aysha came over for breakfast, he'd make it for her, with all of the cinnamon that she could stand. Admittedly, it was a little different since he used sugar-free syrup now.

"Daddy, are you awake?"

"Kitty, you made it." He said, opening his eyes. Aysha could see that it took a lot of effort for him to just say that. "Where's Jay?" He asked, and Aysha noted him trying to move his head.

"Daddy, please don't try to move. Jaylon is here".

"Kitty." His voice was so raspy it was heartbreaking. She was used to hearing the booming voice that called her downstairs in the morning so that she would not miss the school bus, or the teasing voice that joked about her being "wonder woman". This voice was foreign to Aysha, and she could not comprehend that it was coming out of her father's mouth.

Jaylon sensed her distressed, and moved to stand right beside her. He wrapped his arm around her waist, and they both knelt down closer to the bed.

"I have you both here. Kitty, I need you to let it go. "

"Daddy, no... we can talk about this when you get home. Right now, you need

"No, Aysha, right now I need to say what I should have said to you years ago. You, my dear, are the most determined person on Earth. And, I should have stepped in when I saw you use that determination to cut your sister and Jaylon out of your life. Your mom and I watched you do it, and along the way, we even helped you do it. But, baby girl, you must let this go. I know you are hurt. I have watched you push everyone away from you. You gave up your career and went into teaching, and you love those children and they deserve you as a teacher. But, that is not life Aysha. Pouring your heart and soul into other people's children is not your life. You have no secrets from me Aysha, and I love you, but you are gonna destroy yourself. Now, you have been so determined in putting your past life behind you, but I need you to let it go. I need you to stop fighting the past, and forgive your sister and Jaylon and get on with your life. Your mom is going to need you and your sister together, not fighting. And I am trusting Jaylon and Malik with what I love most: You, your mom, and Jada."

"Daddy, don't say that. Mommie has you."

"Kitty, just listen sweetheart. Just remember that I asked you to let it go. Let your sister into your life. Let Jaylon take care of you. I am sorry that I allowed this to go on for so long."

"Daddy, I don't know what you are saying." Aysha could not breathe. Her father was issuing commands to her like this was the last time he planned to talk to her.

"Jaylon, you have been the best son a man could ask for. I need you to take care of my girls. I need you to make sure they mend this. I need you not to give up. You also have my permission to tell her everything. You and my wife can sit her down and tell her everything. There are no more secrets to keep. Aysha, do you understand what I am asking you to do?

"Yes, sir. I love you daddy, but I don't know if I can."

"Oh yes, you can do anything you put your mind to. That has always been true. I love you, Kitty, but now, I am getting tired. Please get Jada and Malik. I need to talk to them.

Aysha leaned down and kissed her dad on the forehead. When she did, he whispered, "Tell him everything Aysha, and both of y'all move on. Together." She was shocked, what was her father talking about. Certainly, he didn't know her secret. She'd never told anyone.

She couldn't remember the last time her dad had actually ordered her to do something. He was more persuasive than forceful. In fact, her mom had handled most of their discipline because her daddy let them do as they pleased. Aysha released her father's hand and stood to look at him. His eyes were closed, and Aysha could tell that he was straining to breathe. She looked at Jaylon, and there were tears falling from his eyes. She nodded towards the door, and both of them walked towards it. She took one look at her father, lying in the bed. She knew that her father was saying goodbye. As hard as it was to walk out of that door, she knew that she needed to go and get Jada and

Malik.

Once they made it back to the waiting area, Aysha collapsed into her mother's arm. She was crying so hard that she could not speak. Jaylon went over to Jada and Malik, and told them her dad wanted to see them. When Aysha finally was able to compose herself a little bit, Jada and Malik were gone, and Jaylon was holding the sleeping Lailani. She was not sure how much time had passed, but her head was starting to hurt from all of the crying. She pulled away from her mother, and sat back in the chair. She was still holding her mother's hand with one hand, and her mother was using her other hand to wipe the tears from Aysha's face. She wanted to speak, but she had no idea what to say. She was about to lose her father, and her mother was about to lose her husband of 37 years. What could she possibly say now?

Aysha looked up, and saw Malik practically carrying Jada. She was crying so hard that she was not walking, but rather her feet were just shuffling down the corridor as Malik held her. She did not even look up when Malik placed her on the loveseat in the waiting area. He walked over to Aysha and her mom.

"Mom, Daddy needs you now. The doctor is there." She hugged her mother before her mom walked away. Jaylon handed Lailani to Malik and walked behind her mother. Together, they disappeared around the corner. Although she was contemplating a life without her father, it did not go unnoticed that Jaylon went in with her mom. Aysha was not clear on what was going on, but it seemed her parents had a very close relationship with Jaylon. She was not sure if she felt betrayed or what. She'd sort those feelings out later, but right now, she was just trying to focus on breathing. At that point, a nurse came out, and asked for Jada and Aysha. Jada sat up on the loveseat, and Aysha stood up and moved to stand by Jada.

"Your mother asked me to explain what is going on.

"Please, no one has given us details. As soon as I got her, I was taken in to see my dad." Aysha responded.

At this moment, Jada reached up and grabbed Aysha's

hand. Aysha tensed up, but she did not pull her hand back. Jada was so wrong if she thought all was well between them. She flashed her father's words to her, and she quickly decided that today was not the day that she was going to start. She'd cross that bridge later. She tried to pull her hand away, but Jada was holding on for dear life.

"Mr. Rutherford had a heart attack. The damage to his heart is massive, and right now he is on a bypass machine to help his heart. During his last checkup, he was advised that he would need a heart transplant if he were to survive long term. The heart attack today has caused irreparable damage. He and your mother have decided that he will not be hooked up to any machines, and currently, they are pulling the plugs".

"Are you saying my dad won't make it?" Jada asked. Aysha couldn't breathe. She almost fell on Jada trying to sit down. She ended up just sitting on the floor next to Jada. Malik walked over to try to console them both, but it was difficult with him holding the baby. Aysha looked around for her purse. She needed Valerie to come and get her. It crossed her mind how many situations Valerie had been there with her for over the years. She'd have to remember to say thank you. She also remembered that she needed to get the title to her car from her dad. As a 32th birthday gift, her dad bought Aysha 3 gifts, a brand-new car, new furniture for her living room, and diamond earrings. Aysha's birthday was two months ago, and her dad insisted on choosing the biggest three items on her list. Her mother wasn't far behind. She paid for Aysha to go to Spain with her sorors, bought Aysha a new designer handbag, and gave her a bag with three of the robin's egg blue boxes inside. It was by far the best birthday Aysha ever had. They'd gone to dinner at Ruggle's and her parents had invited thirty-two of her closest friends. Thanks to Valerie, there were even a couple of her students present.

It hit Aysha that her father would not be around for any more birthdays. She was really too shocked to cry anymore. Jada, on the other hand, was sprawled out on the loveseat. Malik seemed at a loss as to what he was supposed to do. She was crying so vigorously that she was shaking the chair and the table behind her. Aysha thought about what people say about people with the most guilt crying the most. She was going to miss her father tremendously, but she also knew that her dad was too proud and independent to have to be hooked up to machines for life. Certainly, if he couldn't play golf and chess, or go for the morning walk with her mom, he would not consider that life.

"Are there any questions about your dad?" the nurse asked.

"How long will we have once the machines are completely disconnected?" Malik asked.

"I'm sorry, it will only be a matter of minutes once the machines are turned off. Your mother is with him right now. Once it is all done, you may all go in and see him if you would like."

Aysha felt the room spinning again. She was getting light-headed, and the next thing she knew the whole room went black, and she sank to the floor. She came to with Jada cradling her, and a nurse kneeling in front of her. Her mother and Jaylon were standing behind the nurse. While her vision was very unclear, she could clearly see that her mother and Jaylon were alarmed. The nurse was speaking to her, and she could see her mouth moving, but the words were not registering. Aysha looked at her mom and began to speak.

"Daddy? Is he gone?"

Her mother did not respond, but rather she just looked at Aysha and started to cry. Jaylon put his arm around her and walked her to the chair so that she could sit down. He came back and took Jada's place. After the nurse checked Aysha's vital signs, Jaylon picked her up and put her in the chair next to her mother. He had the most solemn look on his face. Her mom reached out and grabbed Jaylon's hand. It did not escape Aysha's attention that everyone in this family seemed very cozy with Jaylon. It had been almost five years since she'd seen Jaylon, but obviously that was not true for her parents.

"Jaylon, can you drive me home please?" Mrs. Rutherford asked. Her voice was so weak that Aysha almost didn't recognize it. Her mother was a very lively person, and yet in this moment Aysha saw just how much her dad had meant to her mother. She'd known they were very much in love. In fact, her dad could not stand to be without her mother. When her mother went on a cruise with her sorority sisters, Aysha's dad found a reason to stay at Aysha's house every night until her mother returned. He would conveniently need to change a filter, or look at a drain. In fact, Aysha's landscaping was a result of her mother's visit to Chicago to be with Jada when Lailani was born in the middle of the season and Jada chose to stay in Chicago so Malik could be there with her. Her dad said he had an appointment that he couldn't miss, so he wasn't able to leave for Chicago until a week after her mother left.

At that moment, Aysha realized the television was on. The reporter was standing in front of the Royal Oaks Country Club, and the caption at the bottom read, "Jaylon Flower's Father Collapses". The reporter was talking about her dad's collapse, but was calling her dad Jaylon's father. What in the world was going on? Aysha stared at the television.

"Hush, so I can hear!" Aysha snapped. After she listened to the end of the news report, she glared at Jaylon.

"Don't you think you have taken enough from me? Jaylon Flowers, I swear up and down that I hate you. "

She spoke the words with so much venom in them, that it stunned everyone in the room. Her mother just started to cry. Jada started to cry. Aysha started to cry also, but grabbed her bag and walked away.

"She shouldn't be alone" her mother said. "Jaylon, get my phone and call Valerie". Ask her to meet Aysha at her house. You can tell her everything or nothing, but she should not be alone. Right now, I can't help myself, let alone, help my baby.

"Yes, ma'am. I will call Valerie". Jaylon actually used his own phone to call Valerie. Unbeknownst to Aysha, he and Valerie were civil. He'd called her several times over the years as he was a major donor to her homeless shelter and he helped out behind the scenes as much as possible. In fact, Valerie had helped him be an anonymous donor to some of the projects Aysha had undertaken at the school. It would probably surprise her to know just how much of her life had been financed by Jaylon. He never wanted her to know, but he knew that he'd hurt her, and he still held out hope that someday she would let him make it up to her.

About six months after the fiasco with Jada, Jaylon had flown to Houston and shown up on the Rutherford's doorstep. He expected them to be hostile with him, but after pouring out his heart, they'd welcomed him in. Having never had a relationship with his own father, he began to spend a lot of time with Mr. Rutherford. They both played golf, so over the last four years, Jaylon made sure to be in Houston as many Fridays as possible to play golf with Mr. Rutherford. If he could count all of the money he'd spent flying to Houston just for golf with Mr. Rutherford, he'd rival his NBA salary. But, that was one relationship that meant more to Jaylon than any other. They'd shared their stories, and Mr. Rutherford had told Jaylon about his own youthful indiscretions and he didn't judge Jaylon. He'd voiced his anger and disappointment, but he'd forgiven Jaylon and that meant more to him than anything, except maybe Aysha's forgiveness, which he wasn't sure he'd ever get.

He'd taken Aysha's dad to every NBA event that he could. They'd gone to every All-Star game together, and this year, Jaylon was able to give Mr. Rutherford his lifelong dream of going to the Super Bowl. He wasn't sure how they'd manage to keep it from Aysha, but her parents never mentioned him, and he never saw her. He did know that Aysha thought that her uncle, who was a Sports Agent, had gotten the Super Bowl tickets. He'd flown the Rutherfords around the world and back, as they were the family he'd never had.

Jaylon looked at Jada. He couldn't believe he'd been that stupid. He couldn't even blame her. They were two adults, and while there was some alcohol involved, no amount of alcohol should make you betray the one you love most. He would never live down that night. Aysha was the one person that had loved Jaylon for Jaylon. She didn't care about the money. She didn't care about his status as an athlete, although she kept up with his stats better than the team could ever track him. She was surprisingly simple. As beautiful as she was, men always paid attention to her. His teammates, coaches, and rivals, all commented on her looks. The friends that had actually gotten to know Aysha always asked if she had a twin. They loved her down to earth nature. When the other guys had to wine and dine their newest fling, Aysha was content with cooking at home. She'd gotten upset with him when he'd spent $3,500 on a purse for her birthday. She tried to make him understand that she didn't need it. He tried to make her understand that with a contract like he had, he could afford it.

Aysha's father was a financial planner, and not soon after he and Aysha started dating, Jaylon hired his firm. However, Aysha's father let his partner handle Jaylon's accounts to prevent any conflicts of interests. Jaylon had no complaints. They kept him on the financial straight and narrow by issuing him a monthly allowance, and forcing him to pay off both of his houses, buy two cars, and save the bulk of his earning. Jaylon had a few endorsement deals, and Aysha's father insisted that he live off of his endorsement money and not his salary. As a result, after 10 years in the league, Jaylon was set for the rest of his life. So much so, that he was considering walking away after his contract expired at the end of the season. He was only 32 years, old, but he was tired of the road, the whole lifestyle associated with being on the road, and needed a place to put down roots. More importantly, he needed Aysha to put down roots with.

Foolishly, he thought that time would heal the wound. The Aysha he knew would never hold a grudge this long. In fact, even her parents were shocked that after nearly five years, she still was nothing more than cordial to her sister. To his knowledge, she never so much as uttered Jaylon's name. As many sporting events that Aysha watched with her dad, she would not have anything to do with any event where there was remotely a chance that she would see Jaylon. Jaylon tried to get her dad to bring her to the All-Star game, and Aysha had not only refused to go, but her dad had almost missed his flight trying to convince her.

Over the years, Jaylon had spent time and money behind the scenes for Aysha. No one thought she was serious when she decided to leave banking to go and teach. Aysha had been in her job for a few years, and her salary and her reputation were both skyrocketing. Still, she'd told her parents that something was missing. She did a lot of volunteer work with Valerie's homeless project, and after two years of being in Houston, Aysha landed role as a Junior High School teacher.

It was said that Aysha had the Midas touch. Jaylon had to admit just how true that was. Everything Aysha touched got better. That was just the impression that she'd left on everyone that she came in contact with. When she and Jaylon started dating, he was on the verge of becoming the league's next bad boy. A couple of run-ins with his coaches, a few missed practices, and a holdout had sent his public image downward. However, once he met Aysha, he wanted to impress her. In fact, everything he did over the next two years was just to see her smile. He couldn't stand for her to be sad, disappointed, or hurt. It almost shut him down completely when he realized that he'd been the source of her greatest pain.

Jaylon knew that Aysha's students loved her. He couldn't go to the school personally, but made sure that each year the school received a visit from the League's MVP or some high-profile player that the children would enjoy. He got Aysha's school put on the league's charity list. They received money, equipment, and programs, all complimentary of the NBA. Last year, they'd awarded an all-expense paid trip to the eight grade Valedictorian to the NBA Finals. He thought about Aysha being stipulated to accompany them, but he didn't want her to know he was involved. Luckily for him, the one player's wife that she kept in touch with from Charlotte was very active in the league's community relations department, and Jaylon was able to leverage his relationship with her to get Aysha's school prime partnerships.

Even the way Aysha handled that situation was a testament to the type of person she was. To this day, she and Jaylon had never held a conversation. He'd tried calling her, but found that her cell phone number had changed immediately. Her friends and family respected her wishes too much to give Jaylon her number. He'd tried to bribe Valerie with donations to her shelter, and although she didn't budge, Jaylon still gave Valerie quite a bit of money each year. He also saw to it that the event that was spawned from what should have been his wedding reception became a big hit each year. He'd attended last year, in hopes of seeing her, and was disappointed to find that she coordinated a large part of it, but had never in five years attended the event. In the last five years, it had become one of the most sought-after tickets among black professionals in Houston. Leave it to Aysha to turn the worst event of her life into a charity function for the benefit of others. That was just another illustration of what he loved about her.

It had been five years since she'd walked out of his life, and he still loved her. He'd had relationships, but none of them ever lasted. It seemed most of the women he met were more interested in his money than him. The one woman that he dated for about a year finally called it quits. She knew all about Aysha and told Jaylon that she would not go any further with him because he was in love with someone else, Aysha. And yet, wishing didn't make something so. Jaylon would admit that he loved Aysha, but never in a million years would Aysha admit that she still loved Jaylon.

He wanted to go and comfort her. He knew how close she was to her father. Over the last five years, Jaylon had become like the son that James Rutherford never had. In getting to that position, he'd had to take the browbeating that came when he finally came face to face with Mr. Rutherford after the fiasco with Jada. He knew just how much of a daddy's girl Aysha was, and he didn't know his own father, so he could not begin to imagine what she was going through. Mr. Rutherford was a solid force in his life the last few years, and he was hurting inside, but he knew that Mr. Rutherford depended upon him to make sure Aysha and her mother and sister were okay. Jaylon had a feeling that he was as much the son he wished he'd had to Mr. Rutherford as Mr. Rutherford was the father that he'd wished for. Jaylon hadn't taken much time to realize the loss that he was feeling. He was going to take Mrs. Rutherford home, and be there as much as he could for the family. Selfishly, he was going to be there for Aysha too. He wasn't gracefully bowing out this time.

THREE-3

    Aysha woke up unsure of her surroundings. The mint green walls and Caribbean décor were not in her home. It took her a minute to process where she was, in the guest room at Valerie's home. It took her even longer to get back to the reality of what had transpired. Looking at the clock that was on the nightstand, she realized it was 6:30 a.m. She wished she'd brought clothing. She needed to go for a run. In that moment, Aysha felt tears starting to well up. Certainly, her father had not died. Certainly, Jaylon was not back in her life. Certainly, all of this was just a bad dream, and yet the pain in her heart reminded her just how real it was.

    Aysha began looking around for her purse. She hoped her cell phone was inside. She needed to check on her mother. Well, it was 6:30 a.m., maybe she should not call this early. As a matter of fact, she needed to get up and go to her mother. That thought reminded her that the two people she loathed the most would be there. Certainly, Jada was staying at her parents' home. And, she was still trying to process where Jaylon fit in with her family. Her dad and Jaylon seemed to have a bond, and her mother had asked for Jaylon to drive her home. In addition to feeling lost in her newfound grief, Aysha was also very confused about the dynamics that were obviously operating behind her back. In fact, maybe she should wait to call her mom, she wasn't sure that she could do so without the conversation drifting to Jaylon instead of her mother's loss. Instead of calling her mom, she sent Valerie a text that read, "Wake up, girl". It was the same text that they sent to each other every morning. After a few minutes, Aysha hadn't received a response from Valerie, so she laid back down.

    Within a few minutes of her getting back under the covers, Aysha heard a knock at the door. It was Valerie, with what appeared to be coffee and cake. In fact, it was Aysha's favorite, white chocolate mocha and lemon pound cake from the Pearland Coffee Shop. That made Aysha smile. Valerie sat down on the bed, placed the coffee on the nightstand and gave Aysha a hug. Aysha seemed to melt. She and Valerie had been friends for so long that usually words were just a formality.

"How do you eat all of that sugar so early in the mornin. And, you are still going to want breakfast. Have you spoken to your mom?" Valerie asked.

"I thought about calling, but it is too early. Anyway, I don't know what to say to her. I mean, what can I say? And then just when I thought I was going to call, I could not wrap my mind around Jaylon's presence. I mean, my mom spoke to him like he was her son. And, my dad. I don't even know where to start with that. I just wish you could have seen him. Even on his deathbed, he wanted Jaylon there. I am so unsure of everything right now. But, in a little while I will get up and go home and change and then head to my parents' home".

"It is a lot to process and there is probably not going to be a better time to tell you this than now. I don't want you to be upset or get mad, but Jaylon has been around. He plays golf with your dad a lot. Your dad travels a lot with him, and I even speak to him regularly".

Aysha felt like Valerie had slapped her. How could the people she loved the most be so chummy with the man she hated the most? Better question, how had they kept this from her all of these years. It had been almost five years since she'd seen Jaylon, but obviously he'd been ever present in everyone else's life.

"And, so why did no one bother to tell me about this abundance of love y'all seem to have for Jaylon? When were y'all going to tell me that my feelings didn't matter and that y'all were going behind my back?" Aysha got up out of the bed. She needed to get out of there. She needed to just be alone.

"Never mind, don't answer. Right now, I don't give a shit. I need to go home. Can you please take me home?"

Since her car was still at the school, she would need to make arrangements to get someone to come and open the gate. "Give me a few minutes to make some calls. I need to see if I can get my car from the school, and then go home. If not, then you can drop me at home and I can drive my old truck." Aysha's dad had bought her a brand-new Lexus GS for her last birthday. In fact, her parents had gone overboard for her last birthday. She sank down a little bit. Did her dad know that his health was failing? Didn't Jaylon tell her that her father had a heart attack at the All-Star game? He'd said "third", she needed to know when the other one happened. Aysha sprang up.

"None of this makes any sense. I mean, my dad. MY DAD!! Him and Jaylon were best friends? Are you freaking serious? "

"Aysha, calm down."

"No, Valerie, I don't want to calm down. I mean, let me get it all out. Just how "regularly" do you talk to Jaylon?" Aysha used her fingers to demonstrate quotations on regularly before folding her arms in front of her.

"And, what is his real relationship to my parents? You should have seen them at the hospital. You would have thought he was the prodigal son returning home."

Valerie almost wanted to laugh. It had been a while since she'd seen Aysha go into a sister-girl rant. She knew that if she didn't nip this in the bud, it could last all day. Against, her better judgment, she decided now was probably not the best time to tell Aysha about all of the things Jaylon had done for her over the years. In fact, most of those gifts she got for her last birthday were courtesy of Mr. Flowers, via the Rutherfords and Valerie. Aysha had gotten a new car, new furniture, a trip to Spain, and more of those blue boxes than Valerie could count. And Valerie was complicit in the crime as well. She gave Aysha a $3,500 designer handbag that she swore one of the wives of the players that supported her shelter gave to her. She also gave Aysha her favorite perfume, and floor seats to see the Celtics play in Houston, Dallas, and San Antonio, again swearing that she got them from Jabari Muhammad, Jaylon's best friend, who did a lot of volunteer work at the shelter with the homeless teenagers. Yes, now was probably not the time to tell her that the only gift she's purchased was the perfume, and the rest of it was from Jaylon. He was like the fairy godfather to Aysha. Yet, Valerie was well aware of how proud and independent Aysha was. The thought that someone else had pulled strings was going to be hard for her to swallow. When they finally told her just how many strings Jaylon had pulled over the last few years, she was going to be livid. Yes, Valerie thought, that could wait a little while longer.

Over the past few years, it was obscenely clear to anyone who ever met Jaylon that he was still in love with Aysha. He never discussed the details of what happened with Jada, but his remorse was always visible, and his love for Aysha was so evident. He'd shown Valerie a copy of a print that he had made. It was a picture of Aysha holding a baby. The picture was from the back so that Aysha's face was not visible, but the baby was drawn from a baby picture of Aysha that Jaylon had gotten from her parents. Just last Christmas, Jaylon had given her parents a copy of the picture and it hung in her father's office. Aysha was told that it was Jada holding Lailani. Only Valerie and Jaylon knew that he'd commissioned it to show Aysha holding the child he still hoped to have with her.

Aysha noticed Valerie was not speaking, and just letting her go on and on. She knew what that meant. There was something that Valerie was not telling Aysha. That silence also usually meant that no matter how hard Aysha tried, Valerie was not going to tell her until she was ready. This only got Aysha more riled up.

"Look, we need to get you to your parent's house, and you certainly can't go in there looking like yesterday. So, cut it out, get dressed and let's go. I will even make you some breakfast".
"Where are my godchildren? They can't know that I am here because they would have been in here by now." Aysha asked. She was godmother to all three of Valerie's children. The two girls and one boy loved their "Auntie A", as they all called her.
"No, when I came to the hospital to pick you up, Derrick took them to his mom's. He didn't want them to see you like that. You know they would have wanted to be right in here with you. You know Aaron is attached to you at the hip, and if he'd seen

you crying we would have had to kill him to get away from you". "Awwww. I feel bad. I put my babies out of their house. I will have to make it up to them".

"No, you won't. Every time you "make it up to them" they come home with something that Derrick and I swore to never buy or you take them places that normal 8, 10, and 12, year olds never see. I still can't get Ashala to quit talking about New York City. Who takes a 10-year-old to New York City for their 10th birthday?"

"Whatever. You are just mad because I wouldn't let you go. Shoot, we brought you back a souvenir"

"Yes, you did. That old Canal Street knockoff bag...."

"Well, you are always the one saying, "I don't need a designer bag.", "My purse doesn't have to be Louis Vuitton. Well, guess what, we didn't get you one. Those LV's on your purse stand for "Luis Vato".

They both started laughing so hard that they had tears coming out of their eyes. Valerie leaned over and gave Aysha a hug. They just sat there for a moment.

"You will get through this. Just like you always tell me about the shelter, 'God doesn't bring you to it, unless he is going to help you through it.' Now get up and let's get going."

After Valerie left out, Aysha finished her coffee, got out of the bed and went into the bathroom. Luckily for her Valerie kept extra toiletries in the bathroom. After she washed her face, brushed her teeth, gargled with mouthwash, and combed her hair, Aysha was ready to go. She thought about changing clothes into what she'd worn yesterday, but she had on some of Valerie's sweatpants and a t-shirt, and she was just riding home. Aysha made up the bed, and grabbed all of her things before heading downstairs. She walked into the kitchen and Valerie was making breakfast.

"Egg white omelets for the skinny girl, and a French toast, sausage and scrambled eggs for me".

"No, you didn't. I eat French toast, too"

"Just kidding girl. I got you. And, I can't eat sausage anymore.

Derrick and I both just had checkups and our blood pressure and cholesterol levels were higher than normal. Nothing to get alarmed about, but we want to start making changes before we have to"

Aysha got sad. The tears started to fall. Everyone knew that Aysha loved French toast, and that she loved her dad's the best. Only, she'd never have it again. He wouldn't be coming to cut her grass tomorrow, and hounding her about going to church. He wouldn't be able to pick up and deliver the food for the events she did for her children. He wouldn't be able to call her up on game night and say, "Hey, Kitty, Kitty, rooting for the wrong city city". He hated the Celtics, and she loved them. She'd planned to go over and watch the playoffs with him. Neither of their teams were playing, and neither was Jaylon's team, so she planned to watch with her dad. The tears flowed uncontrollably. She could not imagine what her mom was going through. She reached for her phone and called her mom. Jaylon answered the phone.

"The Rutherford's home." Jaylon answered.

"Uhm, uhm, Jaylon (she actually said his name out loud), how is my mom doing?", Aysha asked hesistantly.

"Aysha... Uhm, well, she is better than I expected. She is more worried about you and Jada than anything." He got silent. Aysha didn't know what to say either. This was very awkward. She had played out for years what she would finally say to Jaylon, and never did she anticipate that he would be on her parents' phone when the conversation occurred. Before she could gather her words, Jaylon continued.

"Uhm, Uhm....well, I stayed here with her last night, and she stayed up all night talking about your dad. She told me how they met and all kinds of stuff. I can get her if you'd like."

"No, no, wait a minute. I think I would rather come and see her in person. I am at Valerie's but let her know that I am on my way over. And, Jaylon, thank you for being there for my mom".

"No thanks needed, your parents have been here for me. I will tell her you are on the way".

Aysha could have slapped herself. Here she was throwing a pity party because everyone was lovey dovey with Jaylon, and she was oblivious to the fact that her mom had lost her husband of 37 years. Everyone told Aysha that she was a spoiled brat, and she never once saw it that way. Now at 32 years old, it took her father dying for her to see just how immersed in her own world she actually was. Even on his deathbed, her father was prodding her out of her selfish ways. She shuddered at how she'd treated her sister yesterday. No, they didn't have to be best friends, but you would think that with their dad dying that Aysha could have mustered up a little more compassion towards her sister. They could go back to their corners after the services, but right now, she knew that her mom needed them, TOGETHER. She also knew that she needed to put her feelings about Jaylon to the side, for now. He was obviously a part of her family's life, and she didn't want to mar the remembrances and celebrations of her father's life by broadcasting her hate and animosity. She'd put on a good face. She had to. Both her mother and her father's memory deserved that.

Before she could process that thought, she heard the reporter say, "Jaylon Flowers' father passed on yesterday". She looked up to the television and was shocked. Why was this happening? Just when she was willing to call a truce, the news story shattered that. She needed to get to the bottom of this. Her dad's picture showed up on the screen, and the reporter stated that "Mr. Flowers could not be reached for a comment". This whole situation was becoming a bit much. Not only did she lose her dad, but also it seemed like she was losing his memory. To Jaylon. How much more could he take from her? Her sister? Her heart? Her friends? Her family? Her father? That truce was beginning to look more and more outlandish. She had some words she needed to say to him.

Aysha was so engrossed in her thoughts that she cleaned her plate without tasting a thing. In fact, when she looked up Valerie had left the room. She walked back in as soon as Aysha stood to put her plate in the sink. Aysha turned to look at Valerie. She lost the words. She wanted to lash out at Valerie's chumminess with Jaylon, but that wasn't the answer. She was going to get to the root of this. She'd avoided him for the last few years. Today, it would all come to a head. Aysha was well aware that this might not be the right time, or place, but she was going to put Jaylon in his place: OUT OF HER LIFE.

"Valerie, I am ready to go. If you will take me home, I will get changed and then I can go to my mom's." She didn't know which emotion was more powerful right now, the grief or the anger. Perhaps, the grief was feeding the anger, or vice versa.

"Aysha, I know you don't want to hear this".

"Val, don't take this the wrong way, but I don't want to hear it, so let it go. At some point in this process, Jaylon and I will have to air out our past. I left a lot of things unsaid when I walked away from him, but I promise you, that will not be the case this time." Aysha got up and walked out of the door into the garage. Valerie rolled her eyes and went on.

Valerie and Aysha had been friends for a long time. They always would be, and Valerie had always stood by Aysha, right or wrong. This time, she knew the fallout would be big. Aysha had suppressed so much of her pain since she and Jaylon broke up. She'd bought a mansion in denial. She poured the love into the students, she doted on Valerie's children, and she volunteered with any organization that had a smiling baby on its' logo. Aysha ran herself ragged filling those spaces with the love that she didn't have. Her father always refilled her tank. Their French toast breakfasts, Sunday sports games, Friday night fish fry and yearly vacation kept Aysha sane. Valerie could not comprehend the voids that Aysha would have. Despite the amount of time that had passed, she hoped beyond all hope that Aysha would give Jaylon another chance, but Aysha was nothing, if not stubborn.

As they drove to Aysha's place, Valerie looked over and saw Aysha crying. Having lost her dad three years before, Valerie was familiar with the grief that Aysha was experiencing. There were no words. All of the empty phrases that people said were meaningless, and sometimes hurtful. "You'll get over it", "It will be alright", "He is in a better place now". Just reminiscing made Valerie want to scream. She didn't notice the tears coming down her own face at the remembrance of her own loss, and at the acknowledgment of what her friend was going through.

They pulled up to Aysha's home. It was a three-story loft style space in the Heights area of Houston. There were 12 houses, and they were so close together that most people assumed they were townhouses. Valerie had a garage door opener for Aysha's home in her car. She also had a key in case of emergency. She opened the garage and they pulled into the garage next to Aysha's old truck. It didn't get much use since Aysha drove the Lexus that her dad gave her for her most recent birthday.

Aysha went in and took a quick shower and changed clothing. She came out with a black baseball cap, black fitted t-shirt with a rhinestone logo on the front, black cargo, Capri pants, and black sandals. She looked like the new millennium version of Janet Jackson from the "Pleasure Principle" video Valerie took one look at her and started laughing. Her laughter startled Aysha, who walked over to the bar stools where Valerie was sitting.

"Uhm, what are you laughing at?". Aysha asked.
'You." Valerie giggled. "Did you look at yourself in the mirror"
"Yes, what are you talking about? I have on all black. What?" Aysha replied, with a shrug of her shoulders.
"I know you are grieving, and all, but you look like Janet Jackson on break from filming 'Pleasure Principle' or 'Rhythm Nation". Can you put on something with some color? You are going to scare the hell out of your mother if you go over there like that." Valerie kept on laughing.
"Forget you, girl. I am not listening to you. Everybody knows that Mama Val ain't known for her style. So, you know I am not changing a thing."

Valerie got up from the stool and started doing some

dance moves and singing "We're all a part of a Rhythm Nation". She was laughing so hard that she could not do the move. She was able to do a hand movement that Aysha recognized from the 'Pleasure Principle" video.

"I swear I can't stand you" Aysha yelled, as she went back into her bedroom to change her shirt. She ended up putting on a pink and green shirt with her sorority logo on the front.

"Is this better?" she asked as she returned to the living room.

"C'mon 'soror" Janet Jackson. We need to see if your mother needs help with anything."

Aysha just rolled her eyes at Valerie and headed to the garage. She thought about driving but decided against it. With all of the people that were sure to be at her parent's home, someone would be available to bring her home. Worst-case scenario, she could always drive her dad's car. Just last year, he'd bought himself the Lexus LS. He would not let anyone drive the car. He would always say he was going to be dead and gone when he let Aysha and her lead foot drive his car. She almost started crying again, as she realized how true that was.

When they got to the Rutherford home, there were cars everywhere. For a moment, it seemed like a typical summer Saturday when her dad would barbecue and invite the whole world over. Her parents had a large social circle, and her dad had a very large family. Her dad's barbecue was legendary, and her mom's desserts always brought in the most money at bake sales and silent auctions. At least one Saturday a month, they cooked and opened the house to anyone who wanted to come.

When she looked up towards her parents' front door, she was brought back to reality. Her mother was standing in the doorway with Jaylon next to her, and Reverend Pritchett, the minister from her parents' church, was standing there with them. He gave her mother a hug and turned to walk away. He saw Aysha and waved at her. She did not want to talk to Reverend Pritchett. She saw him occasionally when she went to church with her parents on special occasions, and he always tried to recruit Aysha to come back to his church. She'd grown up in the pews of the God's Way Church, been baptized by Reverend Pritchett, but after going away to college, she'd only gone back as a visitor. She knew Reverend Pritchett would use this as an opportunity to try to save her soul. She was not in the mood. She waved at him, and turned and pretended to be talking to Valerie.

"You know I am not going up to the house as long as Reverend Pritchett is standing on the porch". Aysha said.

Valerie started laughing. "You better go on up there and receive your blessing. Sow your seed, and reap your harvest".

"Ain't nobody reaping a harvest but him. I bet that is his black Bentley in the driveway. How much do you want to bet? I told my dad he should be part owner of the church, as much money as my family puts into it".

"Well, I am not complaining. The good Reverend hosts several musicals and revivals and the proceeds go to the "Hazel House". Hazel House was the name of Valerie's shelter. The shelter had grown to include housing for 25 families in a building that resembled the first floor of the dorm Aysha and Valerie lived in when they were in college. It had a lobby and family room, and a community kitchen. There were community bathrooms as well. Each family room had a twin bed, and then a set of bunk beds. Some rooms had two sets of bunk beds to accommodate women with more than two children. Of the 25 rooms at the shelter, five of the rooms were designated for two-parent families.

Aysha finally got out of the car. The morning had given her the chance to put some things into perspective. She had set her priorities. Right now, she had to focus on her mother, her own grief, and burying her father with the dignity that he deserved. She would put her grudges to the side. She would not embrace her sister, and she would hold her venom in check. She would not befriend Jaylon, but she was sure that she could tolerate him for the sake of her father.

She walked up and gave her mother a hug. She seemed smaller than she was on yesterday. Jaylon stood next to her, and

Aysha just looked at him, and did not say a word. He looked like he was bracing himself for her to lash out, and a part of her felt petty because he expected that of her. However, a larger part of her was happy that he was aware of just what she was really thinking about his presence. In spite of herself, Aysha grabbed her mom's hand and walked in. Valerie and Jaylon came in behind them. Aysha was talking to her mom, but she noticed that Jaylon and Valerie went into her dad's study, while she and her mom went into the family room. There were so many people in there. Her aunts, uncles, cousins, neighbors, and her grandmother were all there. There appeared to be 100 people in the room, although logically she knew the number was closer to about 20 people. Immediately, Aysha was assaulted by a barrage of "Hello's, Hi's, "Kitty are you okay". She couldn't distinguish who was saying what, and it felt like she was experiencing an episode of vertigo. Before she could answer, it seemed that her mother was walking her to the sofa. Jada came over and stood over her.

"Kitty, are you okay? You don't look so good". Jada said. Aysha wanted to wave her away, but she really didn't feel so good. The fact that everyone was here, and her father wasn't reminded her of the calamity that was her father's death. She closed her eyes. The tears started to fall, and in a few seconds, she was aware of the domino effect that occurred when one person cried. She tried to stand up, but there were so many arms trying to hold and console her. She opened her eyes to see her mother sitting beside her and Jaylon and Valerie entering the room. She immediately noticed the concern on Jaylon's face. He walked over to her.

"Please get me out of here" She whispered. She turned and looked at her mother. "I am sorry mommie. I came to be here for you, but I can't do this".

"Oh, my baby. Don't worry. We have all been so worried about you. Everybody knows about your relationship with your dad, and we were all just trying to make sure you would be okay."

"I am going up to my room. I will be back down later when I can get it together.

Aysha knew that grief was powerful, but when she got up and leaned into Jaylon and allowed him to lead her out of the family room, she was shocked. She'd planned to bury the hatchet for a few days, but this was more than she'd planned. But, at the moment, her options were few. She knew Valerie would stay with her as long as she needed her to. But, Val had a family and she needed to go and attend to them. Aysha was going to have to take the big girl pill and make it through this week, and as much as she hated to admit it, Jaylon could help her.

"I will be okay. Don't worry about me, Val. Go home and tell Derrick and the children that I am fine. I will come over later this week to hang out with the girls. But I don't want you to worry about me".

"I have been worried about you since the first day we met. But, your family is here, and Jaylon is here, so I know that you will be okay. Are you going to stay over here tonight?"

"No. I will go home this evening. Right now, I just need to get myself together and then I can go and be with my family. One of them will take me home, or I can take my mom's car". She realized that despite her earlier thoughts, she was not going to be able to drive her dad's car.

"Okay, I will see you later. Let me know when y'all go to make the arrangements and all. I will come with you".

"Okay. Thank you and I love you, friend"

"I love you, too"

They hugged and Valerie left as Jaylon walked Aysha up to her room. Once inside of her room, she laid on the bed. She didn't say anything, and the tears started to fall again. Jaylon got up and left the room for about two minutes, and returned with a box of tissue. He handed them to Aysha.

"We need to talk. There are some things that you need to know"

"Jaylon, let's not go there. I need to get through burying my father and then we can have this conversation."

"No, this can't wait. As a matter of fact, it is very, very important that we have THIS conversation before your father is buried".

"Are you serious? My father is dead, and you want to talk about how trifling you and my sister really are."

Jaylon was expecting that attitude. He was also determined not to feed it. As a matter of fact, he would not even acknowledge it. Aysha was entitled to her feelings, and he had waited her out this long, and he had no intentions of giving up.

"Remember in the hospital when your father said to tell you everything. Well, that everything is what we need to talk about."

"Jaylon, can't this wait. I mean, I can't do this right now". Aysha was getting frustrated with this conversation, and regretting that she'd asked Jaylon to escort her upstairs to her room.

"Okay, Aysha, I won't press the issue today, but your mother wants to bury your father on Friday, and we will have this conversation before then whether you like it or not ".

"Who the hell are you to tell me anything? I promised myself that I would be cordial towards you and you are not making this easy. I am putting on a happy face with you and Jada for my family's sake, but don't think for one minute that I have let you off the hook."

"Of course not. Not Aysha. Not the goody two shoes, pristine, perfect Aysha. God forbid she let's anyone off of the hook." Jaylon walked to the other side of the room and sat in the chair. He put his face into his hands and exhaled deeply. Aysha recalled that he used to do that when she was being dramatic.

It had been five years, and not a day went by that Jaylon didn't think about Aysha and how he'd hurt her. He spent more time with her parents than he spent with his mom. His mother and Mrs. Rutherford were good friends. They became friends when Aysha and Jaylon were dating, but after the engagement Jaylon's mother moved to Houston and her and Mrs. Rutherford were like giggling 6th graders when there were together. It hurt her tremendously to know what he'd been accused of, as she was very close to Aysha. It hurt her more that Aysha cut off most all contact with her after Aysha moved back to Houston. They all talked to Jaylon about going on with his life. He'd tried, but at the end of the day, he wanted Aysha. Her dad begged him to go on with his life. He didn't hold out much hope that his 'Lil' Kitty" would forgive Jaylon in this lifetime. Nonetheless, he kept Jaylon up to date on ever facet of Aysha's personal and professional life. Sometimes, Jaylon felt that he was stalking her, but she left him no choice when she refused any contact with him.

"Aysha, your dad asked me to tell you the truth about some things. I will honor his wish. I won't push you today, or tomorrow, but before the week is up, you are going to hear what I have to say".

"Whatever. I don't want to talk to you anymore. As a matter of fact, can you leave my room? Just for the record, I am not perfect. Far from it, but I don't count lying up with my fiancé's sister as one of my sins. So, you can sit over there and call names and puff out your chest because of some perceived authority that my father gave up by sharing his secrets with you, but don't throw stones at me unless you want to shatter that glass house you live in. Now, if you really want to be useful, leave me he hell alone."

Aysha rolled over and turned her back to Jaylon. The nerve of him to try to read her. She was having no parts of it. However, she had to admit that her curiosity was getting the best of her. She did need to know what her dad meant when he told Jaylon to tell her everything. She would have to swallow her pride and talk to him. She had no idea what he would say, but the sooner they could talk, the sooner she would get to the bottom of this relationship that he seemed to have with her family.

She was on the bed for about five minutes, when it dawned on her that Jaylon had not left. She must admit that lashing out at him did not feel nearly as good as she thought it would. At the same time, she wondered who died and left him in charge? But the reality was obvious. Her father had trusted Jaylon far more than she did, and he'd died. Somehow that resulted in Jaylon being in charge, but he was not the boss of her. She still wondered why he didn't leave like she asked him to. Before she could do anything else, there was a knock at the door, and the door opened. It was her godmother, Mrs. Beverly. Mrs. Beverly came in the room, and gave Jaylon a hug and a kiss on the cheek, which infuriated Aysha, although she didn't show it. Then she came over and sat on the bed beside her.

"Hey, Bug, are you alright? Your mom told me that you were up here with Jaylon. I didn't hear any furniture crashing, so I figured I might need to check and see for myself that you hadn't killed the poor boy." Nana chuckled at her own joke, as she often did. Her godmother had a rosy sense of humor, and could find a reason to laugh no matter the occasion.

"Yes, Nana, I am good." She glared at Jaylon, and rolled her eyes. "Just a bit overwhelmed by all of the people downstairs. I came to see momma, and was not expecting everyone, and it just kind of knocked me off kilter for a minute, but I am fine".

"Are you hungry? Jaylon can get you something to eat. I think there is enough food to be a mall food court down there. Mexican food, pizza, chicken, and of course your favorite soul food. "

"No, I ate at Valerie's, but I could use something to drink"

Jaylon left out of the room. Aysha assumed he was going to get her something to drink. Her godmother leaned over and gave her a hug.

"Sweetie, I know you don't want to hear this, but how long do you plan to make that boy suffer? Everyone makes mistakes, Aysha. Sometimes, you have to let bygones be bygones. But, I know love when I see it, and it as plain as day that the boy still loves you."

Aysha didn't say a word for a minute. She was trying to choose her words carefully, and control her brewing anger at the same time.

"Obviously he loved Jada too, hunh. How come I have to be the bigger person? Really, I just wish everyone would let it go. The next stage of my life is going to be hard enough without me having to fend off a million questions about Jaylon. Why is he even here? Can somebody just tell me that?" She rolled her eyes, and fell into her godmother's arms.

"Aysha, baby, you cut Jaylon out of your life. That doesn't give you the right to tell us how to feel about him. Yes, everyone was upset and angry with what happened, but your sister was as much to blame. So, should we hate her too?

"You really want me to answer that. You know what... Never mind. I am going home. Ya'll sit over here with the happy family, but I am just not going to be able to pretend like I am not still hurt by this. Nana, I tried, but I can't do this". Aysha got up to leave. She looked at the foot of the bed for her shoes.

"Aysha, don't go. I will leave. You should be here with your family". Jaylon had come back into the room, and he had brought Aysha her favorite vice, Diet Dr. Pepper.

"And make me look like the villain.... Poor, brat Aysha...... Right. No, you stay and continue to play, 'Captain Save-a- Ho' to my family and I am out". Aysha headed towards the door. What little patience she thought she had when she decided to come here was eroded. All of these people could just kick rocks.

"Aysha!" Her nana never used that tone unless Aysha was out of line. In fact, she'd rarely ever called Aysha by her name, preferring to call her "Bug", as Aysha was known to "bug" people until they gave her what she wanted. She knew that she had crossed the line. But, why couldn't they all understand that she was just not ready to let go of this. It had been five years. There were days when it seemed like yesterday. Why couldn't they understand?

"Look, little girl. You can act all mean and evil with everybody else, but you will show me some respect or we will have a problem. Actually, I don't see why the boy doesn't go on with his life. I wouldn't spend one minute putting up with your spoiled ass, and I don't know why he does. Well, yes, I do, because he loves you. Because he knows that he made a mistake. So, if it makes you feel like the bigger person to walk around with the "woe is me, they did me wrong" victim chip on your shoulder, do it. But the next time you get beside yourself and use that kind of language in front of me, you will need a "Captain Save-a-Ho" to save you. Let me go back down stairs before we have to bury you with your daddy". Her nana walked out of the room before Aysha could respond.

She knew she'd overstepped her boundaries. Her god-mother never got angry with her. The fact that she spoke to Aysha like that let her know just how angry she really was with her. After her Nana left the room Aysha just rolled over on the bed. She was sad. Her dad would have taken her side. Well, maybe no. She was wrong. Actually, her dad had obviously not taken her side, since according to the news report, he was Jaylon's dad. In 24 hours, her whole world was collapsing.

Aysha got up and went downstairs. She was intercepted by her family members, who wanted to be sure she was feeling okay. Every one of them commented on how nice it was for Jaylon to be with her during this time. Was she in the freaking Twilight Zone? Had she really been this oblivious to what was going on? Were they really serious? She walked into the room and sat beside her mom. She leaned her head and let it rest on her mother's shoulder. Only then did she realize that it was Jada seated next to her mom on the other side. She heard her mother exhale loudly.

"If your dad could see this moment, it would have made his day. Too bad it took me to lose my husband to get my girls together". That was the straw that broke the camel's back. Without saying a word, Aysha got up, and walked outside. Then she remembered that she rode with Valerie. She needed to get home, but at the moment she was somewhat stranded.

Jaylon walked out of the door and saw her standing in the driveway.

"Valerie left. Did you ride with her?"

Aysha ignored him. There was no audience, so, there was no need to be nice to him. She'd come to comfort her mother, and to be with her family, and he was the cloud hanging over the storm.

FOUR-4

"Aysha, I can take you home". Jaylon walked towards her. He saw her start to walk away. It bothered him that she suddenly seemed repulsed by him. In reality, Aysha didn't want him to see her crying. She'd cried enough tears because of him. What she really wanted was to be able to call her dad and tell him how horribly wrong this day was turning out, and that reminder of the real reason she was at her parents' home threatened to knock the air out of her again. She walked over to the post in the front yard and leaned on it. Aysha knew her limits. She wiped her tears and turned to face Jaylon.

"Yes, you can take me home. And, you can also tell me what the big secret is." Aysha looked Jaylon right in his eyes. Suddenly, that didn't seem like a good idea. His expression softened in a way that was not expected, and it put a little damper on the rage that was building. She wanted to go off, but it seemed that nothing she did antagonized Jaylon as much as his sheer presence antagonized her. She also knew that she was reaching her emotional breaking point, and a total and complete meltdown was not what Aysha was aiming to have.

"Before I take you home, is there somewhere that we can go and talk. I will tell you everything that your father wanted you to know." Jaylon knew that he should tread lightly, but he was excited at the prospect of being with Aysha. It didn't seem right to take joy in the fact that her grief was the only reason she was letting down her wall, but it had been nearly five years since Jaylon had seen Aysha up close. He'd caught glimpses of her around Houston, and narrowly missed her in passing to and from her parents' home over the years. No matter the underlying circumstances, Jaylon was simply content to just be with Aysha. This time, he was intent that she would not shut him out of her life again, even if that meant taking advantage of her father's death to ensure it.

"No, you tell me. If I remember correctly, you can attract quite a crowd. Is there somewhere you feel comfortable where we won't be bothered by your fan club?" Aysha recalled what it was like to be out with Jaylon. There were so many times when fans would come up to them and interrupt their evenings and outings. Most were respectful, but sometimes they were not. Aysha would never forget the night that they were out with players from the different leagues, football, basketball, and baseball, at the Music Festival in New Orleans. She and Jaylon were on the dance floor dancing and being silly like they always did when they were out together. Aysha noticed one female seemed to be trying very hard to get Jaylon's attention. After a few minutes of being ignored, the female walked right up to Jaylon and opened her dress, and starting gyrating. Aysha turned around and saw the girl, and lost it. It took Jaylon and one of the wide receivers from the Dallas Cowboys to pull Aysha off of the floor. She caused such a scene that Jaylon's teammates called her "Miss Set It Off" after that. Even when she'd run into many of the guys who were in the club that night at the charity events for the shelter, they still never let her live that night down. Yes, she remembered what it was like to be with Jaylon.

"Aysha, we can go to my house", Jaylon offered.

"No, we cannot!" Aysha rolled her eyes and was totally flabbergasted. She had said five words to Jaylon, and he already had her at his house. Was she missing something?

"Jaylon, look. I don't know where you are trying to go with this".

Jaylon grabbed her arm, and Aysha shook it free from his hold.

"Aysha, just think about it. I can assure you that what I am about to tell you is going to be somewhat emotional. Are you sure that you want to be sitting out in the open when I tell you?"

"You might have a point, but I am not going to your house."

"Okay, let's go to Hermann Park. We can walk around the park and talk". Jaylon was grasping at straws. He was not going to let this opportunity to be with Aysha pass over something as trivial as the location.

"In Houston? In May? At noon? Do you have a death wish or something? I know you and my dad were buddy-buddy but unless you plan on meeting him today, Hermann Park is not going to be your best option".

"Okay, I have an idea. I know a bar in the Heights that has a private room. Let's go and see if they will let us use it. If not, we will be close to your place and I can drop you off".

Aysha swung around to look at Jaylon. She was a bit confused. Did he just suggest her neighborhood, and hint that he knew where she lived?

"The Heights.... By my house? As a matter of fact, let's just go to my house. I have a feeling that I am going to need to sit down for this. Where is your car?"

Jaylon motioned towards the Black Bentley that was in the driveway. Aysha rolled her eyes. She should have known. Jaylon wasn't the extravagant type. Despite the amount of money that he had, he was never frivolous. The car told her that obviously a lot had changed about Jaylon since she'd known him.

"Uhm... Bentley. I guess your frugality is not what it used to be".

"Whatever, Aysha. You know I am good about my money. This car was a splurge. A gift to myself. I can afford it. I bought your dad one for Father's Day last year, but he made me take it back. He didn't think he could explain to you how he got it. I was able to talk him into getting the Lexus. That, he could explain to you."

Aysha walked to the car. Jaylon was ever the gentleman, opening the door for her. After he went around and got in on the driver's side, Aysha turned to him in he car. She was in shock. Jaylon bought her dad a $200,000 car? And, he didn't accept it because of her. Wow! Suddenly, she was feeling very selfish. She'd seen her dad fawn over that car at the car shows they attended. He always said that he would buy one, but he'd have to live in it. Her mother was the more practical of the two when it came to finances. Had her dad given up his dream car just to spare her feelings? This day was getting worse and worse.

"What? Wait! Back up. You bought my father a $200,000 car. Why?" Aysha asked. She was beside herself. This relationship between her dad and Jaylon was obviously more than she thought. Way more. It would definitely explain why the media and the rest of the world thought her dad was Jaylon's dad. All-Star games, Bentley's, Super Bowls. Aysha just leaned back in the passenger's seat because her head was spinning, and she felt a migraine coming on.

Jaylon didn't respond to Aysha. He knew her well enough to know that no matter what he said, she would twist it. Therefore, he chose to just say nothing. They drove to Aysha's house in silence. It did not go unnoticed by Aysha that Jaylon knew exactly where she lived. Even with the 12 units together, he pulled right up to the one that was her home. Aysha decided that she would address it all once they got inside.

When Jaylon pulled in, Aysha sat in the car and waited for Jaylon to come around and open the door. Some habits died hard. When they first started dated, Jaylon rarely opened her door. On many occasions, Aysha stayed in the car until Jaylon opened the door. After a while, it became more of a joke between them, and Jaylon never let her open doors when he was around. He came around and she got out of the car without acknowledging him. This was going to be more difficult than either of them thought.

Aysha walked up to her front door, and unlocked the door. The alarms started to squeal and Aysha walked over to the panel and shut it off. Jaylon walked in behind her. He took note of the bright and airy feel of Aysha's living room. The walls were painted a rustic orange color. Jaylon would have never chosen the color, but it suited Aysha. She'd decorated her place nicely. Jaylon notices a few of the picture frames and figurines that he'd given to her parents' for Aysha. Everyone knew that she had a fascination with all things with carousels on them. Jaylon had bought her a crystal carousel that cost well over $1,000. He was sure her dad had not told her how much it cost. He walked over and picked it up when he saw it.

"Please put that down. My dad gave that to me". Aysha walked over and took it out of Jaylon's hand. Jaylon just chuckled. *All things in due time*, he thought.

"Is it okay if I have a seat?" Jaylon asked. He was aware

that what he was about to tell Aysha was going to devastate her. He took out his phone and sent Valerie a text. "All secrets are coming out tonight. Be on standby, Ay is going to need you". Before he could put his phone away, Valerie responded, "Do you want me to come over now?". "No, not yet. I will keep you posted".

"Hmppph. Checking in"

"And if I was?" Jaylon asked. He was done being bullied by Aysha. He'd listened to all of her comments yesterday and today. It had taken him a long time to learn when to let it go with her, and when to stand his ground. Today he was standing his ground. This was the last minute in the last round of the championship fight. Everything was on the line. How things went tonight would determine whether or not he and Aysha would ever have a chance, and if he had anything to say about it he would be victorious.

"You are right, it is none of my business." Aysha felt a sting of jealousy. For real? She was not sure where that came from. Certainly, after almost five years, she did not have any feelings for Jaylon. Well, she did hate him, or she tried to. But in that moment, she was reminded of what her godmother, who just happened to be Jaylon's biggest cheerleader, always told her: Behind anger and hate, there is hate and love.

Aysha pushed all of that out of her head. Jaylon was who he was and had a life and he could talk to or date whomever he wanted. They weren't together and would never be together.

"I am about to pour me a drink, can I get you something?"

"Shoot, if you are offering, I have to say yes. What do you have?"

"Water and Dr. Pepper." Aysha leveled that response with an overwhelming amount of sarcasm causing Jaylon to laugh.

Aysha was still so predictable. Just to humor himself, he said, "You don't have any juice?"

"You know good and well that I don't drink juice. I would still much rather soda to juice. But, there might be a juice box in the fridge from when Val's children come over".

Aysha didn't see Jaylon laughing. He knew she didn't have juice and was just trying to push her buttons. Aysha returned from the kitchen with two glasses of Dr. Pepper.

Jaylon was seated on a bar stool, and Aysha chose to curl up on the chaise lounge that was across the room. The silence was killing them both. Jaylon knew what he had to say, but he didn't know how to say it.

"First of all, Aysha, can we go back to the day you walked in on Jada and me".

The look on Aysha's face turned murderous. What was she thinking? Somewhere inside she thought that after five years she was strong enough to handle this. Right now, she was not so sure. She'd played it out a million times in her head. She'd decided on exactly the caustic words that she would use when she finally spoke to Jaylon, and somehow, now that the moment had arisen, the whole script escaped her. No, today was not going to be the day.

"Jaylon, I am sorry, but this is not going to be a good idea". I can't do this right now. I need you to leave."

"Aysha, just listen"

"No, Jaylon. I can't. I lost my dad yesterday, and right now I can't dredge up that day. I thought I was ready to put all of this to rest and I can't".

"Okay, Aysha". Jaylon could never deny her anything. The hurt and fear that he saw on her face was enough to break him. He'd known that his actions had devastated her, but it was nothing like seeing the hurt in her eyes to bring it home. This was the first time in five years, since that day when she drove by him in his driveway that they had a chance to even talk. She had refused all contact with him, and then to have to resume their communication under these circumstances. This was not how he envisioned his reunion with Aysha. He stopped short of berating himself. God knows he'd done more than enough of that over the years.

"Aysha, just understand that there are some things that I have to tell you from your father, and some things that we have to get straight. The things between you and I can wait, but the information from your father cannot."

"Okay, but not today. I can't deal with this today. I mean, I used to crawl on my dad's lap and tell him all about it, and for the first time, he is not here. I can't do it. Jaylon, I just can't do it". Aysha was borderline hysterical. She was crying so hard that she could barely get the words out. Jaylon was at a loss for what to do. He walked over to her, but she stiffened in a way that let him know that she did not want his comfort. He went back, got his phone, and called Valerie.

"Hey, Val. She's not ready. I am going to leave, but can you please come and stay with her. I will let her mom know how she is doing, but she can't be alone and she doesn't want me here."

Aysha could hear the hurt in his voice, but she was hard pressed to do anything about it. The gulf that was between them was threatening to drown her. She was already teetering on the edge, trying to forget the fact that her father was dead. Trying to pretend that this was all just a dream that she would soon awake from. That, by itself, made her sanity very fragile. With Jaylon dredging up the one moment that, prior to her father's death, was the worst moment of her life, she was not sure how long she could hold on. In fact, she just wanted to close her eyes and forget. Without acknowledging Jaylon, she slid down the chaise lounge and tried to do just that. She closed her eyes, and began the meditative breathing that she'd learned in her hot yoga classes. She needed to be transported to another place. Slowly she felt herself become disconnected from her surroundings, her thoughts, her feelings, and herself. When she awoke, Valerie was sitting on the floor next to her, and Jaylon was stretched out on a rug next to her couch. They both were staring at her with looks of concern. She didn't know how much time had passed, but she was sure that enough time would never pass for her to deal with her current circumstances. Yet, she knew that she could not just close down to the world. Life had to go on.

"Ay, are you up? Can I get you anything"? Valerie asked.

"Naw, you sit here with her, I will get her something to drink", Jaylon said.

Aysha sat up with a new awareness of grief. She glanced at Jaylon as he headed into her kitchen, and she hated him thoroughly, but she wasn't blind. No matter how hard she tried to deny it, he was a fine example of God's work. She still felt a physical attraction to him that was not dampened by the static between them. As he stood, she could only appreciate the whole 6'5" package that was Jaylon Flowers. He'd changed clothing, and was wearing a gray t-shirt, and jeans. How long had she been asleep?

"Val, when did you get here?" Aysha asked.

Valerie responded by telling her that she'd been there for about three hours. Jaylon called her before she went to sleep.

"Why is he still here?".

"He was leaving as soon as I got here, but I asked him to stay. He took a shower, and changed clothes.

"In my house?' Aysha interrupted.

"Uhm, yes."

"Y'all are getting on my nerves with this. Exactly what made you all think that Jaylon showering in my bathroom was going to be okay with me?"

"Well, considering that you have the shower on the garage level that you have NEVER used, I thought that might be okay. Besides, you can get over it, but the boy has some stuff that he needs to say to you and he needs to say it today."

"I thought I told him that I did not want to talk about that".

"Aysha, get over yourself. This is not about you. He has things that you need to hear about from your father. You are going to hear it whether you want to or not and then you can put us both out". Valerie seemed a bit more rattled and wound up than usual. Aysha was going to revisit that later, but right now, she needed to consider what it was that Valerie said. The truth was not going to get any sweeter, and she knew that she needed to just hear Jaylon out. It was past time for her to get an explanation on what had been happening behind her back for the last five years.

Aysha sighed loudly. This was getting more ridiculous by the minute. Didn't anyone seem to notice that her father was dead and she was grieving? She had enough to deal with without all of this. She was grieving and all everyone could think about was she and Jaylon. She was sick of this, and decided that the best way to get him out of her life was to go ahead and let him have his say. Jaylon walked back into the room. She wanted to roll her eyes at him, but in light of Val's last verbal tap, she thought that would be a bit childish. He handed her a bottle of water and a bottle of Dr. Pepper. He was staring directly at her, but she averted his gaze, never looking directly at him.

"Aysha, do you want me to stay while you two talk?" Val asked.

"No. You can go. I know you need to check on your family. There is no need in drawing this out. So, the quicker we get this over with, the quicker Jaylon can go. I am sure he has other things to do". Aysha got up to walk Valerie to the door. She ended up outside in the drive way and they chatted for a few minutes before she went back inside.

Jaylon wanted to respond to remark about him having somewhere to go, but he knew Aysha was baiting him. He knew that as long as she was in this mood she would use every chance to make a snide remark. Five years ago, Jaylon would have played right into her hands. Having dissected every single moment that they had ever spent together, he knew Aysha very well. With this knowledge, he sat quietly and just looked at Aysha. She stared intently at him, and it was obvious she was waiting for him to say something.

"Aysha, what I am going to tell you is going to be a little hard to hear, but your father was adamant that should something happen to him, you were to be told as soon as possible".

"Let's skip the speech. Just say what it is."

"Aysha, you have a sister."

"I know that, and I thought we were not going to bring all of that up".

Jaylon looked away. He moved closer to Aysha, but still made no attempt to touch her. Her eyes followed him.

"You don't understand. You and Jada have another sister. Her name is Mia."

"I am lost. What?"

"Aysha, you have a sister that is older than you and Jada"

"Does my mom know this?

"Yes, your mother knows. She is your mother's daughter".

"Okay, wait. You are trying to tell me that my parents have another daughter. Wait!!! He told YOU this?"

Aysha was in shock. She looked around for her cell phone. She needed to call her mother. She needed some truth from somewhere.

"She is 3 years older than Jada."

"Why didn't my mother tell me this?"

"She knows that I am going to tell you. She gave her blessing for me to do so. Your sister's name is Mia, and she is coming to the funeral. Your mom wants you to meet her before the funeral."

Aysha's brain was spinning, but when it stopped, she had more questions. More anger. More hurt.

"Jaylon, please start over from the beginning. I don't understand. I don't understand any of this. I need to talk to my mom. Where is my phone?" Aysha was very agitated now. Where was all of this new information coming from? She was the main character in a soap opera that did not let up on the drama.

"Aysha, just calm down, please. I have more to tell you."

"Don't tell me to calm down. Not only have you all been sneaking behind my back and keeping secrets for the last five years, but also my parents have been keeping this secret for 30 years. Are you freaking serious? Hell no, I don't want to calm down. And wait! Did you just say that you have more to tell me? Oh, Lord! My daddy sure does know how to die…. Just when we are burying his body, y'all decide to dig up all the family skeletons. Please get my mom on the phone."

Aysha sat up and swung her legs around the chaise lounge. She looked up to the sky, "Daddy, daddy, daddy. I wish you were here so I could go off on you too."

"As a matter of fact, let's go to my parent's house. I need to see my mother and my dear sisters."

"No. You are not going to go to your mother's house and cause a scene. You are not going to go and upset your mother."

"No? No? No? Who are you? You cannot tell me that I am not going to my parents' house." Aysha was ready for the fight. She wasn't quite sure where all of the fire was coming from. She wanted to know if Jada already knew about Mia, and why her mother had neglected to tell her that she had a sister.

"Aysha, you are obviously upset. What good is going over there in this type of mood going to do?' Jaylon was trying to give her a minute to calm down and think rationally. Under normal circumstances, Aysha tended to be the more rational person in most scenarios. However, that logic usually went right out of the window when she was the main character in the story. Aysha was not very good at taking her own advice.

"Oh, y'all didn't care about my feelings when y'all were keeping secrets, but now, you do"?

"You know what, why does everything in the world have to be about you. You know what? For the last five years, everyone tip-toes around Aysha. Nobody wants to upset the princess. No one wants to say anything that might ruffle Aysha's feathers. That shit is old, and I am sick of it."

"You are sick of it". Oh, this was the battle that Aysha had been waiting on, and he had baited her in. In that moment, she remembered everything that she'd ever wanted to say to Jaylon, and she was going to say it all right now.

"I don't care about you being sick of anything. You want sick. I was sick for months after my fiancé' slept with my sister. I was sick for months after you betrayed me with my own sister. Sick... C'mon, are you sure that you want to use that word?"

"Okay, so you will not rest until we go through that. I never slept with your sister. "

"Oh, so what? Y'all were having show and tell in your sleep. Please. Shut up with the nothing. You did it and we know you did it."

"Aysha, think about it. You know what? Don't think about it. I am not going there with you today. This is about what your father needed you to know. Not what almost happened between Jada and me".

"Oh, so y'all ALMOST did. Well, this time ALMOST counts. Because you should never have ALMOST gotten that close." That statement seemed to take the wind out of Aysha's sail. In fact, in that moment, she had a very real flashback of walking into that room. It was like an out of body experience and she was transported back to that day. What snapped her out of it was recalling how she threw the glass bottle she was carrying at the mirror. She was trying really hard to maintain her anger, but she was still reeling from Jaylon's blatant lie about what he'd done with her sister. Why couldn't he just admit it? That would be too easy.

Aysha was folded up around herself. She sat and grabbed the mink throw that was on the chaise and wrapped up in it. It had become her security blanket over the last few years. Oddly, the throw was made out of a mink coat that Jaylon had bought for her for Christmas. While she'd gotten rid of a lot of his gifts, her mom convinced her to convert the coat to something useful. She had to admit that she loved the throw, and a part of her had to admit that it was like having a piece of Jaylon around. Those feelings made her mad. It made her more upset because while she was angry with her family for keeping secrets, and she was angrier because she had one secret that she'd never told anyone. Not even Valerie or Kyra, her best friend since kindergarten, knew this secret.

FIVE- 5

Aysha's head was spinning. She had one sister that she didn't know, and one sister that she wished she didn't know. She had a man that she hated sitting on her couch. Her father was dead. What part of this was real? She wished she could pass out again, but the rational part of her knew that would not change her reality. What she really couldn't understand is why didn't anyone tell her about Mia. There was something that Jaylon wasn't saying.

"Okay, tell me the whole story".
'I told you everything that you need to know"
"Which means that there is something that you don't think that I need to know. Tell me everything or get out. No, you are right. You shouldn't tell me. Let's go to my parents' house. NOW!!"
"Aysha, that is not the best".
"You can take me, you can follow me, or you can stay right here and wait for me to get back. But, you better believe that I am about to go and get the rest of this story from my mother. My dad was wrong to put all of this on you. They should have told me all of this. Somebody should have told me this before today".

Aysha got up and put on her shoes. She went into the restroom, and had to hold on to the counter. What in the hell was happening to her world? Her dad was dead. Now, she had another sister? Yesterday, her world was fine, and today, it was gone to hell. She let the toilet lid down, sat down, and with her face in her hands, she began to cry. She wasn't even sure how long she'd been in there, but there was someone knocking on the door. She was too emotional to answer, and before she could get up and go to the door, it opened. Jaylon was standing there, and when she looked up at him, with her face wet from crying, he came over and kneeled beside her. He took her hands in his own and as much as she wanted to pull away she did not. She couldn't admit it aloud, but she really did need someone right now. She was not sure she needed Jaylon, but she needed someone.

"Come on Ay, I just called your mom. Both Mia and Jada are there, and your mom wants you to come, and she will tell you the whole story".

"At what point will I wake up and realize that this was all just a dream".

"Aysha, just keep an open mind. Remember that we all make mistakes, and sometimes, we make choices that seem okay at the time, but they don't always pan out like you expect."

For a moment, Aysha was comforted. But then, she remembered. This was Jaylon. The man slept with her sister. The man broke her heart. The man stole her ability to even trust herself. What he was saying was definitely the truth, but she didn't want to hear it from him.

"Let's just go. "Aysha sighed. She was at a loss for words, and she was really feeling tired and drained. She wanted to know the truth, but she was at a loss for how much more she could bear.

"Jay, can you call my mom and let her know that I will just come over in the morning. I am emotionally drained and I just can't do this tonight." Tears rolled down Aysha's face, and Jaylon reached out and wiped her tear. He knew the fight had gone out of her when she did not even try to stop him, nor did she retaliate with a smart aleck remark.

"Of course, I will". Jaylon went to the bar to get his phone and call Mrs. Rutherford and let her know that Aysha's plans had changed. They chatted for a few minutes, and he explained that he was worried about Aysha. She could hear him talking about her, but in that moment, she was too emotional to care. Her head was cloudy like she'd had an all-night party at her favorite margarita place. Too bad she hadn't actually had the drinks to go with the headache she was feeling. She could actually use a drink, or two. But she decided a hot shower might be best.

"I am going to get in the shower." Aysha said aloud. She wanted to ask Jaylon to leave but she had to admit that she really did not want to be alone. She would not ask him to stay, but she would not put him out. Knowing Jaylon, he would just hang around, and for right now, Aysha was okay with that.

"Okay, I called your mom, and let her know that we will be there in the morning for breakfast. While you are in the shower, I will find you something to eat." Jaylon turned and walked out of the room before Aysha could not respond.

It was not lost on Aysha that Jaylon seemed very comfortable in her space for someone who had never been in her home. It was not lost on Jaylon that she would be naked in the shower. He should have been concerned about her mental wellbeing, but the mental picture of her very attractive physical form being naked in the shower caused a very physical reaction in him. He was grateful she was already headed into the bathroom and could not see the hard-on she'd left him with.

Aysha stepped in the shower and for the ten thousandth time, she was grateful for the upgrades she'd made in the bathroom. All of those showerheads that she'd installed were worth the price. Her family never understood her fascination with baths and showers. Normal people took ten-minute showers. Aysha, however, usually stayed in the shower until the hot water ran out. She and Jada had many arguments over that fact when they were growing up and had to share a bathroom. Today, the hot water was just what Aysha needed to wash away some of the stress and distress that she was feeling. She took her time taking a shower, and uttered a silent prayer for the battle that she'd had with her father to install a water heater that provided endless hot water after she moved in. She fell to her knees in the shower, and began to cry. The tears mixed with the water and Aysha just cried until she had no more tears. She wanted to scream, but remembering that Jaylon was in the house and would certainly come running to see what happened deterred her from fully venting her emotions. After what seemed like an hour, Aysha knew that she needed to get out of the shower. She turned the water off, and got out of the shower.

Aysha came out of the bathroom with a towel wrapped around her. She was shocked, surprised, and angered when she found Jaylon lying across her bed. She was shocked that he'd had the nerve to come into her bedroom and surprised that he'd had the audacity to lie across her bed. Most prevalent thought, she was angry that in that white t-shirt and jeans lying on his stomach across her bed, he was still, hands-down, the finest man she'd ever seen. Here, she should be grieving and, in that instant, she could only admire his physical form. *Damn,* she thought, *he was fine, and if he were anyone else, he could get it.* It angered her that after every thing that he'd done, that they'd been through that she was still physically attracted to him. Before she could even say a word, Jaylon looked at her and spoke.

"Ay, I was worried because you took so long in the shower."

His explanation took a bit of the steam off of her temperament, but she would not pass up a chance to lash out at Jaylon.

"If you don't get your ass off of my bed…Can you please go back to the living room so I can get dressed in MY room? I am fine".

Jaylon looked up at Aysha. He saw the weariness in her face and could tell that she'd been crying. He wanted to reach out and grab her, but it was obvious that a battle was raging inside of her. He didn't want to push too much, because he knew that if he took an inch, Aysha would find a way to push him back a mile. So, Jaylon stood up, and took a step back from Aysha before extending himself in the widest stretch of his limbs. He glanced at Aysha, smiled, and then got up to walk in the other room. She was still, hands down, the most beautiful woman in the world to him. Wrapped in that towel, she could still elicit the most primal response from him.

Aysha started to get dressed. She did not hear any of the alarm chimes, so she assumed Jaylon did not let himself out and would be waiting for her. She chose some sweatpants and a t-shirt and grabbed some colorful socks to go with them. Looking at the colors on the socks made her smile. If only those socks could help her forget the whirlwind that was gusting through her life. After getting dressed, Aysha sat down on the bed. The ringing of the doorbell snapped her back to whatever world she'd drifted off too. She got up to go and answer the door, but before she could get out of the room, she heard voices. She thought it was her mother's voice, and she was also quite sure that she heard Jada's voice. That heffa was not in her house. Jada and Jaylon in her house. This was getting good.

Aysha turned the corner and saw her mother and Jada. Jaylon was helping her mother to the chaise, and Jada was sitting next to her mother. Aysha was so taken aback by the gall that Jada had to saunter into her home that she did not notice that there was third person that was still standing next to the door until she heard Jaylon speak.

"You must be Mia. I am Jaylon, a friend of the family". Jaylon reached out and gave Mia a big hug and that bothered Aysha. What also bothered Aysha was the fact that she was staring at a face that was very much her own. She'd always heard people say that everyone had a twin, but looking at Mia was unsettling and uncanny.

Aysha wanted to go and hug her mom as she usually would, but in this alternate reality that her life had become she was unsure of what to do. She just leaned on the bar stool and somehow found herself seated at the bar with her head in her hands. It was quiet for a few moments before Aysha could catch her breath.

"Excuse my language, but what the hell is going on here".

"Yes, excuse your language, my dear. But, when Jaylon called and said you weren't coming over, I asked Mia and Jada to drive me over to you. This all comes out tonight. Jaylon, can you please get me something to drink? A glass of wine, preferably, if Aysha has any".

Mrs. Rutherford knew that there was wine in the house just for her. Her mother would come over occasionally and she and Aysha would have lunch, but her mom would drink wine and Aysha would always drink Dr. Pepper out of the wine glasses. It was how they did it when they were little girls. She would allow them to drink their own drinks out of wine glasses. Apparently, Jaylon knew about this tradition, as he brought her mother wine, and three other wine glasses filled with Dr. Pepper.

The silence was broken when Mia tasted her drink and

said, "Oh, Dr. Pepper. My favorite".

Aysha was sitting there stealing glances at Mia. She hadn't wanted to outright stare at her, and her mother had made no move to introduce them properly. It seemed that everyone in the room was just hovering around each other tentatively, like two boxers in the ring afraid to throw the first punch. There was a lot that would be said, but it seemed no one wanted to be the first one to start it. Aysha's patience was growing thinner by the second.

"Mommie, what did you come all the way here to tell me". Aysha asked. There was a sense that this not was not about to get any better any time soon.

Hazel Rutherford seemed older than she'd been on just yesterday. There was a frailty about her that Aysha hadn't re-membered seeing before. There was weariness in her being that had not been there before.

"Aysha, I need to introduce you to your sister. My oldest child, Mia". Her mother said. Her voice was not quite as strong as Aysha had always known it to be. There was a hint of disbelief in the tone, and Aysha knew this was not easy for her mother.

"There is a story that I need to tell you. It is about what happened before and after you were born. Your father and I made certain choices, and this is where we have ended up. We should have done this five years ago. Your father and I, together. But we didn't. So, my darling Kitty, I will do it tonight." Mrs. Rutherford looked nervous, but resolved. Aysha wanted to ask a million questions, but she knew it would be better to just let her mother tell her story. Aysha went over to her favorite chaise lounge, grabbed her blanket and curled up. Before she could say anything, Jaylon was bringing her glass and had the nerve to sit right beside her. He was beginning to annoy her, but she knew she couldn't ask him to leave. Her mom was oblivious to or blatantly ignoring the tension between her and Jaylon, as she started telling her story. Everyone in the room listened as Mrs. Rutherford began speaking.

"Aysha, I first met your father when I was 20 years old,

and in my 3rd year of college. He was already playing professional basketball, and he'd come to North Carolina Tech to visit friends. From the moment I laid eyes on your father, nothing else mattered but your father. He'd come and visit every chance he'd get, and a couple of times, I'd visited him on the road. Two years past, and we were not necessarily together, but we got together whenever we could. In the last semester of my last year in school, I was so excited. I'd found a job in Houston and I was going to move there to be closer to your father. The month before graduation, I missed my period. I didn't think anything of it with all of the stress that was going on with graduation and moving. Then the month of graduation, I missed my period again, and I knew. I knew I was pregnant, and I knew that I had to tell your father. His season was just finishing up, and graduation was near. I decided not to tell anyone until after I graduated.

A few nights before graduation, I met your dad for dinner. I didn't say anything about the baby, but I started talking about moving to Houston. Your father told me that Houston would not be a good idea for me. He was marrying his high school sweetheart, and we could not see each other again after I graduated. I was devastated. I simply stood up and walked out of the restaurant. Your father came behind me, but I made it to the taxi stand and I took a taxi home, and not to my dorm. I didn't see your father again for over a year. After graduation, I had to decline the job in Houston, and I moved back home with my parents. I told my brother about the situation, and my brother and his wife decided that they would raise the baby as their own. They could not have any children of their own, and he was in the military, so I moved to Texas from North Carolina with them. Mia was born on the military base in Killeen. Because of my brother's connections in the military, he was able to get him and his wife put on Mia's birth certificate as the parents, and there was no legal connection between my baby and me".

For the first three months I was with Mia, acting as the nanny, but loving raising my daughter. I guess I loved it too much and my sister-in-law grew leery that I would not be able to leave Mia. So, the day after Mia turned three months old, my brother told me that I would have to move out. He would pay for me to go back home to North Carolina, but I would not be able to stay with them. I was hurt, but I didn't put up a fight. At the time, I figured it was the best thing for all of us. In his eagerness for me to leave, my brother booked the flight out of the airport in Houston. It was a four-hour drive from Ft. Hood to Houston, and my brother took me a few days after we had the conversation. I got to the airport and I saw your father. His team was traveling to their next location.

We spoke briefly and I didn't mention the baby. I just told him that I had been visiting my brother in Ft. Hood, and was headed back to North Carolina. I didn't ask him any questions, I was just trying to get away from there. It was obvious for me at that moment that the state of Texas was not my friend. At that moment, your Uncle Rob saw us talking, and I don't know what he saw in my face, but he intercepted me as I was headed to the plane.

"You know he loves you". He asked as he escorted me to the waiting area for my flight.

"He loves ice cream and grape soda, too", was my response. I'd loved him and it didn't matter. I'd loved my brother and my baby and that didn't matter. I felt so alone and abandoned. I felt wrong." Mrs. Rutherford's voice cracked, and Jada hugged her from the side. Aysha was so transfixed by this story she was immobile. Who were these people? This was not the love at first sight story she and Jada had been told. She didn't know what to say, so she kept listening.

"Your uncle asked for my phone number and if it would be okay if he called to check on me sometimes. I wanted to say no, but your Uncle Rob had always been a gentleman, and I knew that he would do just that. I also knew that he would give it to your father, and I am sure that some part of me, in the hurt, and in the pain hoped that he would. While I heard from your Uncle Rob about once every couple of weeks, it would be over a year before I heard from your father." Her mother paused and just stared. She was remembering the hurt, and details about that time in her life that she would never share with anyone.

When your father finally called, he was in town and asked if I would meet him for dinner. Everything in me said 'no', but I couldn't deny him. When we met for dinner, it was light and very causal. While we were there he asked about my job, and the job in Houston. I told him that I decided to go and teach instead of working at a law firm as I had planned to in Houston. After dinner, he asked if we could go and walk by the fountains. I knew this would be the last time I saw your father. I loved him still and I knew that if we were to meet again, that I would make a choice that was bad for him, his marriage, and myself. During this conversation, your father started to cry, and he told me that his wife had died at the ripe age of 23, due to complications with her bowels after childbirth. They'd had a little girl, and he didn't know what to do. The baby, Jada, was in North Carolina with your Aunt Belle, but Belle was still working and your aunts, the twins, were high school girls and could not be consumed with taking care of a newborn baby. He was trying to hire a nanny to take care of the little girl, but he didn't trust them to stay with the girl while he was traveling with the team. The wife's family didn't want anything to do with the baby, and he asked if I would be willing to move to Houston to take care of his daughter, Jada, so that she could be near him".

"WHAT". Aysha was in shock. She was 32 years old, and she had just found out that her sister, who she didn't want to be her sister, was really not her sister. More accurately, she was her half sister, and she had another sister that she didn't know that was her sister.

"Mom, Jada....". In that moment Aysha forgot all about her grudge with Jada. She looked at her sister, whose face was covered in tears. She looked at Mia and realized that she was crying also. She looked over at Jaylon and he was just looking up at the ceiling, and she realized that he was probably trying to hold back the tears. Her mother also had tears streaming down her face, and had sagged to one side and was being supported upright by Jada.

"Aysha, there is more. As much as I wanted to be angry with your father, I knew that I had love to offer that little girl. I felt like I was forced to give up my child, and her God was giving me a second blessing, which is why I always called her that."

Aysha's head was reeling. Her mother always referred to Jada as her "second blessing". Almost everyone in the family called Jada, "Blessing". That'd always been her nickname. Her mother had always explained that she met her father and was blessed, and then Jada came along and that was her second blessing. Now, Aysha understood that a big part of that story had been left out. She understood why her mother had a bond with Jada that she'd never had with her.

"I asked your father to have a contract drawn that outlined the details of my employment with him, and I simply wanted a house where I would have a separate living space. For me, I was coming to take care of the little girl, but I was not coming for a relationship with your father. Jada was just turning 3 months old when I moved there. For the first two or three months, your father was on the road a lot. When he was home, I would make myself scarce. I'd found a neighborly grandmother who would help out, and when he was home, I asked her to come over more and more. Eventually, things were not as tense for us and when Jada could walk we started doing more activities together. Your father had been playing basketball for 4 years, and hurt his knee and was considering quitting the game. He was accepted to Law School and was weighing his options. He'd decided to go to the University of Texas. Entertainment and Sports Law were not the big draws that they are today, and your father had an advantage because he played basketball, and because he was very active in the player's union, he thought he could make a career. He was leaving to go to Austin for school, and we went to dinner to celebrate him going to Law School, and one thing led to another. Your father started Law School in August, and in November, it was confirmed that I was three months pregnant with you, Aysha. I was afraid. I felt alone, and

I can honestly say that if I knew how to get an abortion that you might not be here. I had to face the music, so I told your father I was moving back to North Carolina, and if he wanted I would take Jada with me so that he could finish school. I was so embarrassed about what happened, and more so because I'd allowed myself to get pregnant twice. You know what old folks say, *You burn me once, shame on you. You burn me twice, shame on me.* That's what I was. Ashamed.

"You father did not understand, and he begged and pleaded with me not to leave. As I was crying and so emotional and trying to figure out how I was going to leave, your father proposed marriage to me. He told me that he didn't want it to end this way, and that he should have done this the first time around and that I was not leaving him and our child. I still hadn't told him about the baby, but when I responded that I didn't want to trap him into marrying me, he kept at me until I told him that I was pregnant. He carried me to the bed where I cried for the next 24 hours straight it seems. I woke up the next morning with him and Jada in the bed with me, and we slept like that every night until you arrived. We decided to go to the courthouse and get married. In the car outside of the courthouse, I told him that I had to tell him something before we got married. I told him about Mia and the situation with my brother. It did not deter him from marrying me, but as soon as we were married, we got in the car and we went home to pack an overnight bag and we drove to Ft. Hood. Your father was not happy that my brother would not allow me to see Mia at all. I'd never told him who Mia's father was, your father was adamant that the adoption was not legal because he did not give his consent. He wanted his daughter. However, on the way to Ft. Hood, I was able to mellow him out. Mia would have been 3 years old at the time, and while it hurt me to the core, I could not rip apart the life she knew. As long as she was healthy and happy, I had to let her stay with my brother. My brother allowed us to visit, and James was able to see Mia. Not long after that visit, my brother accepted a transfer to Germany. He called and told me that he was transferring bases, and he would send information when he could. That was the last time I heard from my brother.

The next time that I got any word about him was when he and his wife died in a car accident and the military was notifying his next of kin. By this time, he had returned to the US, and was living in South Carolina. Mia was 16, and we were complete strangers to her. After careful thought, your dad and I decided not to go to her. We went to the funeral, and I introduced myself to her, but I did not tell her that I was her mother. We decided not to try to reclaim her once I found out that she was living with her mom's sister. It was not until Mia's aunt told her when she was 30 that she was adopted did she seek us out. That was the year before you and Jaylon were getting married. Mia moved to Houston so that she could be near us, her family. Your dad and I were being selfish and we were spending as much time as possible getting to know her while you and Jada were in North Carolina. We had every intention of introducing her to the rest of the family.

The weekend before you and Jaylon broke up, Jada had come to Houston to do some things for your wedding. She surprised your dad and I, and I guess you could say we surprised her." Her mom seemed overwhelmed by sharing her truth, so Jada took over telling the story.

Kitty, I came home and I didn't knock, I let myself in. I saw a car in the driveway, so I knew mom and dad were there. When I got in the house, I saw they were all watching a movie. Mom and Dad snuggled up on the couch and I thought it was you on the floor. I walked in the room, and sat on what I thought was your back. Instead of laughing or saying something Mom looked at me and yelled, "Oh my God, James. What are we going to do"? When I got up, I realized that it was not you, but a face that looked very much like you. They had to tell me everything. I was angry and I flew back to Charlotte. They made me promise not to tell you, and so I didn't. A couple of days after getting back to Charlotte, I went to Tony's house, and I met his very pregnant girlfriend. We'd been dating for one year, and he had a pregnant girlfriend. I was so hurt and angry and I went home. That was when Jaylon came over and the rest is history.

Aysha could not breathe. She had tears running down her face. Her emotions were a jumbled mess. She could imagine if someone illustrated her emotions it would look like a heap of electrical cords tangled together. She wanted to feel sadness for her mom for losing her daughter, and Jada for losing her mom, and Mia for losing both of her parents. Her mother lost her brother. Maybe her mom had understood the situation between her and Jada a lot more than she'd even given her credit for. There was so much loss. At the same time, she was angry that Jada chose to lash out at her by seducing Jaylon because she was hurt.

"So, how have y'all hidden Mia away these last few years that I have never met her or run into her? I have a sister and no one bothered to tell me. Hell, we could be twins, I am surprised no one else told me".

"Aysha, there have been several times when we have just allowed people to think she was you"

"And that was okay with you" She looked at Mia.

"Yes. Aysha, when I decided to seek out mom and dad, I was in a bad place".

Aysha didn't know how she felt about this "sister" calling her parents "mom and dad". But, the rational side of her said that she had just as much of a claim on her parents as Aysha did.

"I had just divorced my husband, who was very abusive. I needed someone or something to hold on to. My sanity was slipping, which was how daddy was able to convince me to move to Houston. So, when Mom explained everything to me, I understood. I don't know if I liked being the best kept secret, but Jada and I developed a relationship, and I spend quite a bit of time with Aunt Belle too.

This whole story was too much for Aysha. She was coming out of the compassionate phase and was quickly heading towards anger. Fortunately, for everyone involved she was just too tired to be anything, and just wanted to go to sleep.

"Mommy, this is too much. I just need to lie down. I am going to go and get in the bed and I will come over later this week. I just need to digest what has been said here tonight, and right now, I am just exhausted. Can y'all just leave, and we can finish this on another day.

"I will, but on one condition." Her mother paused, and bit her lip. Aysha knew what was coming next would be a doozy. "You let Jaylon stay here with you tonight. I do not want you to be alone"

"Mooooommm, of course not" Aysha whined. "I will be just fine."

"Kitty, please don't argue with me on this. The boy can sleep on the couch, or in one of those rooms. But I just don't want you to be alone. So, either that or I can stay, or you can come home with us. Better yet, you have enough beds here, we can all stay". Aysha knew better than to let her mother stay. She would smother Aysha, and that was not going to work. She also was not ready to go play "happy family" so going home with her mother and her "sisters" was completely out of the questions. Having the "Sister Sledge" in her home was also not an option. Aysha figured she could just put Jaylon out later after her mother left.

"Okay, okay. He can stay." She stood up and hugged her mom, and she hugged Mia. She wanted to be mean towards Jada, but after all she'd heard tonight, she knew her sister needed a hug. She still owed her a beat down, but today was not going to be that day. She gave Jada a quick hug, and she was sure her mom smiled. She went back to chaise to sit, and Jaylon walked them out. She heard the door chime, and then a car engine, so she knew they were gone. It took Jaylon about ten minutes to come back inside. Aysha could only hope he'd gone home too, but she knew that was not the case. Aysha surmised that he must have needed to make a phone call in private. She was sure he was calling to check in with some woman. Before she could decide how she felt about that, she heard the door chime and he came back in.

"Hey, you still haven't eaten, so I called and ordered some Chinese food".

"From where? You don't know what restaurant delivers around here"

"I called the take-out taxi service. You used to love P.F. Chang's, so I ordered that".

Aysha did not respond, as she was taken aback by how much of her life he seemed to remember. When the food arrived, they ate in silence. Aysha went back to relaxing on the chaise lounge and Jaylon chose a movie. She thought that she was enjoying the movie, but when she awoke, she was surprised that she was in her bedroom and the clock next to the bed was glowing 3:13 a.m. She reached her arm out across the bed to find that she was in the bed alone. She wondered where Jaylon was, and for a quick second she was disappointed that he hadn't climbed into bed with her. Then again, she knew that she would have been furious if he'd tried. She replayed her mother's story and immediately got weary, so she rolled over and went back to sleep. She was not ready to deal with her truths. A few more hours of sleep and denial were exactly what she needed.

SIX-6

The last week had gone by in a blur. She'd spent most of the time curled up on her couch ignoring Jaylon. He would not leave her alone unless someone else came over, and then he would leave and go straight to her mother's side. He'd handled the funeral arrangements, and according to what he told Aysha, he was taking care of the business and the estate matters, and he would update them on everything once the funeral was done. His main job since her mother and sisters left her home the night they told her everything was babysitting Aysha. To her relief, several of her sorority sisters dropped by, and a few of her coworkers from school. Her aunts had come by to see her, and everyone commented that she was avoiding her mother's house. No one seemed to understand how the grief was suffocating her. It seemed Jaylon was the only person who understood. Mia had even come over and brought Aysha some of her favorite food that people had left. She knew her mom had put her up to it, but she was grateful. Mia was trying to be a sister, and Aysha could at least be open-minded. Her interactions with Mia were not awkward. They actually had quite a bit in common. It was uncanny how she liked many of the same things. It was still a bit unnerving to look at her, though because her face was like looking at herself in a mirror.

Aysha had not been to her parents' house since the day after her father died. Today was the funeral, and Aysha was dreading this. She'd tried to think of how she could get out of attending this funeral, but there was no excuse that she could give for not attending her own father's funeral. Aysha knew that she was the apple of her father's eye, and no matter how she felt about the people around her, she would do nothing IN PUBLIC that would dishonor her father's memory. She'd put on the happy face for the media that had taken an interest in this situation because of Jaylon's association with her family. She was happy that he'd finally cleared up the story that her father was not his father, but a mentor to him. She was not happy that her name had come up because it had been discovered that her father was actually the father of Jaylon's ex-fiancée, her. She was also not happy that she'd had to deal with all of the speculation on why their wedding was called off, what their relationship was in the past, and what their relationship currently was. Luckily, she'd never discussed the situation with anyone other than Valerie, her parents, and her childhood friend, Kyra. She was sure none of them would have uttered a word to anyone. She'd tried to leave that all behind, but it seemed that in the last week, she'd been transported back in time. But she was determined to tune all of the noise out today, and celebrate her father's life. Unfortunately, she'd come to her parents' house late last night, at her mother's not so motherly insistence. She wanted them all to go to the funeral together, but after everything that had transpired in the last week, she didn't feel much like family. In fact, yesterday's debacle had been enough to make her question whether or not she should not bury her relationships with these people when she buried her father. Maybe she could just walk out of that church and never see her "sisters" or her mother again. Yes, maybe she could.

Aysha had never thought of herself as selfish and self-centered, but listening to her mom say how they didn't tell her because of the wedding, and then because the wedding was called off made her feel some kind of way. When her mother told her just how much her father had worried about her mental stability since her and Jaylon had broken up, it brought tears to her eyes, but she refused to cry another tear over that situation. How could she make them understand the magnitude of her loss? It wasn't just Jaylon that she'd lost, it was everything. EVERYTHING! But not today, the pity party would have to wait. She'd need her bravest face to get through this funeral.

Aysha had refused to take part in planning the funeral, and refused to go and view her father's remains with everyone else the day before. Of course, they thought she was being selfish, but she didn't know how to voice that she just could not stand to see her father in that state. Luckily for them all, her father had taken care of most of the arrangements. What he hadn't done, he'd obviously discussed with Jaylon, who'd stepped in and taken the reins. She would have to be sure to tell Jaylon thank you for all that he'd done for her family this past week. She could hate him for what had transpired between them, but she could not deny that he'd gone above and beyond for them all since her father died. He'd been there for her mom, been there for her whether she'd wanted him to be or not, and made sure that everything was prepared for today. Each day, he'd gone to her mother and sat with her as long as necessary. He'd made sure they all ate, and she was sure her mom had not driven a car since her dad died, as Jaylon chauffeured her wherever she wanted to go. It did not go unnoticed to her that for someone that had never had a relationship with his own father, he'd handled this situation as if he was the oldest son in the family. While on some level that bothered her, she did have to acknowledge that this whole week would have been much more difficult without him there. She would definitely have to thank him.

Aysha took one look in the mirror and was stunned by what she saw. There were no remnants or marks to remind her of the explosion that occurred yesterday between her and her family. What had started out as her trying to do a good deed, and be less of the selfish person her family obviously thought that she was had failed miserably. In an effort to start a relationship between Aysha and Mia, and mend the relationship between Aysha and Jada, her mother had taken them on a spa day. They'd also gotten services so that they would be presentable for the funeral, as her mother was adamant that none of them would be wearing buns and sunglasses. Aysha had laughed at her mom for saying they would not walk into the funeral looking like the grief-stricken version of the singing group En Vogue after a bad night out. Unfortunately, it hadn't ended up like she'd hoped.

Aysha had done her best to be cordial to Jada, but it was so much more difficult than she'd expected. So much more difficult, in fact, that Aysha just resorted to her usual disposition, and ignored Jada completely. She understood Jada's issues, but what kind of person lashed out at the world by trying to seduce her sister's fiancé'. She was tempted to ask her several times, so ignoring her was the best Aysha could do. Apparently, this was too much for Jada, and she'd decided not to go to lunch with them after the spa, which resulted in Aysha's mom and Mia ganging up on Aysha and giving her the old "not forgiving is like drinking poison speech". Her father and their pastor would have been proud. This snowballed into Aysha going into defensive mode, shutting down, and then lashing out in anger. She'd called Mia a "Johnny come lately who needed to get some business". Of course, in true Aysha fashion, she'd not stopped there, and continued by telling her mother about how she really felt about the favoritism that she'd shown Jada her whole life. It got even uglier when Aysha had thrown in how Jada was "just some orphan" that her mother felt sorry for and wasn't even her child. The culmination of that conversation was something that Aysha had never expected. In fact, in retrospect, Aysha smiled a little as she had a new respect for her mother based upon her reaction to what Aysha said.

In the past, Aysha had always known exactly what buttons to push to get her mother to leave her alone. Aysha and her mom were close, but their relationship always seemed strained, and it was not nearly as close as the relationship between her mother and Jada. Jada always went to mom first, and Aysha always went to daddy for everything. Aysha was so strong-willed, and her mother tried very hard not to break her spirit, which usually meant acquiescing to a lot of what Aysha wanted to do. In fact, most people relented to Aysha's strong will, but yesterday, she'd miscalculated in a major way.

After Aysha said what she'd had to say and called Jada an orphan, her mom had momentarily dropped her head, and Aysha momentarily felt bad for what she'd said, but she thought that she'd hit her mark and her mother would shrink back. She was wrong. Her mother's reaction was so out of character and was definitely unexpected. Her mom had raised her head, and proceeded to try to slap the proverbial taste out of Aysha mouth. In her 32 years of living, her mother had never raised her hand in anger at Aysha or Jada that she could remember. They got spankings, but they were all well-deserved, and even then, she'd known her mother didn't have the heart to physically punish them. Aysha didn't even notice the other patrons in the restaurant who'd turned to look at them. She'd tried to get up from the table, but her mother grabbed her hand like she was an obstinate five-year-old having a tantrum. She'd looked Aysha in the face and called her an "insensitive ingrate" and continued by telling Aysha that she was ashamed to have reared a child that could say something so hateful. Aysha was stunned to silence, and didn't need to hear anymore. Once her mother released her wrist, she'd gotten up and left her mother and Mia at the table. In that moment, Aysha could not have cared less about any of them. The only reason she was in the house today was because she would not air the family business, and her showing up to the funeral independent of her family would have certainly caused tongues to wag. Already she was ignoring calls and messages from her cousins who obviously had already gotten the story, as her mom kept few secrets from her aunts, who were also not known for their ability to hold water in a cup.

Aysha took a few minutes to look around her room, and was amazed at how little her room had changed. Her mother had updated the bedding, but it looked just as it did when Aysha was there in the aftermath of Jaylon and Jada. She felt a bit sad about that. It was the piercing revelation that this bedroom was the real-life proof that she'd not moved on as nearly as much as she tried to pretend. She started to cry when she remembered her mother telling her that her father's primary reason for not telling her about Mia was that he was so much more concerned than he'd ever let on about her mental stability. Aysha realized that it was certainly time for her to put the past truly behind her and walk into the present. But, right now, she just needed to walk into the living room downstairs with her family and not swing at anyone.

Getting out of the bed and into the shower took a lot of energy, but the hot water in the shower gave her a little spunk. Aysha understood that today was going to be difficult. She slipped on the navy-blue shirt dress that she'd brought for the funeral. Aysha coordinated the outfit with simple silver bead earrings, and the rest of the matching pieces in the set from Tiffany's. She jazzed it up a little with red and blue pumps and red clutch to go with it. After doing her makeup, she was ready. At least she was ready for the funeral, not necessarily to face everyone downstairs. But, she had to leave the room, so she stood tall, and headed downstairs for breakfast.

Aysha walked downstairs and the first person she saw was her Aunt Belle, who stood in the family room at the bottom of the stairs and was dressed up and looking like she should be on the cover of the AARP newsletter. No one was sure how old Aunt Belle was, but she always reminded Aysha of Diahann Carroll and according to all of the stories she'd heard, she'd raised her father and his three siblings after Aysha's grandparents had gone to Chicago to find work, but never managed to come back to retrieve their children. According to the family folklore, Aunt Belle was her grandmother's baby sister, and had just returned from college at Howard University to find that her oldest sister had four children. Her father was the oldest, and her grandmother had no intentions of taking care of them. Aunt Belle had been a school teacher in North Carolina, and progressed to a principal before retiring when Aysha was much younger and moving to Houston after her retirement. Aunt Belle was more like a grandmother to Aysha, but no one would tell Aunt Belle's age, but she was sure that Aunt Belle was at least 10 years older than her father's age of 57, although she still walked 3 miles every day and was the starting forward on her team in the Seniors' Basketball League.

"Good morning, Miss Kitty. Are you hungry, punkin?" Aunt Bell greeted her, and walked towards the staircase as Aysha was descending the last step.

"Good morning Auntie. I probably should try to eat something". Aysha responded, as she stepped into a warm, comfortable hug from Aunt Belle. She immediately smelled that Samsara perfume by Guerlain. Aunt Belle had worn that same scent for at least the last 33 years that Aysha had been alive. In fact, when they were teenagers, they'd always know when Aunt Belle had been over to the house and snooping in their rooms because they could smell the perfume long before she came, and long after she left. Aysha bought her a different fragrance when she was a freshman in college, and to her knowledge, Aunt Belle never even tried it.

"Go on in the kitchen. I cooked breakfast casserole and biscuits already. Your mama and your sisters are in there already, and Jaylon and Malik too". Aysha noted that she said "sisters", acknowledging both Mia and Jada. She looked at Aysha with a challenge in her eyes. Aunt Belle was matriarch of her family and she ruled it with a soft heart and an iron fist. Whatever Aunt Belle suggested was typically law in the family, and she gave Aysha a look to let her know that she expected that to continue to be the case.

"Well, maybe I will eat later. Not really in the mood for a family reunion this morning". Aysha started to sulk. All of the confidence that she'd geared up for today went out of her like air fleeing a punctured balloon. How was she going to get through today with these people if she could not get through this morning? How was she going to keep the peace with everyone if she started the morning with a battle of wills with Aunt Belle? She'd already dug a hole for herself yesterday, and she just did not see how alienating and angering Aunt Belle was going to make that better. At the same time, she did not want to go into that kitchen either.

"Gone in there lil' girl. I heard about yesterday. I ain't your judge, but don't let your pride get you into nothing that love can't get you out of". Aunt Belle responded. "Too much of your daddy in you. That is the only thing wrong with you. That man created a copy of himself with you. Good and bad. Now, gone in there, or do I need to get my 'Belle Bit" out for you"? With that question, Aunt Belle started laughing and hugging Aysha to her side, and started walking towards the kitchen. Aysha had to smile. A "Belle Bit" was a piece of an old leather belt that Aunt Belle had kept close to her when Aysha, Jada, and her cousins had come to visit. In addition, she'd taken it to church, to their house, and to any other place that her nieces and nephews might think to get out of line. Aunt Belle lived by the "whenever, wherever" motto. She'd told them over the years that "Whenever they decided to show out, she would get them right wherever they were." and the "Belle Bit" was the tool she'd used to keep them in line. Aysha's hand started stinging just remembering the number of pops she'd gotten in her hand for various offenses.

Aunt Belle released her and Aysha started towards the kitchen. She had no clue what she'd done to deserve the mercy, but she was given a reprieve from what was going to be an uncomfortable moment when everyone started filing out of the kitchen just as she walked into the room. Her mother walked right up to her and gave her a hug and kissed her forehead. Before Aysha could decide how she felt about that, her mother looked at her and said, "I love you, Kitty". The devil in her wanted to be rude and angry and respond with just roll of her eyes. After all, wasn't this the same woman that had tried to slap her into the proverbial next week not even 24 hours ago? But, since those eyes were now watering up with tears, she could not respond at all. She simply dropped her head and refused to meet her mother's eyes. It would be easier for her if they could just all be angry with each other and get through today. Aysha was so much better at holding a grudge than she was at apologies and forgiveness. Aysha should have known that her mother would never permit that. If she were honest, she would admit that it was her mother over the last five years who had pulled out all of the stops to stop Aysha from waging war on her sister. Her father had given up after the first Christmas when Aysha had stubbornly refused to even acknowledge her sister's presence. But, yesterday was another illustration of her mother's commitment to getting them back on sisterly terms.

Previously, she'd never understand why her mother had been so invested. Well, yes, she knew that no mother wanted her children estranged, and now that she knew that her mother had not ever spoken to her brother after she'd taken her father to see Mia, she actually did understand why her mom could not give up on them. Maybe on some level reconciling the relationship between her and Jada was putting to rest the demons of never having reconciled with her brother before his death.

Jada and Mia stood behind her mother, and Aysha decided to concede by simply smiling at her mother and continuing into the kitchen. She was so wrapped up in her own feelings that she didn't register what anyone was wearing or anything. Her mom had only requested that the whole family not show up draped in black. As she got into the kitchen, Malik and Jaylon were there, and still seated at the table. It did not escape her that Jaylon was sitting in her father's chair. An emotion that she could not quite identify was welling up. She was not sure if she was angry that Jaylon had assumed her father's place, although she was very clear that her father had instructed him, on his deathbed nonetheless, to do exactly that, or if it was grief over the fact that her father would never occupy that seat again. She felt a deep emptiness because she realized that her father would forever be absent from this kitchen, which was the room where she had the most memories of her father.

"Good morning, Ay. Why don't you have a seat and I will fix you a plate?" Malik offered when she walked in. Aysha could not say that she really knew her brother-in-law at all. She'd sat at the table with him on holidays, but in the four years that he and Jada had been together, they'd never had a real conversation. She didn't think they would today either, but she also knew that rebuffing his kindness was not going to be useful in her quest to just keep the peace today.

"Thank you. I would like breakfast casserole and two biscuits". She responded as she sat at the table. She did not sit in her usual seat, which was next to her father's chair that Jaylon was occupying. As she sat down, she noticed Jaylon was just staring at her.

"What?" she snapped. Just that quickly, she'd forgotten that she was supposed to be nice to him. She was even supposed to be conveying her thanks to him. She wanted him to stop staring at her like that.

"I am not sure if I should say this, since we are going to a funeral, but you look nice." Jaylon responded. He reached out and retrieved the bear-shaped dispenser of honey in the middle of the table, where there was strawberry jam, grape jelly, and maple syrup, and handed it to Aysha. She was a bit thrown off that he remembered. That simple gesture, coupled with his compliment, made Aysha feel a bit ashamed that she snapped at him.

"Oh, thank you." She mumbled.

"Uhm, is there anything else I can get for you? Would you like something to drink?" Malik asked. His comment seemed to set the room at ease. She knew the tension between her and Jaylon could be felt by anyone in a fifty-foot radius, and Malik probably knew the whole story anyway. At least she hoped he did. That made her a little sick to her stomach. Both of them were sitting at the table chatting it up, and both of them had slept with the same woman. She'd never understand how men did that. Perhaps if she did, she wouldn't have this battle raging in her as she finally looked at Jaylon when he stood up. All of that man in a tailor-made, black suit that probably cost more than her monthly salary should have been illegal. She wished she could take a picture of him, and as he moved around the kitchen, her eyes followed him. She was so enthralled with watching Jaylon, that she never answered Malik and did not notice that he left the room. Jaylon noticed her watching him and responded to her the same way she'd responded to him when he was staring at her.

"What?" He asked, but not nearly as rudely as she'd asked him a few minutes before.

"Oh, uhm, you look nice also. And, by the way, I just want

to thank you."

"For what?"

"Thanks for everything that you have done for my family. I have been no help to my mom. Actually, if I am honest, I have probably been another problem for her this week. Me and my issues" Aysha gave a half smile when she said the last part. "You know, I don't know if we could have done any of this without your help this week"

"Aysha, I promised your father that I would look out for you all, and I know it is difficult between you and me, and difficult between you and your sisters, but I intend to keep that promise as long as I am able." Jaylon was glad that she was being cordial to him, but he kept his distance. It would have been nice to go to the table and just have a real conversation with her, but he would not push it. The fact that she was even talking to him in a civilized manner, and that she was trying to be nice gave him hope. From the way that she'd watched him in that kitchen, he knew that she was not as unmoved by him as she pretended. He knew he wore the suit well, and he could see the appreciation of his male form in her gaze. Today was going to be hard enough for her, so he would not do anything to antagonize her. He did, however, tuck the remembrance of the smile on her face when she watched him move around the kitchen into his pocket, silently making a promise to himself. This time, he was going to fight for Aysha, even if it meant fighting Aysha, and he would not lose her this time. Last time, he sacrificed her for what he thought was the greater good. Well, this time, greater good be damned. Through hell or high water, mountains or valleys, oceans or ponds, he was getting Aysha back. She didn't respond to him, and he simply smiled at her and walked out of the kitchen.

No one in the world should be that fine, Aysha thought as Jaylon walked out of the kitchen leaving her alone. He was 6'4, 210 pounds, and of course, he kept himself in top-notch shape. She knew Jaylon would be one of those 50-year old men who would still have "it". She watched him walk away and noticed her mother and Jaylon's mother standing in the hallway looking into the kitchen at them. She could only wonder what they were thinking. She'd have to tread lightly. The whole family was already under the impression that she and Jaylon were back together, and she didn't want to put any more ammunition in that gun. It was time for her to move ahead. That meant letting all of her hurts go, wiping her own slate, and the slate of others clean and embracing a new reality for her. Too bad, she had to lose her father to realize just how much of herself that she'd lost.

After she finished eating, Aysha put her dishes in the sink and went into the family room. She wondered who was going to clean the kitchen. Her family had the same housekeeper for the last twenty years, and she was sure that Mrs. Marwa would be at the funeral with them. When she walked into the family room, she saw that her Uncle Rob had arrived. He was the only man that Aysha may have loved and respected as much as she loved and respected her father. He and her dad were two years apart, but she was sure that not more than seven days had ever passed without them seeing each other since her dad had quit playing basketball. This had to be hard for him. For as long as she could remember, her dad and Uncle Rob did everything together. They ran the investment firm together, traveled together, and in their spare time, they played golf together. She wondered was Jaylon as close to Uncle Rob as he was her dad.

She also saw that her twin Aunts, Barbara and Bea were outside. Standing side by side they made a very nice illustration of the number "10". Aunt Bea was always the vain one, and was always overly concerned about her appearance. Aunt Barbara, however, believed in the good life. She was always the life of every party. In addition to her aunts, she looked out the window and saw several of her cousins out in the driveway, and Jaylon was out there talking to her cousin, Greg. Greg was Aunt Bea's only son. His dad, her husband, was killed in a military ambush when Aysha and Greg were in 6th grade. Aunt Bea and Greg moved to Houston shortly after and Greg spent a lot of time at her house with her dad. He and Aysha were more like brother and sister than cousins. She wondered had Greg betrayed her as well, and carried on with Jaylon. Although Greg was in the military, he and Aysha spoke often and whenever he'd come home on leave, he'd always stay at Aysha's place, as Aunt Bea tried to treat him like he was still in 6th grade. She'd even tried to give him a curfew. Aysha was pretty sure that no one else in the family knew that Greg was gay. Over the years, Aysha and Kyra had covered for him in every way. In fact, he and Kyra pretended to date for so long that people were asking when they would get married. The truth was, Kyra was hiding a secret of her own and using Greg as a cover worked just fine for her. Greg never brought up the subject of her and Jada, and seemed to be the one person who understood Aysha's feelings. However, she was clear that he'd maintained a solid relationship with Jada, and was actually Lailani's godfather.

The family car from the funeral home pulled up into the driveway. Everyone began shuffling outside to begin getting loaded up so they could proceed to the church. Aysha was unsure if she could do it, but she picked up her purse and headed outside. As she stepped outside, it seemed all eyes were on her. She was pretty sure that the whole family knew what transpired between her and her mom yesterday. No doubt, her mom and her Aunt Barbara were thick as thieves, and had been as long as Aysha could remember. Aunt Barbara had moved to Houston shortly after Aysha was born to attend college at the University of Houston, and she'd lived with Aysha's family, helping her mom with two busy girls at the same time. Aunt Barbara had three children, but they were all at least 8 years younger than Aysha. She, Jada, Kyra, and Greg used to babysit for them. Aunt Bobby, as they called Aunt Barbara, could always be counted on to have the most junk food at her house. She was not known for her cooking skills, but Aysha loved to go to her house. Her parents rarely let them eat things like frozen pizza, frito pies, nachos, and fishsticks, which were all staples in Aunt Bobby's pantry. It was no wonder that all three of Aunt Bobby's children, and Aunt Bobby herself, were severely overweight.

Aysha headed to her car, as she had no desire to get into that family car. Before she could get there, her mom called for her to come and get into the car with them. As she spun around to answer her mother, she heard Aunt Belle's voice.

"Let me make it very clear that if anyone shows out today, I will show up. Now, I have not spanked anyone in years, but I promise you that I am going to get you if you get up in that church and clown like y'all did at Freddie B's funeral. Y'all shamed me at my brother's funeral, but if y'all think y'all are about to make a circus at James Earl's funeral, you better think again." Everyone dropped their heads, some in shame and some in laughter. Aysha's was a little of both, because they should have sold tickets to Uncle Freddie's funeral with all of the foolishness that went on. Aysha was quite sure if he was in heaven and looked down to see them getting $5 per person he would have been proud.

Uncle Freddie B was Aunt Belle's brother and for as long as Aysha remembered he lived with Aunt Belle, but didn't have a real job. He was like a grandfather to them. Uncle Freddie B's claim to fame was that he was always busy building or fixing something. What they'd love Uncle Freddie for most was that he never told them "no". His usual answer to any question was, "If you like it, I love it". Gregory had the memories of a broken arm from when Uncle Freddie gave him that advice when Gregory asked about jumping off of Aunt Belle's house. The one spanking Aysha could remember Aunt Belle giving her with a real belt was after Uncle Freddie gave her that same advice when she asked could she ride her bike to the snack shop in the next neighborhood, and she'd gotten back well after the street lights came home to Aunt Belle nervous, scared, worried, and angry. As a matter of fact, she realized most of the trouble they'd gotten into at Aunt Belle's house was a result of asking Uncle Freddie.

At Uncle Freddie's funeral, Aunt Bobbie's children put on a show. Aunt Belle walked out of the church when Sha'Tara, the oldest girl started doing a praise dance that looked like she was the headline act at Magic City. That was after Jada collapsed at the altar and Malik had to carry her out, twice. It was also after Quentin, Aunt Bobby's son, did a rap song in Uncle Freddie's honor. And, it was after Aunt Bobby sang a solo in a key that had every stray dog within a 5 mile radius around the church lining up in the parking lot. In retrospect, the fiasco had actually started when they were lining up to go pay their last respects and Aunt Bea started screaming, "Why Freddie, Lord. Why Freddie?" It didn't help when her oldest daughter, Nina, opened her purse to get tissue and a beer can fell out, in the aisle at the church. Luckily, Aunt Belle had never come back in because when they opened it up for remarks, Miss Faye, who'd been Aunt Freddie's "old lady", as he liked to call her, gave a repulsive speech about how she was going to miss having Freddie hold her tight at night, and told everyone that she was going to have to find another tree to climb. Unfortunately, as Aysha remembered, that was not the end of the tomfoolery. Not to be outdone, Aunt Debra, who was legally Uncle Freddie's wife, got up to talk about how Freddie left her well off and that although his shoes would never be under her bed again, he would always be with her, in spirit and in cash. At the cemetery the two of them had gotten into a shoving match, and they said some pretty colorful things to each other. Aysha specifically remembered Aunt Debra saying, "If I have to pull my wig off and beat this bitch in this cemetery, I am just ladylike enough to do that. I will do it for Freddie." So, Aysha was quite clear on what Aunt Belle meant and why she had to say it. In fact, she made up her mind that she was going to tackle any friend or family member that threatened to turn her father's funeral into some type of variety show.

Once everyone stopped laughing and reminiscing on that day, Aysha headed towards her mother to get into the car with her and realized that she could not breathe. She was feeling very light-headed, and began panting. She was having an anxiety attack in the driveway in front of her closest friends and family members on the day of her father's funeral. If she could catch her breath, she would laugh at just how dramatic and how much of a cliché that was. As a child, Aysha was known for being the drama queen, and there was no doubt in her mind that her whole family was looking at her from the perspective of those memories. All of the times that she'd feigned passing out, and all of the times that she'd thrown tantrums for one reason or another were not lost on her. Sadly, this was the real deal, and it was occurring at the most inopportune moment.

Before Aysha could get her bearings, Kyra was on one side of her and Valerie was on the other. She hadn't even noticed that both of them were there. They both held Aysha up, and tried to steady her. She heard her mom call out, "Is Kitty okay?" The responses were lost on her, as the only voice she heard was Kyra's reminding her that she was okay, and she could get through this. Kyra and Aysha had been friends since the first day of kindergarten. When Aysha left for college after high school, Kyra had moved to New York to pursue a modeling career that her overly religious parents did not approve of. She'd found moderate success, and decided to enroll in college while modeling. She'd eventually graduated with a degree in Public Relations from Columbia University, and now worked as the Director of Public Relations for one of the largest financial institutions in the world, and it was headquartered in Charlotte.

When Aysha and Jada lived in Charlotte, Kyra was still in New York, and would visit as often as she could. The third bedroom in their townhouse was as much "Kyra's room" as it was the guest room. It was during one of these visits that Kyra began dating Kenyon Clarke, the very married quarterback of Charlotte's football team. They met at a birthday party that the team had thrown for Jaylon, and many athletes from all sports were present. She and Aysha had stopped speaking for a while because of her decision to involve herself with a married man, but after a few months Aysha softened up. It was not her place to judge her friend. They were adults and Aysha would keep her two cents out it. After her fiasco with Jaylon and Jada, Kyra and Valerie were the only people she'd called and given the whole story. They didn't usually have secrets from each other. In fact, Aysha was probably the only person who knew that Kenyon Clarke was the father of Kyra's three year old son, and Kyra was the only person who knew Aysha's secret. None of that was important to Aysha, she was just happy that her friend was there with her.

As Aysha regained her composure, she realized that Jaylon was standing in front of her. Before she could question his intentions, he stepped in between her and Valerie, grabbed her hand, and said, "I will drive and you can ride with me". She was forever grateful for his presence in that moment. The tough exterior she'd been trying to muster up was disintegrating. She didn't even have the energy to sass him or put up an argument. She didn't even bother to answer, but rather simply allowed him to lead her to his car. She hadn't even gotten to the church and already she was unraveling. Aysha was quite aware that she'd had so many fastballs thrown at her this past week that she had easily wrapped herself in the anger of the family secrets, as opposed to getting pulled under by the grief of her father's passing. In this moment, she was acutely aware of the void that felt like her heart had physically been ripped out. The grief was quickly overtaking the anger in her, and she was on the verge of having a full-blown panic attack.

"You are one of the strongest people I know Aysha. You will get through today". She'd barely noticed that he'd gotten into the car. She hadn't realized that Kyra had gotten into the car also. Too bad Kyra was Jaylon's number one cheerleader and had been, so Aysha should have expected that she'd get her nosy behind in the car to see what was going on.

"I can't do this. I am not going. This is so not fair. I should not be going to my father's funeral today. I should be arguing with him about what he wants for Fathers' Day". Aysha just reclined in the seat, as Jaylon pulled his car behind the family car. Aysha closed her eyes. Jaylon put the car in park, and grabbed her hand, and she was in no position to resist.

"Aysha, I have no clue how you feel today, except that I

know how tight my chest has been since we left your father in that room at the hospital. No words are going to make this easier, but Aysha, I am going to be here, and you don't have to be strong. You don't have to try to hide how you feel. You lost your father, and if you feel like falling out, screaming, kicking, then do it".

"Yep, Aysha, just fall out girl." Kyra added. "I brought my Chinese fan, so I will whip it out and we will still look pretty when I am fanning you. I will fix your hair and everything because you do know that if you fall out your cousin, Quentin, is gonna put it on YouTube. If Sha'Tara does another praise dance we might even be able to charge for the video."

"Hush, girl!" Aysha responded as she started to laugh. The imagery of her falling out on the floor and screaming and kicking was one thing, but a video uploaded on YouTube with 100,000 hits was another thing. Oddly, she was sure that Quentin would have it on YouTube before they left the church. She could just imagine that going viral around her school. Yes, she'd better get herself together. Besides Aysha was sure that despite Aunt Belle's warning, Aunt Bea's children were going to give everyone a show before her mother would have to put a stop to it, or before Aysha would have to tackle someone.

"Well, you know I am just trying to put it all into perspective". Kyra responded and laughed, and Aysha fell back and relaxed in the softest leather seats Aysha had ever sat in. It seemed the pity party kept threatening to go on with her as the guest of honor, as she suddenly felt sad at the knowledge that her dad had made Jaylon return the Bentley that he'd tried to gift him. Who was this fragile, selfish, bitter person that she'd morphed into? This was definitely not the person that she wanted to be, and once she could find her "normal" after this funeral, she was going to find a counselor, therapist, coach, or somebody to get her past this.

"Jay, was this the type of car that you gave my dad?"

"Yes, just like this, but it was a smoke grey color".

Aysha just turned and looked out of the window. She exhaled

and tried to focus on the glass, because any other thought was going to result in her having an emotional meltdown in the car and that wasn't what she needed to happen at that moment.

When they arrived at the church, Kyra immediately got out of the car, almost before Jaylon could park. Aysha looked over to where she was heading, and saw Kenyon.

"Jaylon, why is Kenyon Clarke at my father's funeral?"

"Aysha, your father ran a very successful financial planning firm, and after I signed with him, many of the guys in Charlotte and a couple of other teams did, too. Kenyon was a client. There's no telling which players are going to show up here today. Your father was a good man and a role model to a lot of guys".

"Oh." Aysha and her father rarely spoke about his business. He tried hard to never bring work home, and after Aysha quit the banking industry, she knew he was disappointed, and the conversations about his business were even fewer. Again, she couldn't help but wonder how much she'd miss out on with her family in an effort to keep her vendetta against her sister going. She was keenly aware of the last statement her father made to her the last time he'd broached the subject of her and Jada prior to his deathbed lecture. It was the weekend of Jada's wedding, and she'd elected to hang out with her father, as opposed to going to spend the day being pampered at the spa with the wedding party. He'd told her, "Jada's happy. Her life has moved on. She'd love to repair the relationship with you, but she's not holding her breath for you to accept her apology. You keep playing the martyr and the victim, and I guess you got a right to do that. But, the only person drinking poison is you. The only person hurt and bitter is you. You can carry that around and keep killing yourself if you'd like, or you can put the poison down and move on. I am done with it. Ain't nobody still mad, but you. Ain't nobody still hurting but you." They'd eaten French toast and drank hot chocolate and her father had never even hinted at her and Jada reconciling again.

SEVEN-7

    The funeral went smoothly. Rev. Pritchett was not having any foolishness from the Rutherford clan in his church. He'd made a statement about how he expected a dignified service that proceeded according to the written program. Sha'Tara had to be carried out, but once Aunt Belle walked out to be with her, everyone else was clear that today was not going to be the day to host a family comedy show.

    Aysha left the church with her cousin, Terri. She'd decided that she was not going to the cemetery for the internment. She had no desire to see her father's coffin lowered into the ground. She was okay with the knowledge that it would be, but it was not necessary for her to see it. Instead, her sorors, cousins, and friends had all headed to the Hillberry Bar, which was one of Aysha's favorite hangouts. They had margaritas, Bellini's, and the best fish tacos in the city of Houston. Aysha decided that she'd rather be there than in the house with the rest of her family. Her mom would be furious, but she had decided not to go to the repast with her family.

    Later that night, Jaylon heard the phone ringing, but he didn't know where it was. He rolled over and turned the light on the nightstand on. He'd gone to bed after leaving the Rutherford's home quite late. Mrs. Rutherford had been content with showing Jaylon old pictures of her and her husband. It didn't seem the same without Mr. Rutherford. Not surprisingly, Aysha had not shown up for the repast. In fact, she didn't go to the cemetery either. Every since she'd met Mia, she'd been withdrawn completely from the family. That didn't concern Jaylon so much, but the fact that she seemed to have given up on even hating him concerned him. When he got the phone, he saw a missed call from strange number. Usually Jaylon didn't think twice about strange numbers, but with all that had transpired in the last week, he figured he'd better call back. He quickly unlocked the phone and dialed the number back. Shockingly, a man's voice answered the phone.

"Is this Jaylon?"

"Yeah, it is. Who is this".

"Yo, Jay. It is Devon Ranch. I am at the Hillberry Bar and your girl, Aysha, and two of her girls are in here, and none of them are fit to drive."

"Man, what".

"Dude, your girl is beyond gone, and she is sitting with a group of dudes that don't mean her anything good in her condition. But don't worry, I won't let her leave. I asked her where you were and she said something about not needing you to babysit her, but she is gone. Hell, I sent them three rounds of drinks, and they were here when I got here."

"Damn you Aysha," Jaylon responded. He looked over at the clock, and it was almost midnight. Aysha had left the church immediately after making sure her mom got in the car with Jaylon to go to the cemetery. That was around 2 p.m. Had she been drinking since then?

"Man, I am sorry to call you, but I figured you might want to come get her." Devon said.

"Devon, I owe you one. Her father's funeral was today. That's her favorite bar, so I should have known she would go there. I am on my way. I will be there in about 30 minutes. Please keep an eye on them for me." Jaylon hung up the phone and yelled "SHIT". Aysha always did know how to get herself into some strange situations. He laughed aloud at that thought. Jaylon picked up his jeans from the floor and went into his closet to grab a t-shirt. One whole side of the closet was still empty. It was a room that he and Aysha decided to convert to a closet to suit both of them in a house that they were supposed to share. Even though they'd not married, Jaylon kept the house and moved in. That closet was a daily reminder of just what he lost. Fortunately, he didn't have time for reminiscing about the past Aysha because the present one was giving him enough drama.

Jaylon decided to drive his old BMW. He was not about to let Aysha and her girls hurl all over his Bentley. That was his one gift to himself, and love or no love, she was not puking in his car. Besides, the BMW had enough stories to tell and he was sure that one more would not hurt it at all. There was very little traffic out, and the personalized plates that read "JFLOWS" pretty much assured that he would not be stopped regardless unless he was being ridiculously reckless. Jaylon arrived at the bar in much less than 30 minutes, and was shocked that there weren't more cars in the parking lot. Hillberry was a neighborhood bar and grill that usually had business every day of the week no matter what time you went there. The food was good and the atmosphere was laid back, and the drinks topped it off. The owner was a bit extreme but that all added to the allure of the bar.

When Jaylon walked in, he noticed two things. One, the number people in the bar did not match the number of cars in the driveway. Maybe carpooling was catching on in Houston or there was a city bus around the corner that was missing its passengers. Secondly, he noticed that Sammie, the owner, was sitting at the table wrapped around Jessica, one of Aysha's friends, who was also the realtor that sold him his house. Aysha and Kyra were sitting at the table with them, and there were two other guys. They looked like they were triple dating. In that moment, after seeing Aysha splayed out on that guy, Jaylon got angry, and his logic and reason fled the building. He headed over to the table where she was sitting.

"Aysha, let's go". Aysha looked at Jaylon and she was too intoxicated to even be surprised by his presence.

"What are you doing here?", she slurred. Her mannerisms and demeanor only served to ignite more fire in Jaylon. He looked around for Devon and saw him sitting at the bar. He turned and went to Devon. He walked over and they shook hands and he asked Devon for another favor. They had been rivals in college, but Devon played for Charlotte for three years before getting traded to Houston. During that time, he and Jaylon had become friends. They didn't keep in touch regularly, but they always had a minute and a word when they did run into each other. Devon agreed to take Jessica and Kyra home to Jessica's house, as she lived close to the bar.

By the time he walked back over to Aysha, she'd gotten up and was heading towards him. He was happy that she'd left the table. He and Sammie had a decent relationship, as he'd visited the bar quite a few times over the years, and he didn't want to mess that up, but all things where expendable, even friendships, when Aysha was involved. Without saying a word to her, Jaylon picked Aysha up, threw her over his shoulder and walked out of the club. He would've liked to think that people were shocked by what they saw, but he never turned around to see. Heading outside, he realized that she wasn't protesting nearly as much as he thought she would. In fact, she was giggling and just asking him to put her down, which he did once he got to his car that was illegally parked in the fire lane.

Once he got her in the car, he asked her where was her purse and keys. She said something about Valerie's car. He should have known that Valerie and Kyra would have been wherever Aysha was, but he couldn't believe Valerie would have left her at the bar if she'd known she was that intoxicated. Since she could not get into her house, he decided to just take her to his house.

"No, I am not going to that house. EVER!"

"Well, I can't very well take you to your mom's house like this, can I?"

"I don't care. I am never stepping one foot into my house....I mean, our house...your house"

Tears began to roll down Aysha's face.

"I've lost everything. Everybody. You. Jada. My dad. Every-body." And she silently cried.

Jaylon was not prepared for this. Angry Aysha. Sarcastic Aysha. Caustic and hateful Aysha. Yes, he knew how to deal with all of those. But, drunk, self-pitying Aysha was a creature he didn't even know existed, and would rather not deal with. Jaylon was tired, and didn't feel like arguing with her. She could sleep in the car in the garage, but she was going to his home, their home. Luckily, by the time they arrived at the house, Aysha could not protest because Aysha was fast asleep.

When he got to his house, he parked the car in the garage, and he lifted Aysha out of the car and carried her into the house. This was the first time that they'd actually been in the house together since agreeing that they wanted to buy it. Jaylon understood that he was using this moment to his advantage, but he also knew that he had to do whatever he had to do to get her back. This was probably not going to make her happy, but he was sure that she would be shocked at what she found.

Surprisingly when they got to the bedroom, Aysha started stirring. Jaylon put her down on the bed and reached over to turn on the lamp next to the bed. Much to his surprise, Aysha sat up and then proceeded to get off of the bed. She didn't appear to be very conscious of her actions, but Jaylon stood there as she pulled off her shoes, and her skirt and her shirt. He realized that she'd changed from the navy blue dress that she'd worn to the funeral, and had on a white, cotton button down shirt and a denim skirt. She stood next to the bed in nothing but bra and panties and looked around, as if trying to get a bearing on her surroundings. Then she moved back to the bed. Jaylon followed her. The one lamp was on in the room, and the room was softly illuminated. Jaylon watched in awe as Aysha crawled into the bed and tugged at the covers. She got under the covers in the bed and turned towards the lamp. She was still for about 10 seconds before she reached up and turned the lights off. Jaylon stood there in the dark and could only laugh at what he'd just witness. She didn't even seem to notice that he was in the room.

The bright red digital clock read "2:18" and in that moment Jaylon realized that he was quite tired also. He removed all of his clothing and in nothing but the skin God gave him, he climbed into the bed. Oddly, once he did, Aysha rolled over and put her arm across his abdomen and her head on his chest. He was in both heaven and hell. He hadn't really known how much he'd missed her, mind, body, and soul, until that moment. And he knew when she woke up in the morning with a very naked

Jaylon in the bed with her that he would have hell to pay. But, he smiled as he drifted off to sleep. It was worth it. It was definitely worth it.

Aysha rolled over in the bed, and was immediately aware of the warmth that was coming from beside her. She was afraid to open her eyes. In her last memory she was draped on some guy at Hillberry's, and she was not at all sure if the amount of alcohol she'd consumed had resulted in her going home with someone that she did not really know. One night stands had never been her thing, but she drank an amazing number of tequila shots the day before. Once she accepted that what was done was done, she opened her eyes, and was alarmed because she did not recognize anything about the room she was in. To make it worse, she became aware that she was in nothing but her underwear. She relaxed a little because if she still had her underwear on chances were high that she hadn't done too much that she should be ashamed of. She sat up in the bed, and looked to her left, and was shocked to see that Jaylon was asleep next to her. Like a curious child, Aysha, lifted up the covers and looked under. What had she expected? When they were together Jaylon never slept with clothing on. She thought he could have at least had the decency to put some on since he was in the bed with her. She had a million questions for him, but before she woke him up, she looked under the cover again. She was almost speechless. As fine as he was in that suit, having his unmarred paper bag brown body in the bed with nothing covering him took thoughts somewhere completely X-rated. She even forgot about the small man that was tap dancing in her head, when she was staring at his naked body.

Before she lost her nerve, Aysha reached out and stroked Jaylon's chest. She remembered how sensitive he was to touch. When she did, he began to stir, but did not wake up. That made Aysha excited, and emboldened her to keep going. Before she could even think of where her logic went, Aysha had her hands all over Jaylon. She avoided looking at Jaylon's face, but as he rolled over to lie completely on his back, she knew he was awake. On every level, Aysha knew that she should not be doing this. This was not going to resolve anything between her and Jaylon. It was not going to be the beginning of anything between her and Jaylon. Aysha had not had sex in over a year, and she was about to take full advantage of lying in bed with the finest man she knew. She could relieve some stress and when it was all said and done, she could go back to pretending Jaylon did not exist.

Before she could decide what to do next, Jaylon took over. He reached out for Aysha,'s hand, and positioned Aysha to sit on top of him, and began using his hand to remove her underwear. Aysha was getting impatient, so she stood up and removed them herself, and straddled him. Jaylon grabbed Aysha and flipped them both over so that he was over her. He didn't want to think about what was happening or what would happen after this day. He had Aysha willingly in his bed, she'd initiated sex with him, and he was going to give her exactly what she wanted. Surprisingly, Aysha did not resist him taking control.

When Aysha woke up she was in the bed alone and the clock on the nightstand said 3:10 p.m. She couldn't believe that she had slept most of the day away. Well, she hadn't really slept the day away. But, after Jaylon had given her quite the reminder of what she was missing, they'd both fallen asleep. Now, however, she was in bed alone. She was supposed to be at her mom's house for breakfast this morning. Her mom was already unhappy with her because she didn't go to the cemetery, and now she'd missed the family breakfast. She got up out of the bed to go and figure out where in the hell she was, and where in the hell was Jaylon. Aysha started to look for her clothes, but then decided that she needed a shower. She headed towards the door that looked like it should have been the bathroom, and as soon as she opened the door, she paused. This was Jaylon's house. Her house with Jaylon. She'd never inquired on what happened to the house when they didn't get married, and was somewhat surprised that Jaylon had actually moved into the house. Yes, that shower was looking like more of a necessity.

As Aysha got into the shower, she realized she was a bit sore. She smiled. Jaylon had always been very good in bed, and obviously in the last five years, that had not changed. She wondered if he would be willing to have sex with her one more time. She thought she should call him up to come and get in the shower with her. She could only laugh. Jaylon probably thought that she was losing her mind. She'd gone from hurling insults at him to trying to figure out how to get him into bed. What a difference a day made.

Aysha finished her shower and with a towel wrapped around her, she went into Jaylon's closet and grabbed one of his t-shirts and a pair of shorts. She realized that "her" side of the closet was completely empty. That saddened her a little, but she was determined to put all of that behind her. She was letting Jaylon off of the hook. It was time for her to move on, and she could not do that with the hatred she felt towards Jaylon and Jada. It was time to give it up. She would take her father's advice. It was time for her to stop drinking the proverbial poison because she finally understood that she was the only one still hurting. She was the only one who didn't go one with her life. She was truly the one drinking the poison while wishing that Jada and Jaylon would die. No more. As she dressed, she thought of what she would say to Jaylon. She really wanted to know how she'd ended up at his house. She wondered which one of her traitorous friends called him to come a rescue her from the bar last night.

Aysha came out of the bedroom, and took her time walking around the house. She knew the layout of this place, as she'd been the one to pick it out. Jaylon hadn't cared about anything except having a pool in the backyard, as he was like a fish in the water, and having a separate space for his workout room. Other than that, he'd consented to everything Aysha wanted in a house. She opened the door to the study, and was shocked at the painting she'd seen on the wall. Her father had the exact same painting in his study. It was a painting of Jada from the back holding a baby in such a way that the baby's face was almost visible. Aysha got angry, and started yelling for Jaylon.

Jaylon came to the study, and was breathing heavily as he was alarmed at the tone that Aysha was using. He wasn't sure if she was hurt or what happened. When he got to her, and saw the expression on his face, he knew that he was going to have to tell her the whole truth today.

"Calm down, it is not what you think

"Oh, it is not. Tell me why you have a picture of my sister and her baby in your study. Is Lailani your baby"

"Aysha, just stop. That does not even sound right"

"It doesn't? You slept with my sister once, why wouldn't I believe that you would do it again? I don't know how long y'all carried on before you passed her to Malik. Ugh. That is just nasty. I swear I hate you. And I can't believe that I just slept with you. What the hell was I thinking?

Jaylon did not want her to regret what just happened between them. He was preparing to use that as a springboard to help him get back into her life. This picture was messing everything up.

"Aysha will you just listen. Damn. You get riled up and go off and nobody can say anything. Can you just shut the hell up and listen for a change?

"Okay, then what? Talk. I am shutting the hell up. I am listening."

"That picture is not Jada, it is you, and I gave your dad a copy of it after he saw it in my study and I explained it to him"

"What? That is not me. You lie. I don't have a baby".

"Aysha, I commissioned the artist before we broke up. It was a gift to you. It was my way of saying that I wanted to start a family with you, and that I expected you to be the mother of my child. If you look closely at the baby's arm that is on her shoulder, you will see the shirt has my number on it. That is you holding our baby. Look at the letters on bag. It says "JALA… You do remember what that means?"

Aysha didn't know what to say. When she and Jaylon decided to get married, they decided to wait until Jaylon retired from basketball to have children. Well, actually, Jaylon decided that, and Aysha begrudgingly agreed. They'd always sign anything "JALA" as it stood for "Jaylon-Aysha- Love Always, and they agreed they would name their first daughter "Jala". If what he was saying was the truth, he'd changed his mind and was willing to start a family sooner for her. She was speechless. Before she realized what was happening, Jaylon reached out and wiped the tears from her face. He pulled her to him for a hug, and the fight was gone out of Aysha, and she started crying heavily. She was crying for what she and Jaylon lost, she was crying for the sister she'd lost, and she crying for the father she'd lost. They stood there like that for a few minutes before Aysha pulled away.

"Do you mind if I look around the rest of the house, and then I will need you to take me Valerie's house, so that I can get my purse"

"Yes, go ahead. I got your purse from Valerie already. There is coffee and banana bread in the kitchen, and I will take you home when you are ready".

Aysha didn't say anything. Her head was spinning. Everyone kept telling her how much Jaylon still loved her, and as she walked around his house, she was shocked at the number of her touches that were there. There was a guest room that was predominantly pink and green, her sorority colors. She'd wanted a room that was blue and white with a beach theme, and he'd followed through on it. The kitchen had all of the appliances that she'd picked out. She'd spent a small fortune in Williams-Sonoma and Sur le Table to get all of the things she'd wanted in a kitchen, and it was all there. In the dining room, his mother's china, that was given to Aysha at her bridal shower was tastefully displayed in a china cabinet that his mom had picked out just for her. She'd left the china at her parents' house. It dawned on her that in five years, she had never thought to ask them what they did with it. Aysha was overwhelmed.

She looked up to see Jaylon behind her, and she looked at him, and asked one question, "Why", she whispered.

"Aysha, I always thought that you would come back. I always thought that you loved me enough to forgive me and that someday we would share this house, so I left it the way you wanted it. The only thing I changed was the master bedroom, but everything else is like you planned, or as close to your plans as I could remember. I never thought that this whole situation would be raging all these years. I would have handled it much differently had I known that five years down the line, you'd still hate me".

"You hurt me. You and my sister hurt me". Aysha looked him right in his eyes as she said that. Jaylon dropped his head. There was so much he wanted to say.

"Let's go in the kitchen and eat, and then I will take you home."

Jaylon left out of the dining room where they were and went into the kitchen. He sat one of the barstools, and brewed coffee. He made white chocolate mocha and he made one for Aysha and himself also. A few minutes passed before Aysha joined him.

"I didn't make it to my mom's for breakfast. She is going to kill me".

"Don't worry. I called her and told her that you were here, and not feeling well, so she was not angry. She just said for you to call or come by when you could."

Aysha wanted to go to her mother, but she could not walk in their in Jaylon's clothes. That would set every tongue in the family to wagging, and she did not want to deal with that. She was sure that her mom had gladly told everyone that she was at Jaylon's house. She should probably go over and tell them to cancel the wedding that they were probably already planning.

"Well, I will go over there once I go home and change my clothes, and clear my head. Maybe I will make it by dinner time".

Aysha was surprised that she felt as good as she did-- considering the amount of alcohol she'd had the night before. By her last count, she'd had at least 2 margaritas, and 6 shots of tequila. She ate quite a bit though, as she gorged on fish tacos, tamales, and chicken wings while they were at Hillberry's. When the owner found out that her father died, he'd taken care of their entire tab, and gave them more free drinks. She'd thank him the next time she went in. Aysha also wondered how much her physical release with Jaylon had to do with her relaxed mood. Before she lost her nerve, she walked up to where he was sitting on the bar stool and removed her clothing. Jaylon didn't say a word, he just removed his shorts, sat down on the bar stool, and lifted Aysha to straddle him. She remembered exactly why she'd chosen those barstools, as they were sturdy and made from wood and wrought iron. After another release, Jaylon simply stared at Aysha. She knew that he was questioning her, but she didn't want to answer. She didn't want to tell him that the sex between them was simply a physical release, and that he was a part of her past.

She climbed down off of Jaylon and the barstool, and put her clothes back on. She went back up to Jaylon's bedroom and took another quick shower. She came back downstairs to find that Jaylon had obviously showered and dressed again. He wore a white t-shirt and jeans like no man had a right to. Aysha walked to the bar where Jaylon was sitting and grabbed her coffee and banana bread and moved to a stool at the end of the bar. Jaylon walked over and picked up her coffee and reheated it in the microwave. He was quite aware of the fact that she was putting distance between them, but he didn't comment on it. He knew her well enough to know that she was telling herself that this didn't mean anything. He also knew well enough that she'd initiated sex with him twice in one day, and he was interpreting that to mean a million other things whether she knew it or not. Jaylon was simply bidding his time. Aysha was going to be his wife whether she knew it or not. He was smart enough to know that this was the calm before the storm. Once the truth came out about him and Jada, all bets would be off.

EIGHT-8

It had been two months since Aysha's family had to bury her father. School was out, but her summer was quickly coming to an end. She made a few plans on things she wanted to do, but it was the beginning of August and Houston was hotter than ever. They were in the midst of a 100-day span with no measurable precipitation, and Aysha and her landscaping were bearing witness to the drought. Aysha had declared a truce with Jaylon, and she'd even been a little bit more than cordial to Jada, since she and Malik were going to remain in Houston for the rest of the summer, and return to Chicago in September when Malik had to return to coaching. Her mother was going to go and stay with them for a few weeks when they returned to Chicago. Aysha and Mia agreed that their mom could use a little time away and Aysha had gotten to spend quite a bit of time with her niece, Lailani, and even developed a bit of a relationship with Malik. He seemed like a nice enough guy. Mia was staying with Aysha's mom, and she and Aysha had developed a good relationship. After a few initially awkward interactions, Mia had blended into the family like she was always there. Her mom was skittish about living alone in that huge house, and Mia was making plans to remain in Houston, so the obvious choice was for her to just move in with their mom. Aysha could acknowledge that she was a little jealous. Jada had her mom's attention growing up, and it seems as an adult it was now going to go to Mia. However, she knew that Mia was the best suited to live with her mom. While Aysha loved her mother and sometimes longed for a deeper relationship with her, she understood that the two of them could not live safely under the same roof.

Aysha made the tough decision to not return to the classroom for another school year. Financially, she was fine. After four years of teaching, she'd been able to save money because of the savings she'd had from when she and Jaylon were together. Not to mention, her parents helped with a lot of her expenses whether she'd wanted them to or not. The car for her birthday, for instance was one example of the many things her parents helped with. Each year, they paid for her to go on a real vacation, and if she mentioned needing anything, her dad would have it delivered to her before she could finish the sentence. If Amazon had an MVP, her dad would have been it. Now, with her inheritance as well, she was fine financially, but if she were honest with herself, that was about the only area of her life that was not in turmoil.

She'd been helping Uncle Rob at the firm, and she would help until they were able to hire someone to take her father's place. Aysha missed her students, and she thought that she needed those connections. However, she was keenly aware that her family did need her a lot more than they'd initially demonstrated. She also forgot how much she loved numbers and working in the financial industry. She also loved working with her Uncle Rob, as she was keenly aware of how much he missed her dad. A couple of times, he'd yelled out for "Ford", the name he called her dad, on the intercom. The three sisters tried to divide their time so that no one of them was overwhelmed by her mother's attitude, which had gone from fiercely independent to shockingly needy in the two months since her dad died. They were spared a lot of it by Jaylon, who was at her mom's beck and call when he was able to be.

They'd read her father's will two weeks after his funeral. Surprisingly to Aysha, he'd left the majority of his share of the investment firm to Jaylon and Malik, and left all of his real estate to her mom. While they all shared stock in the firm, Jaylon and Malik were to be primary partners with Uncle Robert, and all of them had gotten a share of the $10 million her father had in life insurance. Her mom had gotten $4 million dollars, and Jada, Aysha, and Mia had gotten $2 million each. She'd been surprised that her father had put Mia in his will and provided for her equally, but apparently, he'd done so not long after she'd first contacted them. Uncle Rob received money as a result of an insurance policy that made the business the beneficiary, and her dad had a separate policy that was for Aunt Belle and his other sisters. Her dad always said that he would always take care of his girls, and even in death, he'd made sure everyone was financially sound. Uncle Rob wasted no time setting up accounts for everyone because he knew that Aunt Bobbie's children would be after her money as soon as they heard about it. He put himself on her account so she could not withdraw anything without his permission. She was waiting on the battle that was going to start when her cousins found that out.

Although she hadn't had a conversation with him about it, Mia told Aysha that Jaylon was planning to retire from basketball after one more season. He wanted to go to law school so that they could expand the financial services to more of an agent relationship and be able to negotiate contracts. He had a degree from Texas State University, and majored in Business Administration, and unbeknownst to Aysha, Jaylon received his MBA degree from the University of Houston in May, and spent the last couple of years as somewhat of an apprentice to her father and Uncle Rob. Since Jaylon had firsthand experience in contracts, he discussed the expansion plan for the firm before her dad died. He intended to keep his word, and Uncle Rob would handle the financial investment side and Jaylon would handle the legal representation and contract matters of their clients. There were also two other attorneys on staff, so they would take a larger role until Jaylon could finish school. Malik would continue coaching, but would work more with marketing the firm to new clients. It amazed Aysha that her father had already set all of this in motion.

Aysha was honest in that she was surprised her father had put Jaylon in his will, but over the last two months she'd found out a lot of things about her father's relationship with Jaylon. While it hurt her that her family kept their ties with Jaylon, she was also happy to know that Jaylon had made sure that the last five years of her father's life were very happy and that he got a chance to do a lot of things that he'd always talked about with Jaylon. The Super Bowls, the NBA finals, golf tournaments, and he'd probably met every athlete that he liked watching via Jaylon's connections. She just wished he could have shared more with her, as opposed to hiding his relationship with Jaylon. But, she was also honest enough to admit that she would have cut her parents off if she'd known they were so close to Jaylon.

When Aysha got to her mom's house, Mia was coming out of the house and she looked flustered.

"What's wrong, MeMe?" Aysha asked. Strange how quickly they'd develop nicknames for each other, as Mia called her "Sha". Aysha couldn't stand to hear "Kitty". Even though many family members called her that, that was the only name her father ever used for her. Many of her family, even Aunt Belle had picked up on Mia's "Sha" and in two months Aysha had a new name. It was still uncanny to look at Mia because she looked like the tanned version of her own face.

"Nothing. Well, not really. I am going to leave and try to clear my head before I say something to your sister that I will regret".

Aysha laughed. "My sister? You can have that heffa all to yourself. And what the hell, tell me what you want to say, and I will say it. I promise you I won't regret it".

"I just get tired of her snide comments. I know that I have not been a part of this family long, but I don't need her to rub it in every chance she gets. Mom is my mother as much as she is yours and hers".

"Well, actually…."

"Don't go there, Aysha. I won't let her go there, and I am not going to let you go there. Our parents loved us all equally. And sometimes, I am sure that mom loves her more."

"Okay, Okay. I was just saying. Where are you going?"

"Momma wants some Frenchy's chicken, so I am going to get some, and hopefully, she and her family will be gone by the time I get back".

"Well, bring me some too, and some peach cobbler. And, no, I don't have any money. I am just a poor school teacher".

"Poor, poor School teacher, hunh" Mia replied and they both started to laugh. Since they'd received their inheritance, Mia and Aysha kept joking about being poor. While they were standing there laughing, the front door opened, and Jada came out.

"What are the two peas in a pod laughing at?"

Simultaneously, they both replied, "You", and then they started laughing harder, and they each turned and went in a different direction, leaving Jada standing there. Aysha headed into the house, as Mia went and got into her car. Jada followed behind Aysha.

"Yall better not have been talking about me." Jada spat out. Her tone of voice was agitating to Aysha.

"And if we were?" Aysha spun around to face Jada as she responded. She'd spent the better part of the last two months being nice to Jada, but there was still an ass-whipping on hold that she owed Jada, and today was as great a day for a beat down as any other.

"It seems you two get your kicks out of excluding me, but y'all still talk about me. I guess if I am all you have to talk about, I should be flattered".

"Girl, please. You really think Mia and I spend a second talking about your raggedy ass. I don't exclude you. I try not to think of you at all. Get a life."

"Me, get a life? No, you are the one my poor, dear, miserable, baby sis who needs to get a life. I got a husband, a baby, and a job. What do you have?"

"I would have had the same if you didn't jump on every dick you saw. I wonder if your husband knows about your 'ho-hopping' ways'. You might be a wife and a mother now, but you are also a whorish tramp. You know, you gotta let a ho be a ho".

"You better watch your mouth and what you say to me."

"Or else what, Jada? What are you going to do? I swear I owe you a beat down already and if you don't get out of my face, you gonna get it today". Aysha turned to walk away. If she started beating Jada, she wasn't sure she could restrain herself from killing her. Her sister had cost her a lot, and an ass-whipping was not equal compensation, but it would allow her to burn off some frustration.

"Ain't nothing between us but air and opportunity" Jada said, spreading her arms out wide to demonstrate.

Before Aysha knew what happened, she turned around and walked back toward Jada. She'd been so intent on hitting her sister in the face that she didn't notice that her mom entered the foyer during their verbal exchange.

"Air, opportunity, and me. You two better cut it out right now before I get in and fight both of you. You know better".

Aysha took a look at her mom, and then back at her sister. She was not by any stretch of the imagination ready to let it go. Jada wanted a fight today; Jada was going to get a fight today.

"I pity you. You screwed your way through college and every place you have ever been. What type of pitiful chick sleeps with her sister's fiance'? Me? Get a life? Interesting choice of word, since for as long as I have known you, you have wanted my life." Aysha was going to just let it go. Their relationship was already irreparable, but she wasn't sure that she could refrain from beating her like the tramp she was, and her mom would never forgive her for doing it in her house.

"Your life? You think you are so freaking special, and you always have. Everybody has to bow down to Kitty. Well, I don't. Yes, I slept with Jaylon, and you should get over it. Now what are you going to do about it?"

Before Aysha could even process the full impact of her words, she ran back and swung at Jada again. This time her fist grazed Jada's cheek. It was her mom's fault she hadn't knocked that heffa into next week. Her mother had gotten between them, but it did not stop Aysha from swinging at Jada's face again. Her mom blocked the second punch, but Aysha still swing again. Out of nowhere, Malik was in the room and grabbed Jada. Both she and Aysha were screaming at each other like two women in the street.

"Stop it. Now, I am sick of both of you. Jada, you were wrong for what you said to your sister. You know good and damn well that you were wrong in every way, and I am ashamed that you would say such to your sister. I don't know what kind of satisfaction you have gotten all these years out of knowing that you were hurting your sister. And you, Aysha, have been no better. You have allowed your hatred of Jada to tear this whole family apart, and your dad and I watched it, but I am not going to have it. Not in my house. Not today and not any other day. So, the two of you can figure out how to get along, or you can both get the hell out of my house right now, because I am not dealing with this any longer."

Aysha was staring at her mom. She heard the words but could not properly digest them. She wanted to swing at Jada again, but she knew if she did her mother might never forgive her. Aysha turned around and stepped around everyone and walked into the family room. She wished Mia had been there. Mia would have let her get at least one or two real punches in before she stopped her. She was sick of Jada. It seemed the more cordial she tried to be to Jada, the more hateful Jada was. She'd always felt like Jada was jealous of her, but she'd always tried to reassure her sister that they were not in a competition. Some of the hurtful things that Jada had done to her over the years resurfaced. Aysha had always played them down. Now, it made her think about the real reason Jada slept with Jaylon. Was it just to hurt Aysha? She was going to get an answer, but after all that transpired; she had no desire to appease Jada. She wanted Aysha to get a life. Well, agitating Jada was about to be a full-time job.

Jada went into the backyard with Leilani, and Malik went back to the family room where he was watching television. Aysha wanted to see her niece, but she'd wait until later. If she went outside right now, she and Jada would no doubt have to go a round or two and she didn't think it was the best idea for Lailani to see her mom and aunt in a brawl. So, Aysha went into the family room and lay across the couch. Her mother came in behind her and sat in her father's recliner and she appeared to be going through mail.

"I am still getting cards from people paying their respects. Your father knew so many people."

"He was a good man, mom. That was daddy. He never met a

stranger".

"Yes, the world is missing a great man", Malik added. Aysha barely noticed him in the room. In the last two months, she'd gotten to know him a little better. He seemed like a pretty straight up guy, and genuinely cared about her sister and niece. Obviously, he had some character, since her dad liked him. Then again, her father liked Jaylon too. Physically, he was quite handsome, she could admit. He wasn't Jaylon, but at 6'0, and excellent physical shape, he could hold his own. He was 8 years older than Jada, making him 11 years older than Aysha. Aysha stared at Malik, and while he was attractive, there was nothing attractive enough to make her cross the line with her sister's husband. She'd never understand how Jada did what she did.

It took Mia about an hour to return with the food, and Aysha was starving. As soon as she heard Mia coming through the front door, she got up to go and meet her. She was surprised to see Jaylon walk in with her. Her insecurities immediately jumped up, and she was speculating a million reasons why Jaylon and Mia were coming in together. She didn't want to appear to care about Jaylon, so she said nothing.

"Look who I found blocking the driveway with the pimp ride of his. I would have hit that raggedy car if I thought he wouldn't sue me." Mia said and laughed. Why certainly no one would call his Bentley "raggedy". Jaylon was behind her carrying the bags of food, and Mia was coming through the foyer to the kitchen.

"Oh, hey Jay" Aysha said and turned around. She'd been nice to him, but she also kept her distance. Since that day that she'd spent sexing him up after her father's funeral, she'd avoided any personal contact with Jaylon. He'd come by to check on her a couple of times, but she'd made sure someone else had been at the house so that they could not be alone. He seemed to live at her mom's house. Every time she called or came by he was there. She was looking forward to his season starting so he could go back to Charlotte.

Aysha went in the kitchen and began setting out all of the

food. She told Mia about her altercation with Jada, and drama-tized her swinging at Jada's face before their mom got involved. Mia was shocked, and was even more shocked when Aysha swore that she was going to do it again if Jada even looked at her wrong. Luckily for the sake of the family, dinner proceeded without an issue. Everyone ate and talked, and while Jada and Aysha didn't say a single word to each other, it did not make din-ner more awkward than normal. After dinner, everyone settled in the family room, and Mrs. Rutherford announced that she'd made cupcakes, and went to get them.

When Mrs. Rutherford left the room, Aysha shuffled out of the room quickly behind her. She rushed to the bathroom, and was head down into the toilet vomiting everything that she'd just eaten. She broke out in a sweat, and just barely had time to close the door before anyone would see her bent over the toilet. Aysha stood up, flushed the toilet, and looked at herself in the mirror. Aysha already knew what was going on. She'd missed her cycle already, and now this morning sickness was coming with a vengeance. Last month, she'd missed her first cycle, but she'd assumed it was the stress of everything. Now, her cycle hadn't come for a second month, and she was vomiting, she knew all too well that those two events together usually signaled one thing. She would need to make an appoint-ment to see the doctor, and if her instincts were correct, she needed to decide what she wanted to do.

There was a knock at the door, Aysha rinsed her mouth with water, and then opened the door. It was Jaylon standing there. When she opened the door, he didn't say a word, he just looked at her. They had about a 30 second stare down and he finally spoke,

"Hey, are you okay. You didn't look so good".

"I am fine. You know fried food does not always agree with me. No worries, I am good.

"Ok, okay. So, there is nothing for me, I mean us to be con-cerned about?"

"Nope. It is just my sensitive digestive system. I don't

typically eat fried foods, so that did not sit well with me. But thanks for checking". Aysha tried to shuffle around him to leave the bathroom, but Jaylon knew she was hiding something. He was pretty sure he knew what that something was. Aysha's tendency to be overly polite when she was wrong was always a dead give-away when she was keeping a secret. He wouldn't push her today, but soon he was going to make her tell him what he already knew.

He'd watched her closely the last month. He noticed that she came to her mom's house and fell asleep almost every day. Aysha was a textbook busybody and taking naps was not her thing. He noticed that she ate things she'd never really liked. Tonight was a dead give-away because Aysha never ate Frenchy's chicken. Her father used to get it all the time, but he would have to stop at Popeye's for Aysha as she seemed to have a vendetta against Frenchy's. She always said it was too salty. Today, Jaylon watched her eat three pieces of chicken with no complaint. He knew exactly what was going on. He also knew that he was about to be in for the battle of a lifetime if he tried to intervene. But, he decided it was worth it.

The rest of the evening was a blur for Aysha. She was so entrenched in her new reality. She was pretty sure that she was pregnant, and she was positive Jaylon was the father. She did not want to have a baby right now. She did not want to have a baby with Jaylon. She had no desire to be a single-mother, and she didn't want to go back and play house with Jaylon just because of this child. Déjà vu. She'd been here before. Aysha had some real choices to make, and based upon the calendar, she was at least 8 weeks along, so she needed to make a choice soon. How did she manage get herself into this situation?

Realistically, she knew that she needed to face her reality. First thing, was setting a doctor's appointment to confirm what she already knew. She needed to think about work. She could still work at the firm, but Uncle Rob would fight her on it. That, she was sure of. Before she could follow this train of thought, she heard Mia saying that her purse, which was on the table by Mia, was vibrating.

Aysha got up and retrieved her purse and phone, and went back to the couch. It was almost 10 p.m., so she wasn't sure who would be calling her this late. When she took out her phone, she saw a number she didn't recognize, and whoever it was left a message. Aysha listened to the message and was stunned. It was from a police officer and they were saying that they had her daughter, Kassidy Rutherford, and they needed her to come down to the Northeast Substation. Aysha was in shock, as she realized that it must have been really serious if Kassidy called her and not her mom.

"Sha, what is it? You don't look good." Mia asked.

"One of my former students is at the police station by the school where I used to work. She had the police call me and told them that she is my daughter. I need to go and see what is going on." Aysha responded as she stood up quickly, which made her momentarily dizzy.

"Are you okay, Kitty? What is going on"? Her mom asked.

"Ma, I am fine, but I have to go and see what is going on."

"Aysha to the rescue. Of course." Jada chimed in. Everyone in the room turned and looked at her. Her mom just rolled her eyes at Jada and didn't respond. Jada shrugged her shoulders like she had no clue what she'd just said was completely inappropriate and unwarranted.

"You know what. You have been trying to push my buttons all day. If I didn't have something more important to tend to than your fat, miserable ass, I would actually stay here and entertain you. But, I am sure you have some ho-hopping to go and do. Go find a dick and sit on it. You are pretty good at that. In the meantime, trust and believe the next time I run into you, I am going to give it to you. I have held back on saying a lot of things to you and about you because I still understand that we were blood. But considering that we are only half blood, all bets are off. Next time, my dear half-sister, you will find out why they really call me "Kitty" because I am going to show you my claws. And I swear up and down that I don't give a damn about whoever is in the room. I am going to read your whole book, from front to back. Just remember you started it. You can take it to the bank that I am going to finish it."

"So, you two are just going to disregard me. Like I didn't tell you earlier to drop it. And Aysha, you just say whatever with no respect to me. Jaylon, drive Aysha to the police station. Malik, drive Jada home. They both need to get out of my house right now before I start reading books from front to back and they will both need to be rescued. Good night". Mrs. Rutherford stood up and left them all there in the family room.

Aysha knew that she was going to have to pay for what she said, but she had some things that she needed to say to Jada, and now, she was more determined than ever to say them. Now, she needed to say it to the world. She thought she was trying to get over it, but it seemed like she was going to be jumping right into it. But, she was wise enough not to argue with her mom about Jaylon driving her to the police station. She needed to pick her battles right now, and that was not worth fighting, especially since she really did not feel like driving at all, and going to the Northside in her current state of mind was not the smartest choice.

NINE-9

Jaylon and Aysha took the thirty-five minute drive from MacGregor Park to the Houston Police Department (HPD) sub-station on Ley Road in Northeast Houston. When they arrived, the situation was so much worse than Aysha could have ever imagined. Kassidy had been arrested for prostitution. To make it worse, her mother had actually been arrested with her. According to Kassidy, her mother had forced her to go to a local bar and forced the girl to solicit herself to the patrons in the bar. Fortunately for Kassidy, HPD Vice had been working that bar that night on the lookout for an area woman who was intentionally spreading the HIV virus to unsuspecting johns. Kassidy and her mother had been separated upon arriving at the station since Kassidy, at 14 years of age, was a juvenile. It helped tremendously that Jaylon had gone with her. His popularity among the officers had gotten them some favors, and Aysha was truly grateful for that. After a thorough explanation of her relationship to Kassidy, and Jaylon's assurance that they would take care of her, the officers arranged for Kassidy to leave with Aysha.

The police officers were able to verify that most of what Kassidy said was true. The officers who worked that area told Aysha that while her mother was a well-known prostitute in the neighborhood, they'd never seen Kassidy. What was unavoidable was reporting the incident to Child Protective Services (CPS). The case worker from CPS was already at the station when they arrived. Luckily for them, the case worker, Justine Washington was an associate of Aysha's, as she handled the cases of several students at Aysha's school. Mrs. Washington agreed to allow her to take Kassidy home with her for the night, and they agreed to report to the CPS main office in the morning. CPS would be investigating the incident, and Mrs. Washington made it clear that even with the few facts that she had, she would be pushing for Kassidy to be removed from the home. Aysha could not agree more, but she had no idea what that would mean for Kassidy and her 6-year old sister.

While they waited, Aysha asked Kassidy about her sister, Kai. Kassidy informed Aysha that her sister was spending the night at a neighbor's apartment. Once Aysha shared that with Mrs. Washington, she arranged for a police escort to take Kassidy to get her little sister. The adults agreed it might be best if Kassidy went and got her little sister, to avoid an emotional outburst from the little girl or a confrontation with the neighbor. Aysha was relieved, as Kassidy's anxiety lessened when Aysha told her that they would pick up her sister

Aysha and Jaylon agreed to wait at the police station while Kassidy, the caseworker, and an officer when to pick up her little sister. They did not want this situation to escalate by having a crowd going to get the little girl. While they were waiting for Kassidy to get her sister, Aysha called her mom. She was honest. She loved children, and she loved working with children, but she was in over her head in this situation. She was more comfortable with taking them to her mother's house, with her mom and Mia, than taking them to her house. Her mom answered on the first ring."

"Kitty, is everything okay".

"Mommie, I need your help. I don't know what to do". Aysha sighed. She was on the verge of tears. She was just beginning to absorb the magnitude of the situation. What type of mother prostituted her 14-year old daughter? She'd felt these emotions before. So many days, as a teacher, she'd wanted to do like Cicely Tyson and Richard Pryor in *Bustin" Loose*, and just get her students on a bus and drive them far away from their realities.

"Yes, baby. You know that I will always help any way I can". He mother answered. Aysha knew in her heart of hearts that it was true. Her mother was the most giving person she'd ever known.

"Mom, I will tell you the whole story when I get there, but I have my student and her little sister. They can't go back home. EVER! I would like to bring them to your house tonight, and we can sort it out tomorrow." Aysha was tired. She had her own situation to deal with. She was still trying to come to grips with that, and now she had two little girls thrust into her life, and although she wasn't sure of what she could or what she would do, she was sure that they could not go back to their mother. God just didn't play fair.

Aysha finished the conversation with her mom, and was oblivious that Jaylon was sitting next to her. She was grateful for his presence. His fame ensured that they were treated with a higher level of respect, and he'd promised to come to the Fun Day in the Park that the officers hosted for the children.

"Jaylon, I know I must make it difficult sometimes for you to be nice to me. But, I truly do thank you for coming with me tonight. I don't think I could have done this without losing it. I am not sure that I am not going to lose it at some point tonight."

"Ay, don't worry about it. I'm always here when you need me, even when you don't want me to be". He chuckled and grabbed her hand. She didn't even pull it back, and they just sat quietly hand in hand until Kassidy and her little sister returned. Kassidy was holding her little sister in her arms, and the little girl was whimpering.

"She is afraid of the police. I told her that they would not hurt her, but she's seen them come to our house to get our mom and they aren't nice about it, so she doesn't believe me". Kassidy explained before Aysha even had a chance to ask. Before Aysha could make a move, Jaylon stood up and took the little girl from Kassidy. She was hesitant to let him touch her, but Kassidy told her it was okay, and Jaylon was smiling and telling her that he wouldn't hurt her, and he would not let the police get her either. When she finally went to Jaylon, she turned her head into his neck, and continued whimpering. It was heartbreaking to watch.

"Mrs. Washington, can we leave? I would like to get them something to eat, and in the bed so that we can be at your office by 11:00 a.m. We signed all of the papers, gave copies of our I.D., and gave contact information for where we will be."

"Yes, Ms. Rutherford, you all can go. But, I need to speak to you alone before you go".

"Oh, okay." Aysha was a little startled, but she was ready to get out of this police station.

"Jaylon can you bring the car around and Kassidy can you go and wait over by the door".

"Sure". Jaylon responded and he tried to give Kai back to Kassidy, but she would not let go of her hold on Jaylon.

"Kai, c'mon he has to get the car. You can stay with me"

"That's okay. She can come with me. I can get her situated in the car. How about both of you come, and then we can drive around and get Aysha."

"Ms. Rutherford, is that okay", Kassidy asked.

In light of them being at the police station because of a prostitution charge, Aysha was surprised by the innocence Kassidy displayed. She was one of Aysha's favorite students. She hadn't been a student in Aysha's class in two years, but not a single day went by that Kassidy didn't come to her classroom. When she could, she would sneak to come have lunch in Aysha's room. She was always asking Aysha about college, and work, and other ways to better herself. Aysha had signed her up for Big Brothers and Big Sisters, and Aysha ended up being selected to be her mentor. One of their monthly activities was to go to the homeless shelter that Valerie ran. Aysha wanted Kassidy and her other students to know that there were people with worse realities than theirs. As a result, Kassidy was often a babysitter for Valerie. Aysha knew that her mother was not the best parent, but she had no idea that her mother would go to this level. Aysha had stopped giving Kassidy money because she knew her mother would take it. In her mind, Kassidy was one of those children that could go far. However, she wasn't going to have much of a chance with a mother who was willing to pimp her out at 14. Aysha was glad that she'd had the thought to call her when she'd gotten to the police station.

She watched them walk out, and then turned to Justine, the case worker.

"Aysha, we've worked together on a couple of cases in the past couple of years, and I know you want to do the right thing. I know you really do. But, when you take these girls home tonight, I need you to know that you are setting up an expect-ation with them. You saw how the little one has attached to your friend already. I need you to consider what role you want to play, and unfortunately, we don't have time to waste. When you come to my office tomorrow, I need an answer. Are you going to be in it for the long haul with these girls, or would you prefer that I find them a foster family to take them in. I have a couple that I know that are really good, and that will keep them together. One in particular will also allow you to visit with them. She is a teacher at North Forest High School, and has been a foster parent for over 20 years."

"Justine, I don't know what I can do. I just knew that when she called I had to come. I am actually taking them to my mother's house, and my sister is there also. We will have to talk about this as a family, but I will have an answer for you when we get to your office tomorrow. Are you sure that this foster home will be a good one? How long will they be able to stay there?" Aysha responded.

"The lady will take them for up to one year. If we do get her mother's parental rights terminated, and that would be after the investigation and court hearing, then, we look for more permanent placement. Kassidy will be 15 or 16 by then, and I don't have to tell you how difficult it is to find permanent housing for a 16-year old. At the same time, I don't want you to commit to something just because you are feeling sad and guilty and not look at the consequences. There will be a long transition process if you choose to do it. I will support you in any way I can, but you work with these children every day, and you know as well as I do how hard it is to undo some of the conditioning they have received from parents. But, we need to move quickly. The longer they are with you, the more attached they will become, and the more difficult it will be to transition them should you choose not to take them in permanently. We don't want to make this any more difficult than it has to be."

"I understand. Would it be possible for us to get a later appointment? I just want to make sure that I am making the right decision."

"What I will do, if you will explain it to them, is allow you all to come in on Monday". Tomorrow is Friday, and they can stay with you for the weekend. But you must let them know that they are just with you for the weekend, and you can come at 10:00 a.m. on Monday.

"Thank you, Justine. Thank you. We will see you on Monday. Good night".

"Good night. Call me if you have any questions about anything. I want to help you any way that I can."

Aysha was grateful, once again for small favors. She didn't know what her decision was going to be, but she had three days to talk about it and get input from her mom, Mia, Valerie, and Kyra. She hadn't left her house tonight with the intent of adopting two children, but she also knew the realities of the foster care system, and she was not sure that she could sleep at night knowing that was what she was subjecting Kassidy and Kai to. She'd had no idea what she was committing to when she'd come to Kassidy's aide, she just knew that she had to go to her. She'd given every student her phone number and told them to call at any time when they needed her. This wasn't her first emergency, but it was the first time that she would get so involved. What could she do? A voice in her head said, *"You can't save them all"*. However, that voice was countered with her heart, which said *"You must save as many as you can"*.

Aysha walked to the front doors of the station, and was instantly annoyed. There was a TV news camera setting up outside. Couldn't people have any privacy? Someone in the station had obviously leaked that Jaylon was here. She was glad they'd gone to the car, and ever more grateful that the car had darkly tinted windows, and with it being nighttime, they would not be able to see inside of the car. The girls did not deserve this, and neither did she. This was certainly a component of Jaylon's life that she did not miss at all. Aysha turned and went back to the Sergeant's Desk.

"Sir, is there anything you can do about the TV camera that is outside.".

"Yes, ma'am. Can you let Mr. Flowers know to come through the gate that is marked "Personnel Only"? You can go out that door, and they won't see your face. They will only see the car as it pulls out."

"Thank you. Thank you so much".

Aysha pulled out her cell phone and called Jaylon. She explained to him what to do, and the officer escorted her through the building so she could go out of that exit. In the five minutes that it had taken, there were two additional TV stations that had gathered. *Vultures*, Aysha thought.

After stopping to get the girls some food, they arrived at her mom's house, and both of the girls were asleep in the back seat. It was almost sinful to wake them, but Aysha needed them to both see where they were, and who they were with. Aysha woke them both up, but Jaylon opened the back door and unlatched Kai's seatbelt and lifted her out of the car. Kassidy was groggily walking behind Jaylon, and she had the bags of food in her hand. Apparently, they'd both gone to sleep without eating.

Aysha's mom was standing on the porch waiting for them. She could see Mia sitting on the staircase, looking tired and annoyed. Before she could say a word, her mom walked up to Kassidy and said, "Hi, baby, c'mon in. I have been waiting for y'all". She put her arm around Kassidy, and Aysha was surprised when Kassidy started crying. Her mom stopped in the foyer and turned and hugged the girl, and let her cry. She was stroking Kassidy's hair and whispering reassuring words. Aysha had never known Kassidy to cry about anything. She was a tough and resilient girl, but something happened tonight that scared her, and before the weekend was over, one of them was going to get the full story out of them.

Her mother walked Kassidy into the family room and sat down on the couch with her. Kassidy stopped crying, but she didn't let go of Mrs. Rutherford. Jaylon sat down, and Kai was curled up in his lap. She was looking around the room, and kept peeking at Mia, but she would not let go of Jaylon. Aysha sank into the sofa that Jaylon and Kai were sitting in. This had been the longest day in a long time. It was now 2 a.m. To her surprise, Kai crawled into her lap and rested her head on Aysha shoulder, but grabbed Jaylon's hand.

"Kai and Kassidy, this is my mom, Mrs. Rutherford. Over there is my sister, Ms. Mia."

Neither of the girls spoke, they remained curled up in their respective laps and seemed a little dazed. Aysha couldn't even consider what either of them was going through. She needed to talk to the adults, and she needed them to eat before they went to sleep.

"Kassidy, why don't you two go and sit at the dining room table and eat your food, and then we can find you something to sleep in for bed. Tomorrow, I will go and get you some clothing and other items you will need."

"Okay. C'mon Kai, let's go eat.

Mia stood up with the girls.

"C'mon, little ladies. We might even have some cupcakes left over. Let's go see, and I can talk to Aysha later".

Mia taking the lead with the girls was a relief to Aysha. Her head was reeling and she needed to tell her mom the details of the situation, and she could tell Mia later. She really wanted to go and take Kassidy's place and curl into her mom's side, but she also needed to get the facts out.

"Mom, you will not believe why she was at the police station. Her mother forced her to go to a club and prostitute herself."

"Are you serious? Some of these people don't deserve children. Is her mother on drugs?"

"I don't think so. Kassidy has never mentioned anything. Her mom just seemed like the type to want to always party, so she was usually glad that I would pick Kassidy up. I know that she would take the money that Valerie and I gave her, but I don't know if drugs are involved. The neighbor has a daughter Kai's age, so apparently Kai stays over there a lot." Aysha answered her mom's questions, and gave her more information about Kassidy. Her mom had heard about Kassidy, but had never met her. She told her how Kassidy had clammed up when Aysha asked too many questions about her mother. Kassidy didn't know who her father was, and Kai's father was in prison for 35 years, after pleading guilty to felony murder last school year. Her mother's family was in Sioux City, IA. Her mom had moved to Houston to go to college, gotten pregnant with Kassidy during her first semester of school, and dropped out, but remained in Houston. Kassidy told Aysha before that they'd only gone to Iowa a couple of times, but her grandmother would come and visit them. She said in Iowa they had a lot of family, but most of them did not work and had lots of children. She'd told Aysha about one aunt who was only 23, but already had 6 children. Aysha would have to ask Justine about getting in touch with them.

By the time Aysha finished explaining everything to her mom, the girls and Mia were coming back into the family room. They both looked a bit more relaxed and Kai started yawning. Aysha stood up and walked to the girls.

"Let's go find you something to sleep in and you can sleep in my sister, Jada's old room. She has two beds in there. So, tell my mom and Mr. Jaylon good night, and I will take you upstairs".

"Ay, don't worry. You stay here with mom and Jaylon. I will take care of them."

"Thanks, sis. Good night little ladies, I will see you in the morning. If I am not here when you wake up, it will be because I went to get you some clothing. Come here Kai, so I can see what size you wear?"

The little girl slowly walked over to Aysha, and Aysha turned her around so that she could see the tag inside of her shirt. It read "6X". Aysha smiled inside. She could remember so vividly when she wore a "6X" and she had to let everyone know that it was "6X" and not just plain "6". She turned Kai around and gave her a hug.

"Good night, little bit. I will see you in the morning". Aysha felt the little girl grip her tightly, and was surprised when she'd actually let go. Then she ran over and gave Jaylon a hug and Aysha's mom, and then went back over to Mia and Kassidy and grabbed both of their hands. They all left out and went towards the foyer. At that point, Aysha yielded to temptation and went to her mom, and sat on the floor beside her and rested her head in her mom's lap.

"Mommie, what are we going to do?"

"What are you going to do, Aysha? I know exactly what you are thinking. You can go to the courthouse tomorrow and finalize the adoption. But, you gotta think with your head and not your heart. Do you really think this is the best time for you to take on two children?" Jaylon asked. Aysha was not amused by the feigned sincerity in his tone. He had his own motives for asking that question. Aysha knew what he was trying to allude to and she was not going to let him bait her into confessing to anything that she wasn't ready to confess to. He also was not about to do this to her in front of her mom.

"Jaylon, I don't know what I am going to do. I truly don't. I just know that I can't send her back to her mom, and I can't walk away. I probably should, but I just can't. I became a teacher to save lives, and if I don't take some kind of action, what will happen to them? The foster care system? You know, as well as I do, that it is a roll of the dice. Yes, there are some good foster homes, but I don't know that I am willing to risk their lives on a "maybe". Mommie, what do you think?"

"Sweetie, you know that I will support you any way I can. How about we let this rest for tonight? We can go and get them some clothing tomorrow, and let's just enjoy the weekend, and try to make it the best for them, and we will all talk about this on Sunday, as a family. I will call Aunt Belle tomorrow, and she can come over too. All of her years in the school system should help her give us some insight. You do have to decide baby, but you don't have to decide right now." Her mom was stroking her hair. The six-year old inside of Aysha wanted to stick her tongue out at Jaylon, and let him know that his plan to entrap her did not work. Emotionally, she was exhausted. After the argument with Jada, and this whole situation, she was ready to go to bed.

"I'm going to go up to my room. Jaylon, I trust you will let yourself out." Aysha said rudely.

"As a matter of fact, I will. What time do you want to go shopping for the girls in the morning? I would like to go with you?" Jaylon responded.

"I will call you." Aysha replied. Both she and Jaylon knew that she had no intention of calling Jaylon. She was tired of him insinuating his way into her life. Although, if she was honest with herself, and she had no plans of doing tonight, she would acknowledge that his presence had been helpful on more than one occasion.

"Okay, I will just wait on your call, and in the meantime, I will be here around nine. I know you won't wake up before that." He smiled.

Aysha could only roll her eyes at him, as she leaned and kissed her mom.

"Good night, mom. Good night to you, too, Jaylon." She was too tired to have a battle of wills and wit with him right now. This was not how she planned for her Friday night to go. She'd planned a vacation, and she was supposed to leave to go to Charlotte to visit Kyra on Tuesday. They were supposed to be going to Atlanta to visit with one of her sorority sisters for a couple of days, and then heading to Myrtle Beach for a much needed vacation. Aysha would have to cancel the trip in light of everything that was going on. But, for now, she would take me mother's advice and simply get through this weekend.

The next morning when Aysha woke up, for a minute, she did not recognize her surroundings. The night before, when she'd come up to go to bed, she hadn't paid much attention to the change in décor in her old bedroom. Her mom had gotten new furniture for the room, and painted over the pink that Aysha chosen for the walls when she was 12. The room looked like it was out of some magazine. She was willing to bet that Mia had something to do with it. They agreed that the house needed some updating, and Aysha wasn't surprised that they started with her room. It was the one room in the house that no one had dared move a thing in since Aysha left for college. She'd have to ask them for her mementos that were in the room. Not that she knew what she was going to do with a trophy from the 5th grade Spelling Bee. The thought of putting that on the mantle at her home made her laugh. Thinking of the mantle, she remembered some of the items that Jaylon had in his home on the mantle in his office. He had several carousels, and he had one that was the exact same as the one her father gave her for her birthday a couple of years ago. She'd have to ask him about that.

Aysha looked in the closet for something to put on. She'd always kept some items at her mom's house, and she was hoping they hadn't discarded them. When she opened the closet, she found that they'd reorganized the closet, and while her stuff was still there, her mom had put robes and other items that made her feel like she was in a five-star hotel. She might have to stay over here more often. Aysha grabbed a black t-shirt with her sorority letters in pink and green on it, and a pair of khaki capri pants. Luckily, she'd spent some time in the salon the day before. Her hair was in spiral curls, and she hoped she hadn't slept too wildly, as she was too tired to try to sleep "cute"   .

After taking a quick shower and getting dressed, Aysha went downstairs. When she walked into the kitchen, she was shocked to see Aunt Belle, the girls, and Mia were already there. Aunt Bell was cooking omelets for everyone, and Mia and the girls were sitting at the table. She was also a bit nauseous from all of the scents coming from the kitchen. She was going to try to eat something, but she was afraid of the speculation that would certainly ensue if she had to rush to the bathroom after another meal.

"Good morning, Ms. Rutherford". Both of the girls looked relieved to see her. Aysha wondered did they think that she'd left them there. She was happy that she'd chosen to stay there and not go home last night.

"Good morning, little ladies. What's for breakfast?" Kassidy started to answer, but before she could get a word out, Kai started explaining that Aunt Belle was cooking for everyone, and Aysha needed to place her order. She offered to let

Aysha go first if she wanted to. The little girl was the cutest little girl, and this morning, she was a lot more active and livelier than she'd been the night before when her whole world was shifting. Kassidy sat back in her chair and rolled her eyes.

"Kassidy, those eyes. What is that about? It is too early"

"She talks too much"

"No, I don't. You never let me talk"

"Because you talk too much. Why don't you just shut up?". Kassidy snapped at her little sister. Kai looked like she was so disappointed. She simply dropped her head, and leaned over and rested her head on Mia's shoulder.

Aysha was angry at the way Kassidy treated her little sister. With everything that was going on, Kai needed her sister. Aysha understood exactly how her mom must have felt all those years listening to her and Jada bicker and fight and argue. In fact, she imagined the frustration that she was feeling after a 30 second argument must pale in comparison to the frustration that her war with Jada had caused her parents to feel. Just yesterday, she was swinging at Jada's face. Although she was disappointed she'd missed, her heart went out to her mom.

"Kassidy, come go to the store with me. Kai, will you be okay with Aunt Belle and Ms. Mia?"

"Yes. I am going to eat, and then Ms. Mia will let me play in her big bathtub and then she will comb my hair. She said we might be able to go to the zoo later. I like the zoo, but we never get to go."

Much later, Aysha thought. Mia obviously was not thinking of the August heat in Texas. Aysha would have to find something else for them to do, because she was not walking around The Houston Zoo in 100° weather. She and Kassidy needed to have a talk right now. No matter what she decided about their future, Kassidy needed her attitude checked and Aysha was going to do it right now. *Circumstance did not excuse poor behavior*, as Aunt Belle often told them growing up.

When they got in the car, Aysha started the conversation. She got right to the point. There was no need beating around the bush.

"So, what do you think about everything that is going on?"

"I don't know. It wasn't right for my mom to do that. If she goes to jail, what will happen to Kai and me?"

"That is a good question. You are obviously worried about her, but look at how you were speaking to her this morning. Sweetie, this is going to be difficult for you and your little sister. No matter what happens, that little girl needs you. You are all she has. So, I need you to watch out for her. You can't let anyone else hurt her, and you can't hurt her either."

Aysha was in no way prepared for what happened next. Kassidy dropped her head, and was crying so hard that she was trembling. Aysha was so shocked that she pulled into the next driveway that she came upon.

"Sweetie, what is it. You can talk to me."

"I am not supposed to tell anyone."

"You know since you were in my class, we have always talked about secrets. There are good secrets that you should keep, and there are bad secrets that you should not keep. I need you to tell me whatever it is. I promise not to get angry with you". For the one millionth time since she'd become a teacher, Aysha wished she paid attention in those psychology classes that she'd been forced to take at the University. It might have given her some insight into how to deal with this situation. She felt like a fish out of water, and her gut told her that she was not about to like anything that Kassidy was about to tell her.

Kassidy sat silently for a few minutes. Aysha didn't want to push her too much, but she was not moving that car until Kassidy told her what was going on. After about five minutes, Kassidy sat up and turned toward Aysha.

"Ms. Rutherford, do you promise you won't get mad at me?"

"Yes, sweetie. No matter what you tell me, I won't get mad at you."

"I only went to the club to protect my little sister."

"What do you mean?"

Kassidy hesitated. She put her head down fiddled with her fingers for a few seconds before looking up and continuing.

"My mom has a lot of men in and out of our house. One of them just started giving me money for no reason. Not a lot of money, but $10 or sometimes $20. Then after a month or so, my mom told me that he liked me. I was scared. I know what you and the other teachers have told us about boys and sex, and about letting people take advantage of us." Kassidy seemed like she was struggling to find the words, and Aysha just remained silent, and let her talk.

"Well, I know what my mom does with those men, and she told me that it was about time that I started making money. I wanted to tell you on the day of the award's ceremony because she came and she brought the man with her. He said that he was proud of me and called me "his girl". He kept saying that I was smart, and that he liked his women smart. It was nasty to me. He is too old to be looking at a child like me, but I didn't know what to do. Over the last few weeks, he is always at our house, and making comments to me, and saying stuff that a man shouldn't say to a little girl. My momma urges him on. She is making comments about me being 14, and that when I turn 16, she is going to give me to him. She said she would sign the paper for us to get married, and she knew a preacher who would do it. When I would say something to her, she would get angry and yell or push me. She would threaten me and she kept tell me that the man paid good money and that I was going to give him his money's worth."

Kassidy started crying really badly. Aysha didn't think that she was equipped to deal with this by herself. While Kassidy was crying Aysha told her to relax and that they needed to get out of this parking lot. Usually, Aysha would have called her parents or Valerie. Her mother had Kai at the house and she didn't want her mom or Mia to leave her right now. She thought of calling Valerie, but she was in the midst of trying to save her marriage and Aysha didn't feel right adding this to her burdens, although she knew Valerie would be spitting nails when she finally told her. Aysha dialed a number, and she called the one person that she never thought she'd call for anything.

"Jaylon. I have Kassidy with me, and we need to come to your house. It is an emergency."

Kassidy started panicking. She started crying heavily and was rocking herself in the front seat of Aysha's car. Aysha was sure that the seat belt was the only thing keeping her from sliding down to the floor. She just needed to get her somewhere where they could continue their conversation.

"No, Mrs. Rutherford. I can't tell Mr. Jay. Please don't make me tell him."

"Kassidy, sweetheart, listen to me. We can't do this in the car. We have to go somewhere and Mr. Jay lives closest to here. Please let me take you to his house. He can leave the room when we talk. But, you saw how he held and protected Kai last night. Sweetie, he won't hurt you, and I promise you he won't be angry with you no matter what you say. Sweetie, please let me take you somewhere safe?" Aysha had started to cry. She had to make Kassidy understand that they needed to go somewhere else, and she didn't know where else to go. She could not risk upsetting Kai, so going back to her mother's house was not an option.

"Aysha, you can't come here." Aysha's feelings were instantly hurt. She instantly steeled herself. This wasn't about her, and she needed to keep her focus on what she needed to get Kassidy through this.

"I'm sorry to have bothered you. Forgive me for actually believing you when you said that if I needed you, you would be there. I hope whoever she is makes you happy"

Jaylon wanted to laugh at this jealousy that Aysha was displaying, but the urgency in her tone told him that was not best. This was not the time to demonstrate his sharp wit.

"Ay, don't hang up. I will help you. I will always help you. I can meet you two, but not here. Listen!! Please!"

"No, that is okay. I will figure out something". She snapped. Before she could hang up, she heard his response.

"Aysha, there are new reporters at my house. Apparently, the fact that we were at the police station last night is the top of the morning news. They have me linked with a prostitution ring, and there are 5 major news channels set up outside of my house. I don't want you, the girls, or your family associated with this in any way. This is the last thing that the girls need right now."

"Oh." That was all Aysha could say. She should have known after they'd had to go out the back door of the police station last night that there would be some repercussions for Jaylon. He had his own storm brewing. Maybe, calling him was not the best option.

"Aysha, are you close to my mom's building?" Jaylon asked.

"Yes, we were heading to Target on South Main, so I am not too far from The Parklane." Aysha replied. The Parklane was one of the oldest high rises in Houston. It was nestled on the outskirts of Hermann Park near Rice University, so was still considered prime real estate. Jaylon had bought his mom two units, and completely renovated them to her specification after his first year in the NBA. His mom had since used her own money to buy more units in the building, and in addition to living there, she was the landlord for six other units. She had become quite the real estate magnate in Houston, and was known for closing some of the largest deals in the city for the most exclusive clientele.

"Go to my mother's apartment. I will call her now and let her know that you are coming. If she is not there, I will call the building's manager and have them let you in. I will be there as soon as I can".

"Okay, we are going. Jaylon, I'm sorry about what I said earlier and thank you".
Aysha couldn't disregard the fact that she'd used the phrase "Jaylon, thank you" quite a bit in the last few months. She shook that thought, and turned to Kassidy.
"Sweetie, we are going to go to Mr. Jaylon's house. Well, his

mother's house. She lives very close to here. I need you to just calm down and trust me. I need you to tell me the whole story, but let me get us out of this car first."

When they got to the building, the doorman was expecting her. He'd given her a tag to identify her car for valet parking, and ushered them into the building. The elevator required a key code, which he kindly put in.

"Ms. Flowers is waiting for you on the 32nd floor."

Aysha hadn't been to Ms. Flowers' home in a couple of years. Their relationship was very strained after she and Jaylon broke up. Ms. Flowers could not understand why Aysha could not just forgive Jaylon and move on. She'd told Aysha to give him hell, but take him back. She could never have a single conversation with Aysha without inserting Jaylon. Her mother and Ms. Flowers were still friends, but Aysha avoided her. *This should be interesting,* she thought as they exited the elevator.

Kassidy had calmed down, and was shifting back into the child that Aysha knew. She seemed a bit more settled, and she knew that Ms. Flowers, who had a very calm aura, would be able to help keep Kassidy calm. Aysha thought about calling Justine, the social worker, also. She needed to let her know about this, but she would call her after she got the full story. There was no need to get anyone else involved unless necessary. She feared she'd already done too much, getting Jaylon and his mother involved.

"I like high rises. One day, I want to live in one. Like on TV".

"Well, you will love this one. Ms. Flowers' place is like a house, but on the 32nd floor. I would not be surprised if she has the whole floor now."

As they stepped off of the elevator, Kassidy hesitated. Aysha didn't push her, but when the doors started to close again, she hit the button to reopen them. Kassidy looked up at Aysha, and then walked out of the elevator. She could see the doubt in her face. In that moment, Aysha was reminded of one of her father's sayings. Whenever something untimely would occur, her dad would say, *"You can't schedule trouble".* Aysha left her mom's house with Kassidy this morning to go and get clothing and toiletries for the girls, and give Kassidy a different perspective on everything that was going on. She certainly hadn't expected to be the one getting a crash course in perspectives.

Before they could ring the doorbell, Ms. Flowers answered the door. It was 10:00 a.m. and Delores Flowers looked like she'd just stepped off the cover of Vogue Senior. Her hair was flawless in a salt and pepper, short, spiked cut. Her makeup was flawless and simple. Aysha often wondered if she didn't have a glamour fairy because no 60-year old lady should look that good all the time. She was dressed in a white linen outfit that consisted of a flowing tunic and harem-styled pants that tapered at the feet. It should have looked cheesy, like an *I Dream of Jeannie* moment gone wrong, but she'd pulled it off with such flair that Aysha said a silent prayer that she could have that much grace and style when she turned 60. It was no wonder her Uncle Robb was after Ms. Flowers with such a vengeance. Word on the street was he was finally wearing her down, after almost 8 years.

"Aysha, it is so nice to see you." Ms. Flowers said and pulled her into a hug. She knew she was telling the truth, and not just being cordial. They'd been really close at one time. She'd planned to enjoy having Ms. Flowers as a mother-in-law, and they'd spent lots of time together.

"Ms. Dee, it is nice to see you too. You look great, as usual".

"Aysha, you know these are just my house clothes. You always have to be prepared. I never know when a tenant of mine in the building or a contractor or something will stop by, so I try to be ready. Who is this little lady?" Ms. Flowers said as she stepped back and looked at Kassidy, who was standing still as a statue next to Aysha.

"Ms. Dee, this is Kassidy. She is a young lady I mentor from the school. Kassidy, this is Ms. Dee. She is Mr. Jaylon's mom.

"Good morning, Miss Dee. Nice to meet you." Kassidy's

voice quivered.

"Aren't you a little doll? Come, have a seat. Aysha, have y'all eaten".

"No, ma'am." Aysha sighed. Breakfast seemed like so long ago. That was where this all started, with Kassidy being mean and snotty with Kai at the table when they were getting ready to eat.

"Well, let me ask Jaylon to stop at Chandra's Deli, and I will call and place an order. It is after breakfast time, but I am sure Chan will still make it for us."

"Are omelets, pancakes, turkey sausage, grits, and hashbrowns okay?"

Aysha started laughing. Ms.Dee hadn't changed a bit. She always loved a big meal, although she was not going to eat half of it.

"Yes, that is fine for me. Kassidy, do you want that or something else?"

"I will eat that. Can I look out of the window?"

"Baby, make yourself at home. You can look out of any window in this house." Ms. Dee answered and walked out of the room. Aysha assumed she was going to order breakfast and so she sent Jaylon a text and let him know that they made it, but she figured he'd get a second one from his mom. She did send Mia a text which read, "I have a situation with Kassidy. We took a detour. I will call you when I can and fill you in. You might want to take Kai to get some clothing. I am not sure how long this will take."

Mia responded by asking Aysha where they were, but Aysha was not giving any details because she knew her mom and Mia would hightail it right to Ms. Dee's house no matter what she said. And, to be certain, she needed to tell Ms. Dee and Jaylon not to call her mother, because both of them would feel obligated to do so.

"Kassidy, do you want to finish talking now, or when we finish eating."

"I want to talk now". She answered, and came and sat down next to Aysha.

Tears started to fall down Kassidy's face. She started

trembling, and Aysha reached out and grabbed her hand. She used her other hand to lift her face.

"You have nothing to be ashamed of. You are a child, and he is an adult. Please tell me everything that happened." Emotionally, Aysha was on a tightrope, and her stomach was twisted in knots. She'd heard too many of these stories in her four years as a teacher, and she knew that she had to maintain her composure and let her get it all out.

"Ms. Aysha, during that week after the last day of school, around when your dad died and I couldn't go to the shelter because I didn't have a ride, my mom kept yelling at me and Kai and telling us that she hated school was out, and what were we going to do all day. Then one day, she came and told me that I could start making money." Aysha wanted to interrupt and ask questions, but she figured the more she let her talk, the more she would tell her.

"I didn't know what she was talking about so I just ignored her when she would say it. Then she told me that he was paying her to sign for me to marry him when I turned 15 in July. I just started crying, and saying that I didn't want to marry him. She grabbed me and just started yelling at me and shaking me saying that she started having sex when she was 12 and that I needed to get all of that 'goody-two shoes' college stuff out of my head. She told me that I should be happy that someone wanted to marry and take care of me and I wouldn't have to struggle like she was struggling to feed us. She made it clear that she was going to do it whether I wanted to or not. She said I needed to learn some stuff first. That day she told me what I was going to have to do. I didn't want to do it, and I begged her not to. She told me that I had to and that if I didn't she was going to put me out of her house. She told me that if she found out that I called you or anyone else that she was going to hurt me."

At this point Kassidy just seemed spaced out. She seemed like she was telling a story about someone else, and not talking about herself. She still held Aysha's hand, but she'd stopped crying and was just speaking in a flat, emotionless voice. Ms. Dee had come back into the room and was seated behind Kassidy and Aysha. Aysha was sure that she could hear Kassidy, but she didn't react at all.

"That night he came over to our house, but he really didn't talk to me. I was glad, and then our neighbor got sick and had to bring Kai home. He was not happy about Kai being there and left. My mom was mad, but she just went into her room, got dressed and left me and Kai there. The next day he came over that morning and he started saying how pretty Kai was. My mom even asked him if he thought Kai was prettier than I was. Ms. Aysha, I was not going to let him do anything to my sister." In that moment, Kassidy's anger was exuding from more like a protective lioness, than a broken child. Her mom had manipulated her using Kai as bait. That was just plain sick, and Aysha's heart went out to her. There was a time when she'd have done anything to protect her sister, so she knew exactly what Kassidy was feeling. She was bothered by the fact that she no longer had that relationship with her sister, Jada, but was buoyed a little thinking of the budding relationship between her and Mia. Aysha was momentarily distracted by her own feelings, but when Kassidy calmed down and started to speak again, Aysha refocused her attention.

"My mom told me that if I wanted him to stay away from my sister, that I should do whatever he asked."

Aysha was sick to her stomach. She was trying so hard not to just scream. It went beyond her every thought that a mother could do that to a 14-year old girl.

"He took me into my mom's bedroom and told me to lie down. I was scared and so I did. He started touching me. I didn't want him to touch me, and I told him to stop, but he just laughed at me. He kept on and then he put his finger inside of me. I screamed, and he laughed even more. Then he sat on the bed next to me, and grabbed me. He said since he knew I was a virgin and not ready for that yet, he would wait, but I would have to do something for him. Before anything else could happen, his phone went off. He got up, looked at this phone and left.

He told my mom that he would be back to get me later."

Every part of Aysha was on fire. She wanted to scream. When Aysha looked over her shoulder at Ms. Dee, she saw that Ms. Dee was crying, but the tears did not negate the murderous look that she had in her eyes.

Kassidy hadn't seen the man since that day, and her mother kept saying that she did something to the man and that was why he hadn't come back around. That night, her mother had gotten tired of waiting for him to come back and told her that it was time for her to earn her place. Kassidy's mother had given her two options: either she was going to go to the club and work with her, or she was going to put her little sister out there with some man. Not knowing what to do, she went with her mom. Luckily for Kassidy, they got arrested after her mother made a deal with a man who turned out to be an undercover police officer.

Kassidy stopped talking and just stared into space. Aysha was shocked in place, and had no idea what to do or say. Part of her wanted to go to the man and shoot him between the eyes, but a big part of her wanted to go to Kassidy's mother and put a bullet in the back of her head. She could not fathom how much money a person would accept in exchange for her daughter. Aysha was completely baffled and confused by what Kassidy was saying to her. Ms. Dee must have sensed Aysha's apprehension and she stepped in by coming over to sit on the other side of Kassidy. She pulled Kassidy into a comforting embrace, with Kassidy's head resting on her bosom, just like you would expect a mother too. Kassidy was hurting and that seemed like the only thing to do. That broke Kassidy and she started crying and shaking. Aysha just sat there shocked, and she heard the door to the apartment close.

"Please don't tell him. Please, I don't want Mr. Jaylon to know".

"Sweetie, I won't tell him, now, but we will have to tell him. I promise you that he will not be angry with you. Let me go and get the food, and I am going to call my mom and Mia, and I need to call Mrs. Justine and let her know what is going on. We are going to protect you, sweetie. You just sit here with Ms. Dee and I will get you something to eat, and we will talk about this some more."

Aysha walked into the kitchen where Jaylon was standing against the counter with his arms folded. When he saw her come towards him, he opened his arms to her and much to her own surprised, she collapsed into his arms. He simply stood there and embraced her and allowed her to cry. He didn't say a word, but wrapped his arms around her, and for a few minutes, he just let her cry.

"I heard everything." He said. He continued to just hold her as she cried.

"Jaylon, I don't know what to say. I don't know what to do. She is hurting and I feel completely useless. This just cannot be real. Who does that to her own daughter?"

Aysha stepped away from Jaylon and grabbed a paper towel from the sterling silver holder on the counter. After using it to dry her eyes, she went towards the white shopping bags with food that Jaylon had put on the counter.

"What do you want to do? Whatever you decide, I will help you any way I can. You just tell me what we can do to help those girls, and I promise you I will make it happen for you". He sounded as if he were holding back his own tears. At that moment she saw the one thing that she had been avoiding. She saw and understood the one thing that everyone had told her from the beginning. She saw the truth of the one thing that she denied for five years. Jaylon still loved her, and there was no way she could keep denying it. But, there was also no way that she was ready to face that either.

"Jaylon, I don't know what I want to do. But I do know that they can never go back to that woman, ever. Whatever that means, then I will do it. We will do it, but they can't go back". Aysha'd resolve was strong. Her family and her would have to work it out, but Kai and Kassidy would be staying with them.

TEN-10

It was after 2 p.m. that afternoon when everyone was emotionally balanced enough to return to Aysha's mom's house. Ms. Dee had come with them, but Jaylon had not. He thought it would be best for him to go home, and let them talk with the girls. Besides, with the publicity swirling around their visit to the police station, Jaylon was needed elsewhere. Aysha'd called Justine, the case worker, and she decided that she would come over tonight and talk to both of the girls so that she would have a better idea of the plan of action they needed to take on Monday. Aysha still hadn't made it to Target to get clothing and toiletries for Kassidy. Aysha's head was spinning. Too many of her days were turning out to be such stark, emotional deviations from the mornings. Aysha and Mia needed to talk. She decided to leave the girls home with her mom and Ms. Dee while she and Mia would go and get clothing for Kassidy and Kai, and anything else that they might need. This was going to be a long weekend.

When they got in the car, it was Mia that started the discussion off. As much as Aysha just wanted to take a few minutes to just forget everything that happened today, that was not a reality. Mia wanted to talk about the girls and she wanted Aysha to think about the commitment that she was willing to make to these girls. Mia threw out lots of pros and cons, and Aysha listened quietly. She knew that she should have been considering some of the things that her sister was saying, but above all else, all she knew for sure was that those girls were never going back to their mother's care if she had anything to do with. She knew what needed to be done, but considering her own dilemma, she was not sure if she had what it took to be a single mother to three children. She knew that she would have all of the support she could get from her family, and she knew that Jaylon was going to be a part of his child's life, and there was nothing she could or would do to stop that. The reality was sobering, and she said as much to Mia.

"MiMi, I just don't see how I can send her back to that. Will Kai actually be safe?"

"But, Aysha, are you ready for the responsibility of two children? I mean, honestly, according to the family, no one even lets you dog-sit."

Aysha knew that Mia was trying to lighten her mood, and she also knew that it was true. Aysha did everything she could for those children at school, but bringing them home was a completely different set of challenges. Would she have to move? Where was the nearest elementary school? What about Kassidy and school? There were a million variables and Aysha was sure her head would explode from trying to go through all of them.

"Aysha, I need to share something with you. I might be being selfish, but I might have a solution."

Every cell in Aysha's mind screamed at her to change the subject. She knew that she was not about to like what she was about to hear. Wasn't she over the limit today for drama? This whole summer was the most emotional one in her life. She'd lost her father, had Jaylon reinserted in her life, had to learn to look at Jada without slapping the taste out of her mouth, and left teaching. Aunt Belle always said, *God didn't give you more that you could bear.* That always sounded so much better when Aunt Belle was saying it to other people. She was not ready for any other drama, and was not sure that she could even stand anymore. However, like a good little sister, she sat there and listened to Mia. What Mia shared with Aysha was as heartbreaking as what Kassidy told her.

Mia had been married when she was 27. She'd just completed her Doctorate in Psychology and moved to Nashville, TN for a job. Within one month of being there, she met a very nice guy, Martin. He was attractive, intelligent, financially stable, and seemed to be everything Mia could have wanted in a man. They'd gotten married within six months of meeting, and Mia could not have been happier. The only downside in her life at that point was that she didn't have many friends because she was new to the city. Outside of her Grad Assistant and one other professor at the University, she'd never met many people, as she'd met Martin so early on in her move. The circumstances that Mia described after the wedding seemed like deleted scenes from the movie "Sleeping with the Enemy".

Mia told Aysha about his jealousy, and his controlling behavior. He started driving Mia to work every day and if he could not pick her up, he would arrange for a car to pick her up. Several times, when Mia asked the driver to make a stop, the driver told her that he'd been instructed to take her directly home. While there was the gradual increase in his controlling behavior, the first time that he'd hit Mia was when she'd told him that she was supposed to speak at a conference in Atlanta. He'd told her that she didn't have his permission to go, and that no wife of his was going prostituting herself with her male colleagues. Mia was shocked and told him that she planned to go anyway, and he could get over it. That had incensed him, and he'd slapped her. He'd told her that if she ever defied him, he would do more than that. That night, when they'd gotten into bed, he'd forced himself on Mia despite her crying and pleading with him to stop. Surprisingly, he woke up the next morning and acted as if nothing had occurred.

Aysha was in shock. Mia was one of the strongest people she knew, not to mention she was one level away from a black belt in Taekwondo. Mia told her that over the next three years, the abuse intensified, including a broken arm, broken ribs, a chipped front tooth, and a cracked eye socket. Mia finally left when she'd gotten pregnant, and suffered a second miscarriage at his hands. The second time, when she told him she was pregnant, he beat her and accused her of being pregnant by someone else. She'd spent two weeks in the hospital because of the internal damage done due to him kicking her in the abdomen. As a result, the doctors informed Mia that she would not be able to bear children of her own.

Mia was forever grateful for a nurse from the hospital and her family. The lady, Mrs. Angela, had gone to Mia's house with her sons, who were police officers, and retrieved some of Mia's things. She'd moved in with them after she left the hospital, and Mrs. Angela had nursed her back to health. She was able to transition to teaching online classes for a semester, while she healed and after staying with Ms. Angela and her family for four months, she'd moved back to North Carolina with her aunt after all of the physical bruises healed. It would be many years before her psychological healing would catch up, and Mia was still not sure that it had. She'd filed for divorce, and left the state and the marriage with little more than a desire to be safe. She was so grateful, that she'd still kept in touch with Ms. Angela and her family. The lady saved Mia's life.

As they pulled up into the parking lot of the Target in Meyerland Plaza, Aysha was in tears. Her sister had gone through so much. She'd been given away as a baby, lost both of her adoptive parents, and been in a mentally and physically abusive relationship. Her story put a lot of things in perspective for Aysha, and left Aysha feeling emotionally overwhelmed. Aysha didn't know what to say, and so she just looked at her sister, and said nothing. She reached over and grabbed her hand.

"Aysha, please don't cry for me. I have cried enough tears. He was the reason that I got into martial arts. I needed to be able to protect myself. He was the reason I moved back to North Carolina, which is when my aunt told me about our parents, and how I finally made the leap to Houston to come and find them. It has all worked out, and now I see a bigger picture."

"What do you mean?"

"Aysha, I know your secret. I know what you are hiding. Well, I know half of it. I know that you are pregnant, and I am going to guess that it is Jaylon's baby".

Aysha started laughing. It was more of a nervous reaction than anything. To hear that aloud was something else.

"Secret. Pregnant. No, I am not."

"Girl, you have run to the bathroom every time you eat something, and it did not go unnoticed that you ate Frenchy's chicken, and you ate 3 pieces. You usually don't eat any, and if you do it is one piece." Mia was staring at Aysha and Aysha refused to meet her eyes. When she did glance over, Mia was smiling like it was picture day in the elementary school.

"Okay. Okay. I yield. It seems I have been doing a lot of this today, but can we go somewhere and talk. I don't want to figure this out in the car. Target stays open late. Let's go to Chik-Fil-A. I would love some chicken fingers and lemonade."

"I just bet you would. I bet both of you would." Mia said while rolling her eyes playfully at Aysha.

Once they got there Aysha was a bit relieved that it wasn't nearly as crowded as she'd thought it would be. Aysha placed their orders while Mia got condiments and found a table. Mia was not going to let the momentum of the conversation lull for a minute, and she started talking before Aysha could even sit down.

"Okay, so give me the whole story, and don't you dare try to leave a single detail out."

Aysha and Mia were both giggling. Aysha was trying to look innocent, but she was having a hard time not laughing. It did not escape her that this used to be the relationship that she had with Jada. That was a lifetime ago, and she was determined to move past that.

"Well, there is not really much to tell"

"Uhm. Aysha Rutherford. Stop playing. You are pregnant by a man that worships the ground that you walk on despite the fact that you pretend to hate his guts. You don't see any issues or discrepancies with this picture? Obviously, there were a few minutes, a good few I hope, when you didn't hate him. At least not all of him"

"What am I going to do with your filthy mind?" Aysha asked jokingly. It was truly amazing how much alike she and Mia were. Their minds worked alike, and she was not surprised that Mia went there.

"Filthy mind? Well, you probably did everything that I am thinking and then some. I must say it is not secret that the boy is fine as wine, so give up the ghost, and tell me what happened." Mia sat back in the booth and folded her arms and smiled at Aysha.

Aysha filled Mia in on the details of her antics the day of their father's funeral, and how Jaylon had to come and rescue her from herself. She told her how she'd ended up at his house, and one thing led to another, and another, and another. Aysha had to admit that the physical attraction was still there, and she had to admit that his skillset went beyond those that he displayed on the court. She also explained to Mia that she had no intention of rekindling their relationship.

"So, does he know?" Mia inquired.

"He suspects it. Yesterday, when I ran off to the bathroom, he followed me. As soon as I opened the door, he was there. He suspects it, but I am not confirming anything"

"Girl, what the hell are you going to do? You won't be able to keep him away once you confirm it?"

"I know. But, I am not sure if I want to confirm it to him. Mia, I have my own secret. I don't even know how to say this, except to say it. I am not even sure that I want to have this baby, except I have been here before. And I can't do what I did last time".

Mia looked a little confused, but she didn't say anything. She just kept looking at Aysha, and Aysha could not believe that she was about to share her biggest secret. She and Mia had shared a lot in the last three months but she was not sure how her sister would feel about what she was about to say, and she did not want it to affect their relationship in any way. Especially not right now. She needed her sister right now. Before she could finish the story, they called her name, and Mia got up to go and collect their order. As soon as she sat down, Aysha started talking before she lost the nerve to tell her. This secret was truly eating away at her, and it was time she let it go and put it to rest along with some other things from her past.

"Two weeks after the wedding was called off, I found out I was pregnant. I didn't tell anyone. The following weekend, I just told everyone I was going to Austin for the weekend, and I went to the Women's Retreat in Austin. I was actually going to Austin to have an abortion. I could not imagine bringing a child into this world, and with everything that I was going through, I chose to end the pregnancy. It haunts me because I feel like I made a selfish choice. Part of me chose to lash out at Jaylon, and part of me was truly just not ready for that responsibility in light of everything else that was going on. I can't say that I regret my choice, but if I had it to do again, I would not have been so rash in my decision."

Mia did not respond. She didn't even look up for a few seconds, and when she did, she had tears in her eyes.

"Sis, thank you for trusting me enough to share that with me. I have never had to make that choice, and I envy no woman who does. It is easy for us to judge when it is not us. I have had a couple of clients who come for therapy and counseling after having terminated a pregnancy, and no matter what the reason, it is something that takes them a while to come to grips with. Did you go and get any kind of counseling?"

"No, when I got back, I moved in to my own place, I went back to work, and I got busy being busy. I spent half of my time hating Jaylon for the choice that I felt like he forced me to make, and I think that is why it is so difficult for me to accept him again. I felt like this whole situation was the result of his choice. In these last few weeks, I have had to look at him differently. He is the person I made him out to be, but he is also the man that I was going to marry, and because God has a sense of humor, he is once again, the father of my child."

"What the hell are you going to do? You lost dad, you quit teaching, you get back with Jaylon, you get pregnant, and now these girls. I swear, sis, when you do it you do it". They both chuckled a little at the irony of the situation that Aysha now found herself in.

"I don't know. I am going to have to tell Jaylon and mom sooner or later. Eventually, they will find out anyway."

Mia gave her a momentary reprieve from her situation. "Well, let's talk about the girls for a second. I know that I don't know them, and that I am just getting settled into Mom's house. I don't want to make a quick decision, and I know we have a lot to sort out first. But, Sis, I would be willing to be foster parents to them. I know that I will never have my own children, and I thought that I was okay with that. Last night, when I was putting Kai in the bed, I could not help but think that maybe this is God's way of giving me a chance at being a mother.

Aysha looked at Mia and was shocked. She didn't know what to say. She was frozen in her thoughts. Mia misinterpreted that to mean that Aysha was upset.

"Sis, I am sorry if I overstepped my boundaries. I am sorry if I am just taking over".

"Mia, no. No. No. Please don't apologize. I am not upset, I am just speechless. I wasn't expecting you to say that. I thought you were going to try to talk me out of taking them in, and try to talk me in to putting them in foster care, and that was not it at all. I'd braced myself for the "you can't save the world" lecture that everyone always gives me when I get one of my ideas." And before Aysha could say anything else the tears just started rolling. " Can we just get out of here? We need to go and talk to mom and Ms. Dee and the girls about this."

Aysha was overwhelmed. This lady who had been thrust upon her in the form of a sister was turning out to be more valuable than she could ever imagine. Especially in light of her current situation, what Mia was offering was priceless. She knew Kassidy very well, and she knew that Mia and Kassidy would do just fine. She was more concerned about Kai. At her age, she would not really understand the magnitude of what was happening and why they would not be able to live with their mom. Already, she'd formed some type of attachment to Jaylon, and Aysha was not sure how all of this would play out. There would be court cases, parental rights, other family rights, and issues they were going to have to get legal advice on. What Aysha really needed to do was to own the drama that was in her life. She had some choices, some tough choices, to make and they weren't going to get any easier. Monday was going to be a day of reckoning. Not only did she have to go to the caseworker's office, but she also had a doctor's appointment to confirm what she already knew was true. Her family of one, was well on the way to becoming a family of at least five. Right now, Aysha really needed her father and his words of wisdom that always seemed to make everything okay. But that time was over.

ELEVEN-11

When Aysha and Mia returned to her parents' home after finally making a stop at Target to get items for Kassidy and Kai, she was not surprised at all of the cars in the driveway. Her Uncle Rob was there, which probably meant Aunt Belle was there too. Surprisingly, or not, Jaylon's car was in the driveway also. Aysha decided right then and there that she was tired of secrets. She was tired of running and hiding from what was going on with her. She would take Mia's suggestion. She would have a conversation with Jaylon, and it was time for her to lay it all on the line. It was time she accepted that no matter what their relationship was, or was not, he was going to be a father, because she would have this baby. She knew that her child deserved two loving parents, and she would bury the hatchet and wipe the slate clean with Jaylon. On some level that thought gave Aysha peace. At least she could imagine that part of her life was together, and yet, she knew that part was just beginning.

When she got in the house, Uncle Rob and Ms. Dee were sitting there chummy and smiling. She wondered for the 100th time what was really going on between them. Uncle Rob had made it plain several times that his life's desire was to marry Ms. Dee, and Ms. Dee usually responded with complete disinterest. It looked to Aysha like Uncle Rob was wearing her down. She glanced over and saw Kassidy sitting on the couch with what looked like Mia's iPad, and since Aunt Belle was sitting right next to her, and was more technologically savvy due to her classes at the Senior Citizens' Center, it didn't even cross Aysha's mind to try and monitor what she was looking at. Aysha was looking for Kai and Jaylon. Her mom noticed the alarm on her face.

"Kitty, they are outside in the pool. Kai wanted to get in the water, and Jaylon was the only one willing to go outside."

Before Aysha could say anything, Kassidy chimed in, "She always wants to swim, but where we live the boys play too much in the pool and she can't swim and neither can I, so we don't get to go".

"Well, maybe we should look for some swimming lessons for both of you." Mia responded.

"Really, I just want to go to the beach and put on a swimsuit, but I guess I could learn, too. Ms. Mia, can you swim?"

"Well, maybe we should look for some swimming lessons for all of us." Mia responded and everyone laughed.

Aysha went around the room giving everyone hugs, and then sat down between Kassidy and Aunt Belle. Kassidy looked at Aysha and huffed, but she moved over and Aysha curled up on Aunt Belle.

"Child, I know something is going on when you get up in my lap. Kassidy, sweetie, why don't you go outside with Kai and Jaylon? Grown folks need to talk." Aunt Belle was going to get the show on the road.

Kassidy didn't even blink, she kept the iPad and walked out of the room, and a few seconds later Aysha heard the beep of the security system acknowledging that a door or a window had been opened.

"Aunt Belle, what are we going to do? What am I going to do?"

"Aysha, we've been talking about it since you left here. This is not going to be easy no matter what you decide. You got a big heart, girl. But, child, you can't save the world."

Aysha looked over at Mia and gave her a smirk, and rolled her eyes. This was the conversation that Aysha expected Mia to have with her, and one that she knew was coming. She hadn't expected Aunt Belle to be the one to say it, but she knew it was coming.

"Well, Aunt Belle, it seems saving the world runs in our veins. Mia and I spoke, and she actually wants to foster the girls, once we get more details. She wants to expedite the process." Aysha responded. She glanced at Mia and she looked like a little girl who was nervous about something she did.

"Mom." Mia started. "If I am fit to foster them, I will get my own place so we won't crowd you".

"You will do no such thing. It will be great to have those girls in the house. They will put some life back in the house, and since

James is gone, this place could sure use that.

"I don't know what to say. Momma, you want Mia and the girls here? Are you sure?"

"Aysha, the second I heard the story I was sold on them coming here. Whether it is for a short time or long time, this house is their home as long as they need it."

Aysha started to cry. She was so overwhelmed with emotions that she didn't know what to do. She couldn't wait for Justine to come over to get more details on the process, and what all would happen. She also needed to talk to Kassidy, as this all hinged on how she and Kai felt about this, but for tonight, they would let this all go. In fact, she decided to call Justine and ask her if she could wait until they came to the office on Monday to get the girls' statement. Aysha just wanted them to be "normal" for a few more hours before their worlds were shattered to the extent that she knew it was going to be once the whole story came out.

Without saying a word, Aysha got up and went out side with Jaylon and the girls. Much to Jaylon's surprise she came and sat down next to him. Kai was in the water, but she was holding on to the side practicing her kicking. At least, that is what Jaylon said she was doing because to Aysha it appeared that she was just spraying water everywhere.

"How is she Jay?" Aysha asked.

"She is fine. I wish I could record some of the things she says. She has such an innocent take on things. She has no idea how wrong some of the things she has witnessed are. Oh Boy!" Aysha wasn't sure she'd ever seen this side of Jaylon. He was very good at controlling his emotions, but he really looked like he was about to explode. He just looked off at Kai and Kassidy who were on the other side of the pool.

"Okay, Kai, stop." He yelled. "Kassidy, can you take her inside and get her a bath and dry, so we can go get something to eat? Alright, Kai, you did well. Tomorrow, we will practice again. You are going to be swimming like a fish in no time."

Kai got the biggest smile on her face, and she shook her head yes. With Aysha, Kassidy, and Jaylon watching, Kai proceeded to climb out of the pool, and Kassidy swooped her up, and all anyone could hear was Kai's giggles. It made Aysha too happy to see Kassidy playing with her sister, especially since her harshness earlier in the day was the trigger for everything that happened.

"You can't take them in, Aysha. You have enough going on." Jaylon said, while staring at Aysha.

"It is actually a bit unnerving for me that everyone's opinion of my potential parenting skills is so low. Aunt Belle just said the same thing, and Mia has already volunteered to foster them. I mean, damn, is there not one person in this house that thinks I might be capable of taking care of someone other than myself?"

"That is not what I meant. You take everything so personally".

"Well, how was I supposed to take it? This damn sure ain't business." Aysha replied.

"I just mean that you have, I mean we have our own situation, and I don't know if we will be able to handle the girls and what we have coming".

"We? We have a situation? Excuse me, did I miss something. There is no "we"! And, "we" don't have anything."

"Aysha, we don't? Wow. Are we doing this again?"

"Doing what? Do you really think that one morning entitles you to a "we" role in my life? Is that what you really think"?

"Well, actually it was one morning and one afternoon... And if you weren't so damn stubborn, it could be a lot more mornings and afternoons. But we will talk on that another day". Aysha could have thrown something at Jaylon's head with the smirk that he had on his face. But, if she was honest, it was one morning followed by one hell of an afternoon. But considering the repercussions of that day, she was not reflecting in a "glass half full" type of way.

'Don't flatter yourself Jaylon. Even if it was a whole week, it doesn't give you any say so in what I choose to do. Besides, I don't know what you think you know. There is nothing to choose, anyway." Aysha got up to leave. This was not how this conversation was supposed to go. Why was he able, without even trying, to push her buttons every time?

"Well, you can get upset if you like. You can deny what we both know is true. But, we have some things to talk about and some choices to make."

"No, Jaylon, we don't. I will make my own choices, and if I feel so inclined, I might let you know."

Jaylon stood up and walked towards Aysha. There was a look in his eyes that made her uneasy. She always knew when she was walking into the lion's den with him. It was the look that he had when no amount of begging, pleading, bargaining, or whining was going to change his mind. He strolled over to her and stopped right in front of her. She momentarily got lost in his form, as no matter what he wore, he was still the best specimen of a man that she'd ever seen. He was 6'4, like her father, and no matter what he wore, he looked like he was getting ready for a photo shoot. How could she be attracted to him at a moment like this? Jaylon looked Aysha in her eyes and for a few seconds he didn't say a word. Aysha didn't feel physically threatened by him, but she was not comfortable with him in her face either. Before Aysha could ever get a word out, Jaylon started talking.

"Aysha, I have spent the last five years keeping my distance and taking some high road that I don't even really understand where you are concerned. I have not intervened in your life. In retrospect, I took some poor advice from some people who loved us both, but, if you think I am going to sit by and watch while you abort another one of my babies, you have got another thing coming. If I have to kidnap you and lock you in a room, believe me when I say, you, me, we are having this baby".

Before Aysha could even blink, Jaylon had turned and walked into the house. Aysha had to lean on the doorjamb to keep from falling. What Jaylon said completely knocked the air out of her. Her head was spinning. How did he know about the abortion? What else did he know? She could not think, and her natural reaction was to just scream as loud as she possibly could. However, with the house full of people, Aysha knew that would get her more attention than she could deal with at this moment. She decided to do what she always did. Aysha would just leave.

It took her a couple of minutes to compose herself and walk back into the house. She went over to her mom and gave her a hug. She was on the verge of tears, but simply told her mom that she was tired and the grass outside was getting to her. Since they could hear the mower at the neighbor's house that seemed like a plausible excuse. Aysha gave everyone a hug, and said that she was going home and would be back in the morning. "Jaylon, walk her out please." Uncle Rob said.

"Uncle Rob, I have been walking out of this house for over 30 years, I don't need him to walk me. "

"Yes, Kitty, but I need him to. So, humor an old man. Gone on, young man, and walk her out."

Aysha simply rolled her eyes and walked to the front door.

"Aysha, I am sorry for what I said. Well, no I am not. I am sorry for how I said that. But, I need you to understand, that I can't let you do that again. I didn't have say last time, and but I swear if I have to follow you around for the next two months to make sure that you don't, I will."

"I can't talk about this right now. "

"I know. That is what you always say, but I am not going away. This is not going away"

Jaylon grabbed Aysha's car keys, and opened her door.

"Aysha, I am not going anywhere. You can take as long as you need. But, you are carrying my child. I am not going anywhere."

Aysha's head was reeling. Tears were coming down her face, and when she looked up at Jaylon, he had tears coming down, too. She had a million questions, but she couldn't even answer one. She simply got in the car and held her hand out for her keys. Jaylon handed her the keys and closed the car door. Just like she knew when not to push him, he knew when pushing her would do no good. They were well past that point. Without looking at him, Aysha pushed the button to start the car. Just as she put the car in drive, Jaylon stepped back, and even though she was mentally shaken, she drove off.

TWELVE-12

It was still dark outside when Aysha woke up. It had been almost one month since she'd last seen Jaylon. She'd made sure that she checked with Mia to see when he was at her mother's house. He'd been very interactive with the girls, who were granted permission to stay with her mother and Mia until there was a resolution with their own mother. In fact, they were due in court today for their first formal hearing, which was why Aysha was up so early. Her nerves had gotten the best of her and her sleep had been very restless. If she were honest, she would admit that her sleep had been restless since she'd started avoiding Jaylon. Unfortunately, that hadn't stopped him from visiting her in her dreams. She dreamt that she and Jaylon were married, and it was a dream that she had many times. It seemed to be on repeat. Nonetheless, while she had time to spare this morning, lying in the bed and brooding over the past was not going to change the current reality.

The caseworker had already prepped them that today was going to be a challenge, so, with a few minutes to spare, Aysha decided a good workout might help calm her. So, after a 50-minute spin session in her workout room, Aysha headed to the shower to start getting dressed. They'd decided that Aysha would meet her mother, Mia, and the girls at the Child Protective Services office, as opposed to going to her mom's house first. When they'd gone to the CPS office initially, the caseworker put Kassidy's story on the record, and Mia was granted temporary custody of the girls. Their mother was in jail, and additional charges had been added for other outstanding cases that she had. The last few weeks had been pretty tame compared to the last few months. She'd avoided Jaylon as he'd gone back to Charlotte, since his season started. He called her every day, and they got to a place of calm. She still hadn't officially confirmed that she was pregnant, but she'd stopped denying it, and to keep the undeclared truce, he'd stopped asking.

The girls were settling in nicely with her mother and Mia

and Aysha went over almost every day and had dinner with them all. On the weekends, they'd gone to Kemah's Boardwalk, the Houston Aquarium, the Children's Museum, and quite possibly every mall within a two-hour radius of Houston. Since Kassidy was headed to 9th grade, Mia thought it was a good idea to start thinking about college, so they'd also gone to a couple of University of Texas and Texas State University football games. Mia might have been older, but Aysha was challenged to keep up with her energy, and being pregnant did not help that.

Aysha played a million scenarios in her mind and every single one of them came back to those girls coming home with her. She respected what Mia had gone through and was appreciative of her offer, but she also knew in her heart that she wanted Kassidy and Kai with her. She knew that Mia would be heartbroken, and that her mother would be a bit disappointed, but it was what she wanted and what she thought was best. Her doctor had confirmed that her pregnancy was progressing well. There was some concern about her cervix, which meant she had to go for an update with the doctor each week, but other than that, she was fine.

Just yesterday, her mother had Kassidy on the computer picking out decorations for her room. She could still get those decorations, but they would be at Aysha's house. The place would be little tight for them, and maybe she should call Jessica and get her started on looking for another house. It wasn't like she could not afford it. In fact, speaking of what she could afford, she needed to contact the bank that held the account that Jaylon had set up for her when they were dating. Against her wishes, he'd started an account for her with a monthly deposit. She'd never used much of the money, as she'd had a decent salary at the bank, shared housing expenses with Jada, and Jaylon usually took care of anything else. That money was what she used to buy the house that she was in, and at the time, there was about $20,000 left in the account. She'd not touched it in the last five years, but that money would be instrumental in her purchasing a new house. She'd vowed not to live off of her inheritance, and now that she was back working at her dad's firm with her uncle, she had an income. She was aware that Uncle Rob paid her more than he should have, but she knew that he was just happy to have Aysha there. When she was younger, she would always talk about coming to work with her father and Uncle, and being one of the first female sports agents. She was sure her uncle was just happy to see her chasing that dream again. Aysha smiled, she was a true daddy's girl.

Aysha heard "Not Afraid" by Eminem, and went in search of her cellphone. When she got to it, she saw a missed call from a number she didn't recognize, and before she could put it down again, the phone rang again. She answered it and was shocked to hear Jada's voice.

"We need to talk"

"About what. Why are you calling me? You know good and damn well that I don't talk to you".

"Well, you need to. We need to talk about these girls that momma and Mia have taken in. They can't do this".

"What? Why?"

"Aysha, they don't know anything about these children, and they could come with a whole lot of problems. You have got to talk momma and Mia out of this. They can go to foster care."

"So, let me get this straight. You think the mother that married our dad to keep you out of foster care, and the sister who does counseling for abused children are going to let them go to foster care. I knew you were selfish as hell, but this is a lot, especially coming from you".

Aysha simply hung the phone up. Everything that she wanted to say to her sister was vile and hurtful, and Aysha was going to take the high road. There was no way that her mother and Mia would allow those girls to go to foster care. They'd been at her mom's house for the last month, and she didn't know who enjoyed them more, her mom or Mia. Replaying Jada's words, she knew there was a showdown that was going to occur between her and Jada, but it was not going to be over Kassidy and Kai. She also knew that it was going to happen sooner than later.

Today was going to be a big day for everyone. Hopefully, they could put some type of stability in place for the girls. According to her calendar, she was four months pregnant, and she was going to go ahead and tell everyone today. She was finally accepting that life as she knew it was going to change completely.

When Aysha arrived at her mom's Kassidy was already dressed and in the dining room eating breakfast with Aunt Belle. There were pancakes, breakfast casserole, smothered potatoes, fried bread, and more. Aunt Belle had it looking like it was Christmas morning. Aysha knew that Aunt Belle cooked when she was nervous, and it unnerved her that Aunt Belle was not calmer about the day's impending situation. Her mom was also in the kitchen, but it was unusually quiet.

"Good morning, everyone. Breakfast smells amazing. Aunt Belle, I am glad I am hungry". Aysha said as she moved around the room and gave everyone a hug, and then settled in the seat next to Kassidy.

"Good morning, Kitty. I made plenty, so eat up".

"Where is Kai and Mia?"

Here mom just put her head down, and Kassidy started fidgeting. No one answered for a few seconds.

"Kai had a really bad night last night. She kept having nightmares that strangers were coming to take her from here. She ended up sleeping in the bed with Mia, and I let them sleep a little later, so they are still getting ready".

"Nightmares. Momma, why didn't you call me? I would have come over. "

"Aysha, we all know that you need your rest right now, and we didn't want to bother you. We knew you were coming this morning. Besides, Mia and I have to get used to caring for these girls, and you have your own life, so you won't be able to run over and save us every time something happens.

"Ms. Aysha, she was okay. She just says how much she likes

it here, and it is not like at home where we don't have enough food, or clean clothes, or people going in and out. She loves the pool, and Mr. Jaylon promised to take us to Disney World when his season is over. She misses my mom, but even at her age, she realizes that we have it so much better here.

Aysha leaned over and put her arm around Kassidy. What Kassidy said had hit Aysha in a way that she hadn't expected. Just a couple of hours ago, she was hellbent on the girls going with her. She'd not even thought about the attachment that the girls had with her mom and Mia. Maybe leaving them here was the best idea. At a minimum, she should get their perspectives before she made a choice.

"Kassidy, what do you want? Do you want to go back with your mom? Or, is there a family member that you want to go with? It is important that we know what you want before we go to court. And, it is your choice. Your choice and Kai's choice".

"Ms. Aysha, I agree with Kai." And she started giggling. "She is right. We have it better here. I miss my mom, but I know that it was wrong what she did, and I know that if I go back, she might do it again. I like living here with Gigi and Mia. I like my school, and I like when you come over, and when Mr. Jaylon calls us. I like Aunt Belle's cooking, and even though Gigi won't let the housekeeper clean my room, and she makes me do it, I really like it here, and I don't want to leave."

Well, that settled it. If the girls wanted to be here, and her mom and Mia wanted them there, she would not even bring up the subject of them living with her. She gave Kassidy a hug, and then reached for a plate.

"Well, since we go that out of the way. I have something to tell you all".

Her mom and Aunt Belle froze and looked directly at Aysha.

"I am pregnant".

"Lord, have mercy. You are what? Jaylon is going to be devastated." Her mom responded.

"Seriously, momma. I tell you that I am pregnant and

you are worried about Jaylon's feelings. Wow. Who are you and what did you do with my mom?"

"Aysha, I am so happy. I think. Are you happy? I mean, I already knew something was going one. You are filling out a little bit, and every day you come over here and eat like you are starving. How did I not know that?"

Aysha noticed that Aunt Belle hadn't responded. She knew Aunt Belle was not going to be to excited about her having a baby out of wedlock. As liberal as Aunt Belle could be, she could be equally conservative.

"How far along are you?" Aunt Belle finally asked.

"4 months."

FOUR MONTHS!" They both said simultaneously.

"Aysha Jamia Rutherford. You mean to tell me that you are four months pregnant, and I am just hearing about this. You come to my house every single day, and you hid this. I ought to put you over my knee."

"Ms. Aysha, congratulations. Can I babysit?" Kassidy asked with the biggest smile.

"Of course, Kassidy. You will be the first person I call to watch my little bean for me."

"But I am going to charge. I have to start saving money for college." They all laughed. Kassidy had no clue that money was no longer a concern for her and Kai, but Aysha was happy that she wanted to work for her money.

"So, back to my original point. Have you thought about what you are going to tell Jaylon?", her mom repeated.

"Uhm. Nothing."

"What do you mean nothing? Until the day that boy left for Training Camp, he chased you around this damn city like a sick puppy. Shuttling everyone in this family from place to place, in hopes of being able to sit next to you. Every time someone mentions your name he perks up like a puppy. I am sick of both of you. Nothing. You are gonna tell him something. If he had good sense he'd leave your crazy ass alone, and go and find him someone else".

"Aysha, that boy has done everything we asked for and more since your dad died. I know you keep trying to hate him, but I see it in your eyes. Obviously, whoever this baby is by is not that important, or we would have at least heard his name in four months. So, I am with your mother, you are gonna tell him something. Unlike your mom, though, I think ya'll are made for each other, and I am sure this baby is not going to change that."

"I am trying to figure out how Jaylon has managed to hijack yet another event in my life. Daddy at the hospital was about Jaylon. Even when the girls came, the media made that about Jaylon. And today, I tell y'all that I am pregnant, and y'all have made this about Jaylon. I swear, I can't do y'all right now."

Aysha pushed back from the table, and moved to get up.

"Sit down. We are not done" her mom said sternly.

"UGH!!!! Kassidy, can you fix me a plate of potatoes and breakfast casserole. At least I can eat while I get yelled at. We wouldn't want to cause the baby any distress".

Aysha's mom rolled her eyes at her.

"You are truly pressing your luck this morning, lil' girl". Her mom responded. Aysha knew that tone. Whenever her mother called her "lil' girl, she was not in a playing mood.

"And let me just clear this up before you two get any more riled up. I haven't told the father of the baby yet, and I am not sure when I will." Aysha decided she'd ride this little joke out as long as possible. She knew the whole family would probably throw a parade to find out she was pregnant by Jaylon. Since her dad died, no one bothered to try to keep it a secret that they wanted her and Jaylon back together. She didn't know how they would feel about her not getting fitted for a wedding dress anytime soon. Co-parenting was a lot different from marriage.

"Y'all young people get on my damn nerves. How are you not going to tell whoever he is about his child? Please explain how you think that makes sense. Kassidy, go and tell Mia to hurry up so they can eat before we leave."

Kassidy handed Aysha a full plate of more than what she'd

asked for, as she headed out of the kitchen. She could hear her calling out to Mia and Kai. It took a lot for Aysha to keep from smiling. She would give them a hard time, but she'd tell them that Jaylon was the father, and it was time for her to confirm to Jaylon that he was going to be a father.

"Aysha, you have got to set an example for these girls. Do you really think getting pregnant is the best choice right now? And, by someone that you don't even talk to".

"Well, obviously, I was talking to him at some point."

"Alright, little girl. I am still your mother. Act like it."

"Mom. I got pregnant the day of daddy's funeral. This was way before the girls. It is not like I went out and just decided to sleep with a random stranger, and got pregnant."

"Well, you know where babies come from and you obviously didn't use protection, so you knew what you were doing"

"Look, before we go too far down this road, let me just say one thing"

"Aysha, I am surprised. Of all of the girls, I just didn't expect this from you. And, you are 33. So, I can only guess that you knew what you were doing, and having a baby out of wedlock, with no father, must be what you planned."

"My child will have a father. UGH. Can y'all just stop? Jaylon is the father. Okay, Jaylon. Is. The. Father. So, how do you all feel about that? Does that make it better?".

Aunt Belle walked over to the table and sat down. Her mom just looked at Aysha. Neither of them said a word. Then her mom started smiling.

"There is still hope for y'all. Where is my phone? I need to call Dee and let her know that we are going to be grandmothers". She could see the happiness in her mother's face.

"Mom, please don't. I haven't told Jaylon. He suspected it before he left, but I avoided seeing him. I talk to him on the phone, but I haven't seen him since the weekend when Kassidy and Kai came. I want to be the one to tell him."

"Child, Dee can keep a secret, and she is going to be pleased as pie about this. I have a grandchild, but this is going to be her first one, and unless that boy gets through to your stubborn behind or get some good sense and go find somebody that deserves him, probably the only one".

Aysha cocked her head to the side to just stare at her mom. Did she just suggest that Jaylon get somebody else? Aysha'd been hoping that he might, but hearing that aloud didn't sit well with her. Her mom got up and left the room. Aysha could only presume that she was going to call Ms. Dee despite her objections. She figured she'd better get to Jaylon sooner than later because someone was going to let it slip and she thought it best coming from her. Once she ate, she'd call him so they could talk. She didn't exactly want to deliver this news over the phone, but he was in Charlotte as his season had already started. Aunt Belle walked over to Aysha and gave her a kiss on her forehead.

"Glad to see you got tired of drinking poison. Time has passed for you to forgive that boy and your sister, and get on with your life. You can't love this baby with that kind of hate in your heart. You and Jada gonna hash this out. If it is the last thing that I do on this earth, I am going to mend this family. It is what your daddy would have wanted".

Tears welled up in Aysha's eyes at the mention of her father. She also knew that there was a cavern between her and Jaylon, and the Grand Canyon between her and Jada.
It was time to work on both of them. Over the last month, she and Jaylon had spoken quite a bit. He'd helped her get Kassidy and Kai settled, and as far as she knew he called the girls everyday. He and Kai had some type of swimming lessons going on, and he'd promised Kassidy that he'd fly her and her friends to a game in any city if she made the honor roll in school for the first semester. She was eyeing the Boston game in January because she'd never seen snow. Aysha was a little jealous because come January, she'd be 7 months pregnant and the chances of her going anywhere were going to be zero percent.

Aysha knew that Jaylon had truly done everything she'd asked. He didn't even ask about the possibility of her being pregnant. The last time she saw him, she'd only gained 6 pounds, so it wasn't enough for him or anyone else to see a change, but some how he'd known. It dawned on her just how much he must watch her and know about her to have noticed such subtle changes in her. She'd tell him. She'd honor her father. She'd be the bigger person. She'd mend this with Jaylon, for the sake of their unborn child. More importantly, she'd honor her father and Aunt Belle, and she'd work on her relationship with Jada.

THIRTEEN-13

They'd finally gotten to the courthouse, and everyone was nervous. The girls were fidgeting, Mia was biting her nails, her mom had gone to the restroom three times, and Aunt Belle was rocking and humming, which was usually an indicator that she was worried about something. In just a little under an hour, they would get the word on whether or not they would be able to keep the girls, and if their mother's parental rights would be terminated. Aysha was a little sad that they girls would not be coming home with her, but she knew that she'd always be a part of their lives. She'd just be Auntie Aysha instead of "Momma Aysha".

As they sat there waiting for the judge, Aysha's attorney walked in. Roxanne Nelloms was a good friend of Aysha's. Actually, Aysha'd met Roxanne through Jaylon. When he was on a mission to be the NBA's bad boy, Roxanne had represented him in a couple of mediation and arbitration cases that never quite made it to ESPN. With Jaylon's travel schedule, Aysha'd ended up negotiating settlements on his behalf, and she and Roxanne had become friends. She was the first person that Jaylon called when something went wrong. Her firm, Nelloms & Garrett, handled all of Jaylon's legal affairs.

Roxy spoke to everyone, and gave the girls a hug. She spent a minute talking to them, and making sure that they knew what was going on. Kai seemed a little sad, but Kassidy was more focused on Roxanne than the information she was giving her.

"Mrs. Roxanne, I want to be like you. I want to go to college and Law School and represent like you do."

"I will make you a deal, you keep your grades up and in the summer, if Mia is okay with it, you can come and work at the firm with me. When you go to college, you can work in the summers. If you still want to be an attorney, then you will have the same offer when you get into Law School".

Kassidy was thrilled. She was 15 years old, and she had a summer job for the next eight years with one of the top law firms in Houston.

"Auntie Aysha, did you hear that? OMG!! OMG!! I have to text Rania and Alisha. They are not going to believe me. Mrs. Roxanne, can I get that in writing? That is what an attorney would say, right?"

Everyone started laughing. Aysha was so happy that Roxanne's offer seemed to lighten the mood for everyone. Before she could respond, she looked at the door, and Jaylon walked in. She was surprised. He was supposed to be in Charlotte. He wore a suit like no one else could. Aysha's mind flashed to the afternoon in his bedroom, and she started fanning herself. He walked right next to her and sat down, of course.

"Hey, everybody. Hey little bean and big bighead." Jaylon looked right at Kai and Kassidy. Before he could say anything else, they both jumped on him.
"Whoa! Whoa! Y'all are going to mess up my good suit". Jaylon said laughingly and grabbed the girls in a hug. He grabbed Kai and sat her right next to him between him and Aysha.
"You didn't answer the phone when I called you last night." Kai said. The look on her face was one of sheer disappointment.
"Well, little lady, I was busy trying to get here in time to surprise you this morning. You didn't think I was going to let my favorite girls go to court and not be here? Will you forgive me?"
"Forgive is what you said and Mama Mia said that we have to do when people are mean to us, right? Like we have to do for our mom." Kai just leaned over into Jaylon and he put his arm around her, and he knew that all was forgiven. If only he could make gains with Aysha that quickly. But he wasn't worried. Over the last month, she'd been a lot more talkative. He'd called her almost every day and each time they had a decent conversations. He was enjoying getting to know her again. He didn't bring up the baby, all things in due time. He knew she couldn't hide it too much longer, and he was pretty sure that this time there was no threat of her aborting the baby. Well, with Aysha, he knew anything was possible, but he was hopeful.
"Aunt Belle, would you take the girls outside for a minute. I

want to tell Roxanne and Mia something before the judge comes in."

"Good morning, sweetie. Of course, I will. C'mon girls. Let's go and let these young folks talk. Aunt Belle and the girls stood up and scooted out of the aisle and headed towards the door.

"Roxy, I know a big hurdle has been the judge trying to decide if the girls' mother should have her parental rights terminated, or if they should just be placed in your home under foster care. Well, this piece of paper should help." Jaylon reached inside of his jacket and handed Roxanne an envelope.

No one said a word. It seemed that no one was even breathing awaiting the unveiling of the contents of the envelope. Although only two minutes passed, it seemed like an eternity for everyone as they were waiting.

"Jaylon Flowers, how in the hell did you get this?" Roxanne asked with the most incredulous look on her face. "I could not even get her to agree to meet with me".

"What? What is it?" Mia asked. She was fidgeting and the look on her face was one of strain and worry. She was twirling her hair, which was usually Aysha's nervous habit.

"Their mom signed away her parental rights." Roxanne answered.

"What? What does that mean? Roxanne, please explain." Mia asked nervously. She reached out and grabbed Aysha's hand.

"This means that there should be no obstacles to you adopting the girls. If, and I say that tentatively, if we can get this admitted." Roxanne replied. "Jaylon, do I want to know? "

"I will tell you everything later, but I promised you that I only did what was in the girls' best interest. We can't afford to draw this out. They deserve a normal life, and some closure. They are both so worried about having to go back. Everyday, I have to reassure Kai that she is staying with Mia. They just need normal, so I did what I needed to do." Jaylon answered. Aysha was pretty sure that he did not answer Roxanne's question, but if that letter allowed them to legally adopt the girls, then she'd accept any explanation legal or not.

Her mother and Mia both had tears coming down their faces. Mia stood up and motioned for Jaylon to get up and he did. She hugged him and cried for several minutes. Aysha was speechless. Who was this man who always seemed to ride in on a white horse just when they needed him? She was having a hard time remembering exactly why she hated him. Maybe it was the hormones from the pregnancy or something, but she found that she was softening more and more. At the same time, fear was setting in. What if she opened up to him and he was moving on? Her mother and Aunt Belle both said that they thought he should. She was not sure that was what she wanted. He'd made a mistake, a grave mistake, but it was truly time for her to put the past in the past. This baby was proof positive that they would always be tied together. Maybe, she should consider making that tie a little bit stronger. Before she could process another thought, a very attractive lady came up into the room and came over to Jaylon.

"Jaylon, I don't mean to rush you, but we have to go if we are going to be on time." She said. Jaylon released Mia, and turned to look at the lady. He started to smile.

"Everyone, this is Carly. Carly, you hear me talk about my "other" family a lot. Well, here are most of them. The girls are in the hallway." Jaylon said.

Carly spoke to everyone and waved, and smiled. Everyone was very cordial in speaking Aysha, however, felt as if the wind had been knocked out of her. Just a few seconds ago she was thinking about him moving on, and it seems that he had. She didn't know what to do or to say. Her brain was quite muddled and that moment, and she was focused on just trying to keep her facial expressions straight. She couldn't really blame him. It had been almost five years since they'd broken up, and she couldn't expect him to stay single forever. She felt no need to get to know Carly today. Certainly, as they shared custody of their child, she'd get to know Carly. She was devastated and grateful for the world's greatest poker face at the same time. The last thing she wanted was to break down in tears in front of everyone, but especially in front of Jaylon. She just kept reminding herself that it was the "wrong time, wrong place" to fully express what she was feeling.

"Everyone, I am so sorry, but I have to go. We have a game in New Orleans tonight, and I have got to catch a flight. I actually flew in with a layover just to make sure that I gave you those papers in person and that I saw the girls today. Carly is going to take me back to the airport so I can get to New Orleans in time to go to practice." He went around and gave everyone a hug, and when he got to Aysha, he whispered in her ear, "We need to talk sooner than later". Aysha was unable to give any type of response and despite the fact that she cringed inside when her hugged her, she let nothing show on her face, but her heart was hurting.

A few minutes passed as Jaylon made his way out and the girls and Aunt Belle came back in. Aunt Belle was watching Aysha closely, but Aysha was sure not to give anything away.

"Uncle Jay said that we can stay. That the judge will let us stay." Kassidy said with a questioning tone.

"We will see. We will soon see". Mia said, as she grabbed Kai in a hug. Everyone seemed oblivious to the huge pink elephant that was now walking around the room, and Aysha was quite okay with pretending everything was okay. Afterall, she was an adult, and could deal with her feelings. Right now, the focus needed to be on those girls and their future.

The judge finally came in and Mia, her mom, and the girls went to the table with Roxanne. The judge asked a few questions of the girls, primarily about where they would like to live, and if they wanted to be with the Rutherfords. The girls responded in the affirmative, and the judge asked questions about long-term and whether the family was prepared to adopt the girls once the fostering period was complete. When the judge asked that question, Roxanne stepped forward and produced the letter terminating the mother's parental rights, and asked that they be given leave from the proceedings to prepare the proper adoption paperwork in light of that. The judge agreed and adjourned the proceedings, with instructions for them to appear in court within 180 days to make the adoption final.

Everyone was so happy and there were tears of joy everywhere. Anyone that was not crying already certainly did start when Kai looked at Mia and said, "I am glad that you are going to be my new mommie." Aysha was pretty sure that even the judge and the bailiff appeared to tear up when that happened. It was a great day for the girls, and Aysha was happy that at least one thing in her life had been resolved. Now, if she could just tie everything else up so nicely, she'd be happy.

FOURTEEN-14

It had been two days since they'd gone to court, and the girls knew that they were officially staying with Mia. Against Aysha's wishes, her mom and Mia had indulged every whim the girls had. While it was only October, her mom's house looked like it was the day after Christmas with boxes of shoes, bags of clothing, bedding, pictures, and electronics everywhere. They'd taken the girls shopping to get the things that they needed to finally feel at home. Kassidy had gotten a laptop, iPad, iPods, and headphones with the name of some rapper. Aysha was glad that she owned stock in Apple when she saw the amount of money her mom and Mia had spent. Seeing her mom with the girls reminded her of her own upbringing. But then, her dad had always been the one that was willing to splurge on her and Jada, and her mom was always fussing about the number of pairs of shoes that they needed or the amount of clothing they had. He'd told them a million times how he had two pairs of shoes growing up, church shoes and school shoes, and he went barefoot if he was not going to church or school. Aysha smiled just remembering him tell that story. She missed him dearly. It was because she missed him so much, and seeing her mom with the girls that she knew that she had to do what she had to do, and she had to do it sooner than later.

Once the girls were off to bed, Aysha hung around to speak with Mia. Since Mia was a trained psychologist, and her sister, she wanted to get Mia's input on the best way for her to approach mending the fence with Jada. She still felt like slapping the taste out of her mouth at times, but she knew that it was time for her to bury that hatchet. Maybe they should do some of that therapy where you put on the bodysuits and wrestled. Aysha chuckled at the thought. Although she'd only gained 8 pounds to date, much to her doctor's chagrin, she knew in a few months, she'd look like she'd put on a bodysuit anyway.

"So, it is just you and me, so I am not going to pull any punches, I am just going to come out and say it. What in the hell are you going to do about Jaylon?" Mia asked as she plopped down on the sofa right next to Aysha.

"Uhn. Uhn. Not today. I can only deal with one situation at a time. When I told you I wanted to talk to you, I meant about the other "J", Jada-- not Jaylon. I can't do that right now."

"Aysha, you can't pretend like the situation is not occurring. You saw the woman that he was with. I mean, did you ask him who she was? Do you even care who she is? That is the father of your child. What are y'all going to do?"

"I, me, Aysha Rutherford is going to discuss with you, Mia Garrett-Rutherford, the best way to approach talking to Jada. I, Aysha Rutherford, will not discuss anything about him, Jaylon Flowers, with you, Mia Garrett-Rutherford today. One day, one situation. Tomorrow will be a different day, and a different situation. Deal?" Aysha responded. She was honest. She could not get sidetracked. She needed to steel herself towards the Jaylon situation because he was intertwined in the Jada situation. If she didn't keep a one-track mind, and keep her mind on forgiving and moving on, she knew that the introduction of Ms. Carly could cause this whole situation to blow up, and she was tired of that. She needed to close the gaping hole in her family that her relationship with Jada had caused.

"I just need you to tell me how to approach it. I have been so angry with her for so long that I am not even sure how to not be angry. It seems that now I am just numb towards her. I need this to be resolved. I am truly tired of carrying this anger. I can't do this."

"Then let's call her right now."

"Now" Aysha asked incredulously.

"Yes, there is no time like the present". Mia responded and before Aysha knew what was happening, she heard a phone ringing.

"Hello". Aysha was nervous when she heard Jada's voice. She had no clue what she was going to say or how she was going to say it.

"Hey Ja.... It is Mia and Aysha. "

"And Aysha", Jada said hesitantly. "Uhm, is everything

okay"?

"Yes, everything is fine. We are just calling you. Is now a good time?"

"Oh, okay, and you said Aysha?" Jada was obviously surprised that Aysha was trying to speak to her. She'd pretty much given up hope her sister would ever come around. In fact, she'd found a bit of joy in their separation.

"Yes, I said Aysha. Although she is sitting here like the cat got her tongue, but she is here".

"Oh, uhm, okay. I just put Leilani to sleep, and Malik is on the road as usual." It was apparent from her reaction that Jada was not expecting a call from Aysha, just as Aysha hadn't been expecting to call her.

"Jada, uhm, I am not even sure how to start this, but I do know that I am tired of hating you. I don't know if we will ever go back to where we were. I am not sure that we ever could, but can certainly go forward."

There was complete silence. For at least 30 seconds no one said a word. Mia was shocked that Aysha just said the words, and she was pretty sure that Aysha was just as shocked.

"Aysha, I can appreciate that you just want to move on, but I have some things that I need to say to you. Just because you are ready to be over this does not mean that I am necessarily ready to be over this."

"What? What did you just say? You are over what? You were the one that laid up with my man. So, help me, exactly what did you have to get over?"

"Once again, you think the world revolves around you. So, for the last five years you have treated me like I don't exist and then you just call me up on the phone, and say, 'let's be besties' and somehow that is supposed to do what? Get me to tear up, and we can laugh and sing "Kumbaya". PUHLEEZE. Get over yourself. No one is giving a damn about you being mad. Stay mad."

"You know what. You are a 1,000% correct. You are, and always have been a miserable bitch, so why would I expect anything from your simple ass now. But since I have you on the phone, and you want to keep this feud going, let me put some gas on the fire for your dumb ass. You always have been jealous of me. You think I didn't hear the comments you made. You think I didn't know how you undermined me. You think none of your so-called friends came to me wondering how a sister could do some of the things you did? You hid nothing all these years, and I have pitied you more than been angry with, and to find out you were an orphan only me made me pity your sad ass even more."

"Aysha, you wish I was jealous of you. You wanted to go to the same university I went to, but you didn't get accepted. You moved to the same city that I moved to. Worked at the bank I worked at, but I was jealous."

"Yes, when you laid up in the bed and slept with Jaylon, you certainly were. You were mad because the NFL was passing you around like a basketball on the court, from player to player, and nobody wanted your nasty ass for keeps. You were jealous because I came into the bank and did in two years what you hadn't done in five. So, you can be slick mouthed all you want, we both know the truth."

Jada started laughing. "Truth, you want the truth Aysha. The truth is I never slept with Jaylon. Your knight in shining armour was just that, a knight. That night, before you found us in bed together, I'd just returned from Houston from arranging stuff for your wedding. Except when I got there to our parents' house, they weren't expecting me, and Mia was there. They had no choice but to tell me the whole story, except, as usual, no one wanted to tell our dear Kitty anything. They were worried about messing up your wedding. My whole life was in shambles, and all our parents could think about was your freaking wedding. They didn't care that I'd just found out that our mother was not my real mom. They only cared about Aysha. Kitty this, and Kitty that. So, yes, I flew back to Charlotte, and when I got to our townhouse, Jaylon was already in your bed sleep. I had every intention of sleeping with him, but he was too drunk and never woke up, and I finally fell asleep next to him after try-ing. The next morning, after you shattered the mirror when you caught us, I never said anything to him one way or the other."

Aysha felt her whole world just go black. She had no clue what happened next. She wasn't even sure if she'd passed out or blacked out or what had occurred. She just finally came to with Mia's arms wrapped around her.

"Mia did that really happen? Did my sister just tell me that she allowed me to believe that my fiancée slept with her as some sort of revenge? You mean that I threw it all away for nothing? I aborted my baby for nothing? How do I live with that? And, you mean that our parents likely knew this five years ago? Who the hell are you people, and where is my real freaking family? What kind of games have you all been playing? Playing with my life." Aysha yelled, and then she started hyperventilat-ing.

She was distraught and crying hysterically. No matter how bad she thought the situation was, this was a million times worse. How could her own sister hate her this much? She was clear that there was always animosity on Jada's part, but Aysha just took a lot of that as sibling rivalry. She'd known over the years that Jada had done shady things to her behind her back, and she took it all in stride. She was honest. She actually pit-ied Jada growing up. Although Jada was the "big sister" she was always in Aysha's shadow. Aysha got the good grades, Aysha was the one everyone doted on. Only now was Aysha seeing the blackness in her sister's heart, Aysha was ready to move on and her relationship with Jada was no longer going to be her bur-den. She'd discuss this with her mother tomorrow. Right now, she needed to know where Jaylon was, and she was about to do whatever she needed to do to make this right. She didn't know what right was, but she knew she needed to get to Jaylon to fig-ure it out.

She'd heard rumors of things Jada said and did. She knew that Jada was quite competitive with her, but Aysha just thought all sisters were competitive. She also remembered Jada dating guys that Aysha liked, but Aysha always deduced that Jada was their type she never considered that her sister was going after them. Looking back over their years together, Aysha began to see a pattern. Her sister may have loved her on one hand, but she was very envious of Aysha on the other.

"Sissy, you have to calm down. Think about this baby, and you have got to calm down or I am going to wake mom up. I need you to calm down".

"I need to talk to Jaylon. I need to see him. Can you call him?" Aysha was acting very erratic. Her breathing was still not as calm as Mia would have liked, but mentioning her mom seemed to have calmed her instantly.

"No, Aysha I can't. I need you to calm down, and let's talk about this. Let's be rational, and think about what your goal was. You wanted to bury the hatchet with Jada."

"Now, I don't care about her at all. Actually, now I want to bury a hatchet in her. How do you do that to your sister? It was one thing to think that she slept with Jaylon, but the fact that she let me believe that she did is something totally different. That is just evil, Mia. Just, evil". She wondered did Jaylon even know the truth? She'd find out.

Aysha got up to get her bag and when she found her cell-phone, she called Jaylon's number.

"Who are you calling?"

"Jaylon." Aysha responded. She turned to face Mia, and Mia could tell from her stance, posture, and tone of voice that she was not backing down.

"Hey, Jay, do you have a minute."

"Unh, Aysha? Yes, a minute. Carly and I are getting ready to go and get something to eat".

"Carly? She travels with you?"

"Did you call me to discuss my travel plans?"

Aysha lost her courage. Her heart shattered into a million pieces. He'd truly moved on. There seemed nothing left to say. The past didn't matter anymore. Maybe the best way for her to forgive and forget the situation was simply to forgive and forget it.

"Jaylon…", her voice broke as she was speaking, "never mind. You and Carly go and enjoy your dinner. I am sorry for bothering you. Good night." Aysha disconnected the call without even waiting to hear a response. So often, she'd thought the pain that she felt when she'd finally faced the reality that she'd lost her sister, left Jaylon, and aborted her child was the worse pain imaginable. She knew now how wrong she was. Everything inside of her seemed to hurt, and she truly felt as if her insides had been shredded. At the same time, she realized that her life was no longer just about her, and that her unborn child deserved better than she was giving. She was determined to get through this. She'd have to face Jaylon soon enough, and they would have to come to some agreement to co-parent this child. She'd just started warming up to the idea that maybe they could start over, even if just for the sake of their child. Tonight's events had doused those ideas.

"Mia, I am going home."

"No, you are not. You can go and sleep in the guest room, and stay here tonight, and tomorrow will be another day. You are not alone, and I am not about to let you do it. You run away when things get rough. Well, too bad. We are going to help you through this. If you have to move in with us until the baby is born and old enough to drive, then we will all be one big happy family". Mia was very serious. She couldn't imagine what Aysha was going through, but she did know that she was not letting her go through it alone.

"I don't have any fight left in me tonight, sis. Please, just let me go home. And make me one promise. You will not say anything to Jaylon. I want to be the one to tell him all of this. We have to figure out what we are going to do going forward. We have to parent this child, but Mia, please, just let me go home."

"Nope, you may as well go on to the guest room. I swear I will wake Mom up if you try to leave this house. Go to sleep, Sis, and we will deal with it all in the morning". Mia responded. She could see that Aysha's spirit was broken. Why wouldn't it be? The truth of the last five years came out, she finds out about Jaylon and Carly. Maybe if Aysha thought that she was really losing him, she'd do something about it. What a tangled web that Aysha'd woven.

"Whatever. I am over all of it. All of you." Aysha mumbled and headed to the guest room. For the one millionth time, she wondered who were these people and what happened to her real family. Maybe she was the one that was adopted. She was going to take a shower, but exhaustion took over once she sat on the bed. She got undressed, and looked in the mirror. She was four months pregnant, and it seemed like her belly had popped out since she got dressed this morning. The weight of the future, of her child was just too much. She got in the bed expecting to fall fast asleep.

Unfortunately for Aysha, sleep did not come easily. She'd left her phone in the den with Mia. She probably should have turned the ringer off because she was pretty sure if Jaylon called back Mia would talk to him. She loved her sister, but no secrets were safe with the all-charming Jaylon. She knew firsthand how he could charm a priest into telling confession secrets if he wanted to. In fact, that charm was one of the reasons she'd avoided him completely. She always knew that the right words, the right smile, the right moment, and she would be all over him. Well, her current situation was a testament to that, and if she recalled he didn't even say much. But, Mia was right about one thing. Aysha needed rest, and she could deal with life tomorrow.

The next morning Aysha was awakened by a knock on the door, and when it opened, it was her mother. She knew this must be serious. Everyone knew Aysha was not a morning person, and if her mom was coming to her this early, something grave must be happening. Her mom walked in the room and crawled into the bed with Aysha. She wished she'd had a camera. This was a memory worth recapping. At the same time, Aysha knew that her mother was about to drop a bomb on her.

This was too much sweetening of the pot going on.

"How are you feeling? The baby?"

"Fine. Tired all the time. I just want to sleep. I was expecting some weird cravings, but all I seem to crave is a nap". And Aysha leaned in and rested her head on her mom's shoulder.

"Like mother, like daughter. When I was pregnant with you, I could not get anything done. If I sat down for five minutes, I was sleep. And trying to chase after Jada, who was two at the time was already a task." They both giggled.

"I have something that I want you to do for me. Kitty, we are taking the girls to San Antonio to see Jaylon play tonight, and I want you to go with us. I want you and him to sit down and I want you to talk to him. Mia told me about Jada. I think your dad figured it out a long time ago. I think he was hoping that you never had to know. It broke a part of him to know that you and your sister were not speaking. The last thing he asked me was to make sure that I fix our family."

At the mention of her father, tears started falling from Aysha's eyes. Her mom reached over and wiped her tears.

"No sweetie, your dad would not want this. He would want us laughing at his memory, and that is what we will do. The best way you can honor our father is to bury this mess with Jada and Jaylon. It is not just you, now. It is this baby." Her mom said.

The fight was gone. All of the anger that Aysha felt over the years seemed to just dissipate. Where Jada was concerned, she felt nothing but pity for her sister. Where Jaylon was concerned, she didn't know. She'd loved him more than she thought was possible, and it was shattered.

"Mom, he has moved on."

"Now, Kitty, you know I have never told you to compete for a man, but baby, this boy has done everything in the world he could to get your attention in the last five years. Your daddy and I didn't buy that car, he did. The glass carousels that you love so much, came from him. Aysha, he won't even sell that house because he is convinced that you are going to come home.

The painting in our dad's study is not Jada. That is Jaylon's idea of you and his child. So, do you really think that if he is with this girl, Carly, that he won't give that up for you and his child? The boy can have almost any woman he wants. Hell, if I was 20 years younger I might be in the running."

Aysha raised up and gave her mom "the Look".

"Girl, I am old, not blind. The boy is fine as wine. I tell him to find him someone to appreciate him, and he always tells me that he already has."

"I don't know what to say. I don't even know how I feel. I am angry because no one told me this years ago. I made certain choices based upon something that didn't happen. And, for whatever reason, my own father didn't see fit to tell me. My own sister hates me so much that she let me destroy my life, and even now, all she can do is gloat about me not being so "perfect". I just don't know Mom. I don't know that I can do it tonight."

"Well, they play in Texas for the next week. They go to San Antonio, Dallas, Houston, and back to San Antonio before heading back to Charlotte."

"Since when did you become ESPN, keeping up with the basketball schedule."

"Since the girls got here. You know Kai has to know where Jaylon is at all times. Her class is doing a project on U.S. Geography and Jaylon sends them postcards and mementos from every city. They track him on a map in the class, and at the end of the season, he will have the class come to a game".

Aysha couldn't help but think how much life had changed for those girls. That would always be one thing that she would be so proud of her family for. Although she still wished the girls had wanted to live with her, watching them get settled in was a great joy. Once again, she'd have to thank Jaylon. From the moment he'd driven her to the police station, and picked Kai up in his arms, he'd been there for her. She called him everyday, and if you asked her, she would tell you that Jaylon was her best friend. She'd decorated her bedroom with all things representative of the Charlotte basketball team. Jaylon had helped by having life-sized cutouts of all the players made into stickers that she could put on the wall. He even got her a custom jersey, and from what Kassidy said, she wore it every time she could. She could not thank him enough, and she realized that she did not have to.

She had a secret that she needed to tell him, and without that, there was nothing that she could do until she'd come clean with him. She would call him and arrange to see him when he came to Houston in four days. That would give her enough time to get her thoughts together and the courage to do what she needed and to say what she needed.

"Mom, I am not going to San Antonio with you all, but I promise I will go to the game and talk to Jaylon when he is in Houston this weekend. As a matter of fact, I will call him and leave him a message this morning."

"A good try is all I ask. You two can make this right. That boy loves you. I don't know why, but he does. Make it right, Kitty. For your dad. For him. For my grandchild. But most of all, baby doll, make it right for you." Her mom gave her a deep hug, and Aysha felt like crying, but it was time out for the tears, and the hiding, and the running. It was time for Aysha to face the mess that had become her life.

FIFTEEN-15

After her mom left the room, Aysha just laid there in the bed replaying the last 5 months of her life. It seemed like she'd been put in a blender and chopped up and mixed up. When she came downstairs, Aysha was grateful that it was a Sunday. The girls were already gone to church with her mom and Aunt Belle. Her mother taught Sunday school, so they usually left for church around 8:00 a.m. Mia was in the family room on the computer, and she looked up at Aysha when she came into the room.

"Good morning. How did you sleep?"

"Surprisingly, like a baby. Straight through the night, no problems. Well, except for Mr. Robertson. He has cut that damn grass every Sunday morning at 9:00 a.m. for as long as I can remember. I guess the more things change, the more they stay the same."

Aysha decided that she would go to the game and she would have a talk with Jaylon. At five months pregnant, there was really nothing that she needed to say. If she wore the right outfit, he'd think she gained a little weight, but if she wore anything with any shape it would be obvious. Although he was on the road a lot, he deserved to know about his child. She was tired. The anger, the bitterness, the hurt, and the grief of the whole situation with Jaylon had finally run its course. This baby would mend a lot of wounds, at least she hoped so. She had no illusions about a relationship with Jaylon, and based on what she'd seen and the comments that Mia and the girls made, Jaylon had finally moved on with Carly. She wasn't as optimistic as her mom and Mia that he would just drop everything for her, and she wasn't sure that she wanted him to do that just because she was pregnant. She'd had a doctor's appointment and she'd heard the baby's heartbeat. She actually felt guilty that she'd robbed Jaylon of that opportunity. No matter how she felt about him, she wanted him to experience some of this. At the next appointment, she would find out the gender of the baby. She would Skype him in or something, but she would make sure that he found out at the same time that she did.

She'd not told anyone about her heartache. The day before Jaylon was due to leave to report back to Charlotte for training camp, Aysha went to tell him about the baby. She knew she should have called first, but she arrogantly believed he'd want to see her. She had pulled up to the house, and as she was ready to turn into the driveway, she saw Jaylon and a woman, presumably Carly, embracing in the driveway. She'd kept going, and went home. She was pretty sure Jaylon didn't see her, and she had no recollection of driving home. She'd told no one about what happened, and she knew that he'd actually moved on. She'd cried and let it go. Let him go. She wouldn't complain. After all, it had been five years, and based upon what she was finding out, he'd held out hope as long as he could. She would not hold it against him that he was finally pursuing his happiness, even if it was not with her.

During the game, Aysha spotted Carly. She was sitting in the section where the player's families sat. Aysha never wanted tickets in that section, as she found a lot of the wives to be competitive and the girlfriends to be quite catty. She'd always chosen to sit behind the visiting team's bench when she went to the game or in the section behind the basket. She'd kept her distance from most of the player's wives, and when they'd split she was glad that she had. That was one less tie she had to cut. Tonight was no different. Jaylon had gotten them seats behind the Rockets bench, which was alright with her. She was a hometown girl, and didn't mind cheering for the team. She noticed a couple of times during the game, when there were breaks in the play, Jaylon kept glancing her way. She didn't think he'd paid Carly as much attention. Then again, he could see her when he got home. She wondered did Carly travel with the team or did she live in Houston. Aysha'd met Jaylon on the road a couple of times, but his coach was not happy about it because he broke all of the team rules to make sure Aysha enjoyed whatever city they were in. To appease the coaches and keep Jaylon out of trouble, she only traveled with him a couple of times. She had work also, so she couldn't go as often as Jaylon liked, but she went to as many of his home games as she could. She was pretty sure her jersey with his number was packed up somewhere. That would be a great keepsake for their baby, hopefully a little girl. This was the first time that she'd seen him play in four years. He was still the most magnificent illustration of a man. Though she would never admit that aloud, she could not deny herself the guilty pleasure of watching him. She'd always been attracted to him physically. No matter what he ever did, the image of him was always enough to elicit a very wicked smile from her.

At the beginning of the fourth quarter, Aysha was getting a little restless. She and the girls had run the poor waitress to death. Aysha was as bad as the children. She'd eaten nachos, turkey on a stick, popcorn, and pizza. Sadly, she was still hungry. Her doctor had advised her to be careful because as the baby would be growing a lot during this time, her metabolism would pick up and she would want to eat more. She'd cautioned her to make good food choices, and usually she did. The combination of the stadium atmosphere, spoiled rotten girls, and nerves was overriding her good sense. She'd make up for it tomorrow, as she was still running, or fast-walking if she were honest. She'd also go to her mom's house and get a good swim in as well. She looked up and thought it was the waitress standing next to her, as she was seated on the end of the row as there was uneven seating, but she was surprised to find that it was one of the Charlotte trainers. He handed Aysha a note, and she was scared to open it. Jaylon used to send her notes during the games that she attended. It started from her telling him how the star of another team had sent her a note with his phone number on it. She'd never told Jaylon exactly who it was, but after that he would always send her random notes at some point during the game. She was pretty sure they were packed up somewhere as well. She hadn't been able to throw them away, but she also hadn't been able to even open the boxes that held those memories. She put that on her list of things to do. There was no way she could let go of the past, if she was content with holding on to all of the memories. She smiled on the outside, but she was so nervous, she almost dropped the envelope. It was red, and that too sparked a memory.

"Thank you" she'd managed to mutter, and without responding, the trainer turned and left.

"Meet me at Vic & Anthony's after the game. Give me an hour. We need to talk." There was a heart with a Jay in it. That was how he'd always signed anything he gave her. It was a logo that they'd joked about using to start a business. Tears welled up in her eyes, and Aysha was trying hard not to cry. At the same time, her mom, sister, and nieces were all badgering her about the note and what was on the paper. She didn't say anything, but handed it to Kai, who was sitting next to her, as they were sharing their second plate of nachos."

"Auntie, are you going? Oh my God, will you eat again? Your stomach is going to hurt." And Kassidy laughed and passed the note to Aysha's mom. Mia leaned over Kai and looked at it with her mom. They were both smiling, and turned to look at Aysha.

"Chickens come home to roost." That was all her mom said before she turned her attention back to yelling for the team. Aysha didn't realize her mom was such a groupie, but she knew all of the players on the Rockets' team, and most of them seemed to know her too. Aysha couldn't help but wonder exactly what she had missed out on for the last few years while she was nursing her wounds, as it seems her mother was quite popular amongst the players. She heard "Mrs. Hazel" more than once from the players, coaches, and trainers.

In the end, the Rockets won the game and Aysha was happy for the team, but she could not be happy that Jaylon lost. She told her mom not to worry, as she planned to take a taxi down to the restaurant as it was close to the stadium, and her mother was adamant that they would drop her off on their way home. Aysha was pretty sure that based upon the stadium traffic, Jaylon would get there before them.

"Will you take the girls to wait outside of the locker room to see

Jaylon?" Aysha asked Mia. He still maintained his connection with them, and in their minds "Uncle Jay" walked on water.

"No, he came by the house and had breakfast with them this morning. They flew in last night, and after breakfast, he'd dropped them off at school. I am sure that went over well when Kassidy pulled up to school in a Black Bentley. I am glad Kai's schoolmates don't know that much about cars." Mia replied. "Seems this night is reserved for you." Mia said with a glint in her eye.

"Girl, please. I guess there is no getting around what I need to tell him, or show him at this point, but that ship has sailed. I guess it is time for me to admit that. I hope Carly makes him happy." Aysha said, and tried to hide the sarcasm in her voice. She'd not realized just how much she still loved Jaylon until she realized that someone else also loved Jaylon. She couldn't hold it against him, and she just hoped that Carly was the type of woman that she wanted around her child. It wasn't her choice, and that was a fight she didn't ever want to have, and she'd make that clear tonight. They would always do what was best for her child, their child.

"You can say that to anyone else, honey. But, if Jaylon was my man, and some heffa got close, I swear I would claw her eyes out. You want Carly to make him happy. You are a better woman than I am." Mia rolled her eyes at Aysha. The plan seemed to be working. She just hoped that Aysha would not be too upset when she finally told her that she'd exaggerated all things Carly, and made sure that the girls and her mom saw Carly just enough to make sure that they also reported back to Aysha. The reality was that Carly was the marketing manager assigned to Jaylon as a result of his contract with a shoe company. No one had bothered to tell Aysha that, nor did anyone bother to tell her that Carly was dating Jabari, Jaylon's best friend, and was more like a sister to Jaylon. Both Mia and her mom thought that Carly would push Aysha into being jealous, and forcing her to admit her feelings for Jaylon. What they hadn't expected for Aysha to admit her feelings, and then give up. She hoped Jaylon would fix it tonight. This had been a long year for their family, with lots of changes. She just wanted to go to bed one night and know that everyone was well.

"Well, like Mama said, 'the chickens will come home to roost' tonight. I will put it all out there and we will decide how to move forward for this child". Aysha replied. She wanted to admit that she was afraid. She knew Jaylon would be angry that she'd kept the baby from him. She knew that he'd be angry about the Jada situation. She knew that he'd be angry about the baby that she aborted those few years ago. She just didn't know where they would be after it was all said and done, but tonight it was going to be all said and done.

SIXTEEN-16

Aysha got to the restaurant in plenty of time. She was sitting in the foyer waiting for the hostess to return, and looked out of the window. She was pretty sure that she saw Carly standing at the valet stand. God had a way of testing your resolve. How was she supposed to be the bigger person if this girl was going to be visible so much? Who was she kidding? Carly was beautiful, tall, and obviously what Jaylon wanted. She loved Jaylon and always would. She wasn't liking this chicken and roosting at all.

When the hostess returned and asked for her reservation, she was unsure if she even wanted to stay. Maybe she should just leave, and send Jaylon a message that something came up. But, she was tired of cowering and hiding. She was just ready to go forward, with whatever forward looked like, so she gave Jaylon's name. She was pretty sure that he'd put the reservation in his name. The hostess looked at her and smiled, and then said, "Ms. Rutherford, please follow me." As Aysha walked through the restaurant, she was reminded of her father. This was one of her favorite places, and it was not lost on her that Jaylon chose this setting to finally clear the air. The hostess walked up to a set of wood doors that were exquisite. Aysha was not much into decorating, and certainly not old English décor, but the magnificence of the doors caught her attention. The hostess pushed the right door open, and looked at Aysha and said, "After you." Aysha was a bit caught off guard, as she didn't know what to expect. She'd been to this restaurant at least once a year, if not more, with her parents, but she'd never been in this room that she remembered.

When she walked in, she was immediately overwhelmed. The room seemed to be covered in orange and peach roses, her favorites. There was a very large carousel that looked like it belonged in a display case at FAO Schwartz in the corner of the room. It was easily three feet high, and was the most amazing thing that Aysha'd every laid her eyes on. She wanted to run towards it and just touch it, like a little child on Christmas. There were three horses on the carousel. One was done in orange, sage green, and gold, the colors Aysha planned for her wedding. One horse was done in pink and green, her sorority colors. The other horse was done in Crimson and Cream, Jaylon's fraternity colors. She didn't realize it but tears were falling from her eyes. The painting from her parents' home, the one that Jaylon had in his home also was displayed. There was a slideshow playing with pictures of her, Jaylon, and the two of them together. She wondered who'd helped him with this. She was pretty sure he didn't do all of this by himself. There was a table that held so many little blue boxes that she couldn't count. Jaylon would buy her Tiffany's jewelry because he said he got such joy from watching her open the boxes. She was pretty sure there was an empty store somewhere in Houston. It was like a dream, and she was trying to take it all in. In the corner, was her father's jersey on a stand, next to a Charlotte jersey with her mom's name on it. There were smaller stands with jersey's with Mia, Kai, and Kassidy's name. They were grouped together in a small huddle. That made her really cry. Who was this man? This room had everything in it that represented so much of who she was. As she wiped the tears away, she looked up, and saw Jaylon walk from behind the carousel. Even through blurred, teary, eyes, he looked amazing. The candlelight-dimmed room cast a shadow on him, but it was not enough to hide him. He seemed to have a golden aura around him as he walked towards her. He did not say anything, he stood in front of her, and his eyes dropped to her stomach. She took a deep breath, and did not exhale. She didn't know if he would be angry or not. He simply reached out and touch her stomach, and with questioning eyes said, "Mine?". Aysha didn't think she could speak, so she simply nodded her head. He simply turned and walked away. Aysha was unsure of exactly what that meant, and in that moment, she truly realized how petty and unimportant it had all been. She realized just how much damage she'd done to herself over the years carrying this stupid grudge. She truly understood the magnitude and depth of Aunt Belle saying,

'Don't let your pride get you into something that love can't get you out of." She loved Jaylon. She always had. She loved him so much that even hating him could not destroy the love.

She walked to him and wrapped her hand around his forearm. His back was still to her, and when he turned to face her she saw the tears on his face. He'd always told her that he never wanted to be the reason she cried. She felt that now. She felt hollow because she knew that her stubbornness, her hard-heartedness, her grudge, her secrets, was what had caused all of this. She felt the anger welling up in her towards Jada, but she was determined to put all of that behind her. She looked at Jaylon, and then turned to look around the room. She looked around the room, and marveled again at how much thought and detail had gone into every corner. She could not imagine how he'd arranged it all. And, to think, he'd arranged it all before he knew for sure that she was pregnant with his child.

She turned back to face him, and saw him pull a handkerchief from his pocket and wipe his eyes. He then came over to her and used the handkerchief to wipe her face as well.

"No more tears, Aysha. No more tears." He said, and grabbed her hand and walked her to the table. "Please have a seat. We have so much to talk about."

"I am sorry, Jaylon. I am so sorry for everything."

He looked at Aysha and then he started smiling.

"Always straight to the point. One minute, and then we can talk about whatever you want to talk about." He motioned for the server to come. Aysha was so lost in the moment that she hadn't even realized that someone else was in the room with them. She looked around again. The carousel was absolutely breathtaking. Where was she going to put that? It certainly would not fit in her loft, but maybe it could go in the family room at her mom's. Who buys a 3 ft. tall carousel? It was absolutely breathtaking. The roses, the carousel, the Tiffany's table, the painting, the jerseys, and the slideshow were all overwhelming.

Aysha dropped her head, just as the server walked up. Jaylon told the server that he could cancel the champagne. Obviously,

Aysha was not going to be able to drink it with him.

"What would you like to drink instead?" The server asked.

"Two glasses of sparkling water, please". Jaylon responded. The server turned and walked away.

"How did you know that I would come?".

" I didn't. I actually had all of this planned for last week in San Antonio. Luckily, your mom let me know in advance that you weren't coming to the game, and I was able to have the company deliver it all to Houston, for a small fee of course."

"How did you pull this off? The pictures, the flowers? Jay, just tell me who helped you. I promise not to be upset with them." Aysha said, but she was smiling.

"No. No. No. I can't reveal my sources. But, while we are talking about help, how is it that I speak to Kassidy and Kai almost everyday, but neither of them mentioned you being pregnant. Not that I wasn't suspicious since the day at the pool. Not only did you eat Frenchy's chicken, which I had never known you too. You took a nap, which you never do. Your mom mentioned that you came over a couple of days and took naps each time. You never sleep during the day. I knew. I get why you didn't tell me, but I can't believe no one else did."

"Jaylon, when I found out how close you were to my family behind my back, I was hurt. I felt betrayed. I have been adamant that if anyone said anything to you that I would cut them off completely. Unfortunately, I'd done it before, to you, so everyone knew I was serious." She dropped her head. She had so much that she needed to tell him. She'd come with the intention of just calling a truce so that they could figure out how to raise this baby. Her current reality was so far removed from what she had in mind. "The girls," she continued, "were easy. I simply told them that it was a surprise for Uncle Jay and that they could not ruin the surprise. Getting my mom not to tell your mom took a whole lot of convincing. Getting Mia and Valerie not to tell you took pure and unadulterated bribery. I think my inheritance might be gone." They both laughed at that. "So, before tonight is over, I think we should call your mother, and I will go by and see her in the morning."

"Well, if it is alright with you, I would like to go to my mom's place after we leave here. It will be late, and she will not be happy that we are waking her, but I am pretty sure that after she takes one look at you, she will forgive us." They both laughed. Aysha had to admit that being with Jaylon without all of the anger and the secrecy felt good. But, she didn't want to be too presumptuous. One look around the room said it all; however, there was one question she needed to ask. She'd hold off on the question; there was so much more that she needed to say.

"Jaylon, I have some things that I need to say to you. I came here tonight to get it all out in the open, and let you decide where we go from there."

"Aysha, don't you get it? Look around this room. Do you think I did all of this so that you could come in and say some thing that would make me walk away? There is nothing that you can say to me that will change how I feel about you. It has been nearly five years, and I still think of you every day. I still remember what you ordered at every restaurant, I remember every store you like to shop in, I remember that you like popcorn, and I still have the popcorn machine in the garage that you had to have. I took my vows to you a long time ago, and I gave you up because I thought that I made a mistake. And, even once your dad figured it out, and told me the truth, I thought that it would only be a matter of time before you came around, but your dad never knew how to tell you about your sister. I didn't think it was my place. Had I known that it would take this long for you to find out, I would have told you myself. I doubt that you would have believed me though. I love you Aysha. With every thing that I am."

"But you don't know everything. You don't know what I did."

"The abortion, Aysha. Yes, I know. Your father told me about that. When I came to him and just set aside my pride and begged him to just hear me out, he told me that there was some thing I needed to know and accept if he was going to give me the green light to come to you. You did what you felt like you needed to do in that moment. Was I hurt? Yes. I never thought that you would abort our child. But, I don't judge you. I don't hold it against you. It was your choice, and you made it. It is in the past, and we have wasted enough time. It is time for us to move forward."

Aysha just teared up. She'd held all of this in for so long. She'd tortured herself for making such a spiteful choice. She'd told herself over and over that Jaylon would never forgive her for that choice, and all along it was her who hadn't forgiven herself. She'd used the baby that she'd chosen to give up as the fuel for her anger, and in the end, he loved her anyway. She almost felt cheated, as she realized just how much time she'd wasted being angry and hurt and vengeful and petty, when it seemed everyone else was moving on. She'd truly been drinking poison, waiting on everyone else to die, when the reality was she was only hurting herself.

She didn't know what to say. She wasn't sure what all of this meant. She didn't have a chance to process any of it, as the server began bringing food. They hadn't ordered so she assumed Jaylon must have put all of this in motion.

"I took the liberty of ordering some of your dad's favorite foods. I know this was his favorite restaurant, and I chose it because I thought with his memory, this would be the perfect place for us to start over."

Aysha wasn't sure if it was the hormones, the words, or the scents from the roses, but her eyes watered yet again. She was pretty sure that any minute, she would wake up in the intensive care unit of one of the hospitals in Houston's renowned Medical Center and find that the last few months of her life had been an elaborate dream. However, as the waiter placed the Lobster Bisque and Crabcakes in front of her, Aysha was reminded of just how real this was. She and Jaylon sat in silence for a few seconds as the server delivered the Calamari and Lobster Bisque to Jaylon. He reached over and grabbed her hand as the server left, and they both bowed their heads to say grace, as they'd always done before any meal that they shared. So much had changed between them, and yet it seemed that so much remained the same. "It seems I have been the only one in the dark this whole time. Why didn't anyone say anything to me? I just don't understand why no one saw fit to tell me."

"Aysha, your father wanted to tell you but he was sure that you would forgive Jada and repair his family. I don't think either of you realized what this whole situation did to him. He was really hoping that you would never find out what Jada did. He felt guilty for not telling her about her mother, and he felt like maybe he was to blame for the way that she felt towards you. He thought that maybe it was all of the years that you were obviously his favorite."

"I can understand that, but Jaylon, she was my mom's favorite. Even after everything that happened, or well, at this point, did not happen, do you know that my mom flew to Charlotte and stayed a week with Jada. As if Jada was the one that needed comfort. That is still something that I know that I need to let go of, but I hold that spot against my mother. When I needed her to just be my mother, she went to Jada, and left me with my dad."

"Aysha, there is something else you need to know."

"Oh my word. Can someone just call a freaking janitor and clean all of the skeletons out of the closet? I feel like I am starring in a daytime soap opera. Erika Kane has nothing on me. I don't know if I can take anymore." Aysha was exasperated. She'd taught that word to her seventh graders, and had a hard time explaining exactly what it meant. Now she knew that it meant being tired of being tired.

"Aysha, your sister attempted to commit suicide. That was the reason that your mom flew out to her."

Aysha was shocked into complete silence. It was only when she had to gasp for air did she realize that she was not even breathing. Her big sister. Her idol. Jada was one of the strongest people Aysha knew, and she'd attempted to take her own life. They'd never told Aysha that. She just knew that her mom had told her that she was going to Charlotte to check on Jada. How'd they manage to keep all of that from her? Why? Well, she was determined to stay in the light, and that meant being honest. If her parents had told her that Jada attempted suicide at that time, she probably would have prayed for her to die. At that time, she'd felt nothing but hate and contempt for Jada, and she probably would have used her mother's phrase, "Chickens come home to roost" instead of feeling any pity. She thought of the conversation that she had with Jada, and all of the anger that Jada directed towards her. She didn't have to have Mia's doctorate in psychology to know that it was a cover for something else.

"Aysha, when your mother was in Charlotte, we spoke. Jada was supposed to go work, and when she didn't show up, they tried calling you. Your number had changed, so they looked at your file and called your emergency contact, which was me. I was in Charlotte, getting ready to go to Disney World and The White House after we won the championship. She hadn't called me in two days, and when I tried calling her cell and the phone at your house, there was no answer. I still had the key, so I drove over. I thought I would find her just being ornery and trying to get attention. When I got there, she was in her bridesmaid dress, and laid across your bed, and there were envelopes addressed to you, your parents, Terrence Creighton."

"Jaylon, are you telling me that you found my sister and she'd tried to kill herself? I don't know what to say."

"I called 911, and then I called your parents. I told them that I would stay there until they got there. Your dad and your mom wanted to come, but your mom convinced your dad to stay with you."

Once again, the weight of the world came down upon Aysha. As Jada said, she really did think everything was about her. She'd held it against her mom, and even felt some kind of way when Mia came into the family thinking that once again her mother had chosen someone else over her. All of the while, it seems that they both needed their mom a lot more than Aysha did. She felt ashamed. She wished she could apologize to her father. She'd said some very selfish things to him about her mom when she found out her mom was leaving to go to Charlotte.

"Jay, did she say why she did it? Why she tried to kill herself?"

"Well, she did and she didn't. All your mother said was that she felt like she messed up everything. I did find out later that Terrence had her involved in some really foul situations, and that there were videos floating around of some of the things that she did with different players at his request. She thought they were in a real relationship, and he was just using her to fulfill his fantasies, and from what I have heard some of them were pretty graphic."

Jada never made the best choices, and she always held it against Aysha when her choices came with some terrible circumstances. Over the years, Jada was always the one that was very gullible and believed everything that people said. Just like their mom, she saw the best in everyone. Aysha was very much her father's child and distrusted everything until proven. That had gotten Jada into many situations, and it seemed Terrence was no different. Aysha told Jada on many occasions that Terrence was not what he presented himself as, but Jada couldn't hear her. She was determined to make Terrence into the man that Jaylon was. With the information she had now, Aysha was pretty sure that was her catalyst for trying to sleep with him. Jada needed to prove to herself that Jaylon was like the men that had done her wrong. Sadly, she'd resorted to lying to preserve her reality, which made Aysha wonder how she'd gotten with Malik.

"Aysha, are you going to eat anything?" Jaylon asked. The server had come and removed the appetizers, which neither touched, and was bringing their main courses.

"My stomach is in knots right now." Aysha said in response to Jaylon, and turned and looked at the server. "Please package it all to go."

"Dessert also, ma'am."

"Yes, whatever he has ordered, I would like it all to go. I am sure that I will be hungry later." Aysha said and rubbed her stomach.

"How long did you plan to keep this from me?" Jaylon asked. She could tell that he was feeling emotional, but she couldn't peg if it was anger, fear, surprise, or what.

"Well, I came by your house the night before you left to go to Charlotte." Aysha was unsure if she wanted to continue, but this was the proverbial wash that everything was going to have to come out in. "I passed by and was unsure if I wanted to turn in the driveway but I saw you and a woman, that I assume was Carly embracing. I was sad. Well, I know that I kept saying that I did not want you, but I wasn't quite ready to see you moving on with someone else. That is actually what I came here to tell you tonight. I was not expecting all of this. I was not expecting any of this. I just wanted to clear the air with you, so that we could figure out how to parent this child together."

"So, if I would have told you that I was with Carly, you were going to be okay with that?"

"I had no choice but to be okay with that. Everything that you have told me tonight has more than confirmed just how selfish I have been, and truly for the first time in my life, I was thinking about someone else. I was thinking of only what is best for the baby."

"Aysha, let me make this clear. There is nothing between Carly and me. In fact, Jabari would probably kick my ass if there were."

"Jabari, why?"

"Carly is his fiancee'. She works with the shoe company and my management company to keep me on track for engagements and promotional spots. She is trying to open her own promotions company, and I am working with her to get athletes signed by using the connections that your dad and Uncle Rob built."

Aysha smiled. She was happy to know Carly was not in his life. She was definitely glad that she did not have to be the bigger woman because she was not sure how long a hormonal, pregnant woman who had been scorned would have been able to do that.

"Do you know what you are having, yet?"

"No. I didn't want to know. Well, I didn't want to know without you. I want you to go to the doctor with me. If I need to schedule the appointment with a doctor in Charlotte, I can if that will make it easier. I know that you leave in the morning. But, I don't want you to miss this."

Jaylon just put his head down into his hands. This was truly a side of him that she'd never seen. He was so overwhelmed right now. He wanted to just grab her and hold her and never let her go. He wanted to scream and tell her how much he'd missed her. He wanted to shout to the world that the woman that he loved was having his baby.

"Aysha, I need to ask you one more thing. I know that we can't just jump back to where we were, but I need to know if you are willing to try. I don't want you to try for the baby, I want you to try because you still love me or you still want to love me as much as I love you. I don't want to co-parent this child. I want our baby to grow up with two parents that love each other as much as we love him or her, and the siblings to come. I don't want to take it slow. We have wasted more than enough time. We need to speed-date now."

"Jaylon, I don't know. With everything that you have told me tonight and everything that has happened, I don't know."

"You don't know what? You don't know if you love me? You don't know if I love you? You don't know if we have wasted enough time? Look around this room Aysha, and tell me that you don't know that I love you and that I would give anything for you. Would you like for me to retire? To quit, okay, I will after this season. I will be there for you and for the baby all of the time. But, I am not walking away. I am not quitting, and I am not running."

"You don't know what you are asking."

"Like hell I don't. I am asking you to give us another chance. I am asking you to reclaim what we allowed everyone else to take from us. We sacrificed for your family and your sister, and now I am willing to sacrifice it all for you."

Aysha could not stop the tears. Hadn't this been what she'd wanted to hear. She'd steeled herself for him to tell her that he moved on with someone else. Instead, he'd told her that she was the only one for him. She saw all of the faces flash before her eyes. She saw her dad on his deathbed telling her to fix it. She saw Aunt Belle warning her about that pride. She saw Uncle Rob telling her to go for it. She saw her mom saying make it right. She saw the faces of Kai and Kassidy when they heard that she was going to see Uncle Jay. She heard Valerie telling her to make it right. Most importantly, she saw the face of the unborn child that she was sure was a little girl telling her that it was what she needed to do.

"Yes, Jaylon. I love you, and I am willing to give us another try."

"Aysha, I am going to ask for something, and I know that you are not going to like this, but I would like for you to move to Charlotte with me. I know that my schedule is going to make it difficult for you, but I want to be as involved with you and the baby as I can, and I can't do that if you are here. I know you are going to want your mom and Mia around, but I am asking you to come with me. Can we start building a family together, now?"

Aysha inhaled. This was all too much. She was getting lightheaded. Where was that server with the champagne? She wished she could have just one glass, or maybe a shot of tequila. She just needed to relax, as she could feel that her nerves were on edge. She was so wired up that she didn't even know how to relax.

"I can't answer that today, but I will answer. Right now, can we just go? I would like to go to my mom's. I need to talk to her. Oh, well, we agreed to go to your mom's first. Can we just go? Please."

Jaylon signaled the server as asked him to bring their food, and have his car brought around. He stood up, and helped Aysha out of her chair.

"Who is going to move all of this stuff? I want every single rose. EVERY SINGLE ONE!! That carousel? Where am I going to put it?"

"It is taken care of. They will come and clear the room out tomorrow, and the roses and boxes will be delivered to you. The painting will also come to you, and the carousel is going in my house."

"Your house? What?"

"You are welcomed to move in, too, if you need to be close to it." Jaylon started laughing at the face Aysha was making. He put his hand on her stomach, and the baby obviously liked it because the baby started moving. Aysha smiled at him, and he leaned down and kissed her softly on her lips.

"New beginnings, Aysha, new beginnings."

EPILOGUE

This was truly the fairytale ending that all little girls dreamed of. Today, she was flying to Houston with her three-month old son. Her mom, Aunt Belle, Mia and the girls, and Jada had all been there with her in the delivery room. She'd tried to hold off because Jaylon was on the way, but there was no stopping the little boy who was on his way. Jamaal Jabari Flowers was born two hours before his father arrived at the hospital. Jaylon missed the next two games as he refused to leave the baby's or Aysha's side. The team actually threatened to suspend him for missing the game. He didn't care. He'd stayed with her in the hospital until she and the baby were released, and he only went back to Charlotte on the condition that she stayed with her mom, Mia, and the girls. It had been the longest month of his life, and Jaylon was truly considering retiring at the end of the season.

On that night of reckoning, after all truths had been told, Aysha and Jaylon went to see his mother, who gladly told them that she'd already known about her first grandchild. It seems Aysha's mom hadn't kept the secret from her friend after all. From there, they went to Aysha's mom, and she was prouder than a peacock to see Aysha and Jaylon together, and it seems that the word spread like wildfire, as Aysha turned off her phone after she kept getting "About time" messages from her family. Her cousin, Quentin, was the one exception, as he asked Aysha could she get him and his boys some courtside tickets to the game since she was "back in good with Jaylon". She was about to tell him that she would, but nixed it when he asked if he could video her wedding for his YouTube channel.

"I only wish your father could have seen this. This was all that he wanted for you. This was all that he wanted for both of you." Those were the words that her mom said, and the word that she held dear to. Uncle Rob and Aunt Belle both said the same thing.

Aysha and her mom had flown up to Chicago to go and see Jada. They'd spent a week there, and surprisingly, the last two nights, Aysha stayed at Jada's house. It was important to Aysha that she and her sister move forward in something other than hate and hurt. She was going to bear the brunt of whatever occurred in the past, just to be able to put it to rest. It was what her father tried to do in protecting Aysha from the whole situation, and it was what she would do to mend her family. Aysha was pretty sure they would never be best friends again, but she was glad that they'd buried the hatchet. Her mother made sure that they were sisters again, even if they would never be friends.

Aysha and Jaylon would stay in Houston to finish the plan for their wedding, which would take place the last weekend in June—the same weekend that it should have been five years ago. Jaylon's season would be over in few weeks if they didn't make the playoffs, and two months if they did, as it was looking like they would. They hadn't told anyone, but they got married in the office of the Justice of the Peace in Charlotte a couple of weeks after she'd arrived. They both agreed that it was what they wanted to do, and they wanted to do it before the baby arrived, but Aysha was adamant that she was not wearing a wedding dress while looking like she ate one of Jaylon's basketballs, and they hadn't even told their mothers. She knew they'd take a lot of heat for that choice, but she was glad that they did. They didn't bother with rings, as the decision was made for them, and not the world. Jaylon had surprised her by giving her the exact same ring that he'd planned to give her initially. Another secret, was that her father had given it back to him after his second heart attack, when he'd made Jaylon promise to never give up on Aysha. Her father always knew what was best, and she just wished she could tell him one more time that she loved him, and that he was right. She was pretty sure he knew.

The last few months had been great. They'd picked up in some areas like they had never been apart, and as they lived together, she'd learned some new things about Jaylon, and she was sure he learned some new things about her. They'd bought a new house in Charlotte, as Jaylon lived in a townhouse that was close to the stadium, since they'd always planned to live in Houston. Now with the baby and all of the baby's stuff, she understood why Jada stayed in Chicago during Malik's season and came back to Houston in the offseason. Aysha had most of her furniture from her place in Houston shipped to the new house in Charlotte, and she'd ran herself ragged before the baby was born trying to decorate. She was planning to finally decorate the one place that she swore she'd never live, Jaylon's house in Houston, which was now her home in Houston. As she'd talked Jaylon out of retiring, she would be with him in Charlotte during the season, and they'd come to Houston in the offseason. She knew that he loved playing the game, and when the time came, he could assume his role in her father's firm, but now was not that time.

As Aysha got into the car to head to the airport, she reminisced as Jaylon strapped baby Jamaal into his car seat, and she couldn't help but smile. This time last year, she'd been a different person. She had been hell-bent on being hell-bent, and decidedly unforgiving. Now, she was in the midst of what could only be a dream life. She truly had it all, and she had to thank God that she finally got worn down by the anger and the hate and opened her heart to forgive. In light of everything that had occurred, and all of the truths that had come out, she understood why elders said grudges were like poison. She'd given up drinking the poison, and had a fairytale to show for it. She'd have to look Devon up and thank him for calling Jaylon to pick her up from the bar that night. That was truly the pebble in the pond, and she was grateful for the ripples. God had a sense of humor, and she was pretty sure he was smiling at her right now. Gratefully, she was smiling too.

THE END

Made in the USA
Monee, IL
05 December 2020

50991980R00125